# Saving GiGi

## A Samantha Steele Mystery

### Sandra J. Howell

1

# Saving GiGi

Published by West Ridge Farm Publishing

Copyright © 2013 by Sandra J. Howell
First Edition 2013

ISBN 978-0-9845582-3-0
Library of Congress Control Number: pcx69043
Printed in USA

Cover design: Amy Rooney
Editor: Deb Koske
Insignia: Tina McDowell - www.tinascanvas.com

Also by Sandra J. Howell
Spirit of a Rare Breed, a Samantha Steele Novel

# Dedication

This book is dedicated to my grandmother Minnie, my mother Dorothy, my aunt Doris, and their best friend Dottie. I have been blessed by having each of these loving, lighthearted ladies in my life.

# Acknowledgements

As always this book was made possible by the love, encouragement, and support of family and friends. So powerful is the love for, and from my family, that I consider myself a most fortunate woman. Life is always fun when we are together.

To my beloved husband Dennis. You are my diligent proofreader and my best cheerleader.

To my veterinarian friend, Doctor Michael Stewart, for his advice and consultation.

To my editor and cousin, Debbie Koske. Your unwavering belief in me and generous assistance helped me to bring this novel to fruition. You are the best! Thank you.

To my cousin, Fred Pokrzywa. You are amazing with your artistic design and creative ideas. I love this cover for 'Saving GiGi.' They say "the eyes tell the story," and you have proven this truism.

To horse lovers everywhere! A high-five to those who provide Therapeutic Riding Programs for children and adults with either physical or emotional needs and kudos to all of the Equine Rescue Programs. You have saved so many wonderful horses that, without you, would have gone to slaughter.

To Betsy Lirakis, a friend and horse woman I greatly admire. Your work with American Curly horses and their use in your Therapeutic Riding Program makes me proud.

# Prologue

## Saving GiGi

Lyla Bernhart was in a frenzy. She felt like she was being chased by the devil himself. Her hands tightly clutched the wheel of her rusted old pickup. If she lost control of her truck her frantic attempt to escape would end in a violent way. She knew she was driving too fast for the conditions of the dirt road, but fear had taken over her usual timid personality. Her brain screamed "run" and she was too scared to care. Sweat trickled down her forehead and into her eyes. She blinked to relieve the burning, and pressed harder on the gas pedal.

"Damn!" she cried as she hit the breaks to avoid another deep pothole. Lyla quickly glanced in the rearview mirror and prayed there were no headlights behind her.

"None so far," she thought as she took in another deep breath. Lyla's whole body shook as a surge of adrenaline coursed through her veins.

The dark winding road coiled around boulders and snaked through the dense forest. Tall, massive trees lined the dirt road, and it was filled with ruts and stones. The unkempt road was dangerous to drive at slow speeds, and on a good day it could be tricky. Tonight it was downright dangerous. Unfortunately, it was the only road to and from the barns that Lyla had come to hate.

Bam! She hit another pothole and it just about knocked her breath away.

Lyla let out a deep gasp. She squeezed the steering wheel so tight her fingers began to cramp.

"Calm down, breathe deep!"

The sound of her own voice yanked her back to reality, and her hand instinctively shot out and grabbed the tiny foal lying on the seat next to her.

"Oh my God!" she shrieked. "Stay put. Don't fall."

Each time she hit a rock or swerved to avoid another rut, she was slammed forward in her seat, and once or twice her head almost hit the truck ceiling.

She prayed the old Ford didn't break an axle as it hit the deep crevices. Careening down the dark, dirt road at a high speed wasn't something Lyla had planned on when she impulsively picked up the chocolate colored foal, wrapped it in an old blanket and ran to her truck. To make matters worse, it was pitch black outside and the only light piercing the darkness came from the headlights of her truck. The moon was hidden behind heavy cloud cover and a drizzling rain slopped on her windshield.

Her instinct to flee made her take risks that were foreign to her. If someone had told her yesterday that she would be driving at a dangerously high speed down this dirt road with a foal on the seat next to her, she would have laughed at the outrageous idea.

"Faster, faster," Lyla screamed out loud. "Come on. You can do this!"

Her mind was racing and her lungs felt like they were going to explode. She willed herself to take in another breath. Lyla hadn't been able to catch her breath since running away from the dreaded farm.

Luckily, she was familiar with the twists and turns of the road as it wound its way through the thickly leafed forest. On her numerous trips to her job at the farm, she had checked the speedometer and she knew she was half way to the end of the dangerous road before she met the hard pavement of the highway that led down the mountain.

Lyla's dark red curly hair was swept behind her in a loose ponytail and her bangs hung down almost to her eyes. For a moment, she wondered if she looked as crazy as she felt. She was a wild woman! Her blue plaid flannel shirt was covered with hay and her ragged jeans were splashed with mud. She hadn't taken time to brush herself off or to think about anything except to run as fast as she could.

Lyla's eyes darted once again to the rear view mirror. So far no headlights and she let out a huge sigh of relief as she blinked her tired eyes. She prayed no one saw her at the barn, but she wasn't sure. Maybe no one would notice the foal was gone until morning chores.

"What will they do when they find GiGi is missing?" she thought.

GiGi was special and everyone knew it. Lyla had seen firsthand what happened to foals born on the secluded farm nestled in the wooded mountainside of Vermont.

She shuddered as the truck hit another deep rut and bounced her up and off the seat. Again, she grabbed the foal

9

just in the nick of time. The hard jolt had thrown GiGi to the end of the seat. Lyla knew a healthy foal would try and stand, but GiGi was too weak to make the effort.

She quickly pulled the blanket back over the foal. The fear of injuring GiGi snapped her into reality, and finally common sense replaced fear. She willed herself to slow down as she reached another bend in the road.

Suddenly looming in front of her was a large object blocking her way. She had been so lost in thought that she hadn't realized she had reached the end of the road until her headlights revealed the gate. Just in time she hit the brake and barely missed smashing into the rusty old piece of iron. She put her truck in neutral, jumped out and ran quickly to move the gate. The gate was attached to a crooked post which caused it to sag and lean into the ground, making it difficult to pull open. She reached down and put both arms under the round rail. It was stuck in mud and for a moment she wondered if she would be able to lift it. Giving it all she had and with extraordinary effort, Lyla picked it up and dragged it backwards and off the road. Leaving just enough space to drive through, she ran back to her truck, put it in gear and hit the gas pedal. The tires kicked up stones and mud as she tore off the dirt road and onto the paved highway.

Her hands were shaking and although it was a cool night she was drenched with sweat.

"Okay," she said aloud, not only to reassure herself but to be sure she could still speak. Her mouth and lips felt dry, and she wished she could reach the bottle of water rolling around on the floor in back of her. "No time for that," she thought. "You can do this Lyla. You're safe. Just keep on driving."

Lyla felt a slight smile come to her lips. She realized she had done the impossible. She had saved GiGi's life.

# Chapter 1

## Philadelphia One Year Earlier

A light rain had fallen on the empty city sidewalks. The soft rain had cleansed the pavement between the large brick buildings. Small puddles lay spattered on the sidewalk and the smell of spring filled the air. The early morning sun was just beginning to peak out from the scattered clouds that floated east on their way to the ocean.

During the past twenty years, The South End, the name of the old part of the city, was left undisturbed and lost in time. Nothing had interfered with its decline until a few investors with foresight, realized that a jewel was sitting just waiting for its time to shine again.

The rows of brick buildings had once been home to a generation of Italian immigrants. As the immigrants moved to the suburbs, crime and decay had slowly crept into the once thriving community. With prudence and planning the city poured money into redeveloping the old neighborhoods. Little by little, the rows of apartment blocks had been bought up and refurbished by new owners. To promote tourism and build on the needed tax base, the mayor and chief of police had dedicated themselves to making this part of the city safe for new tenants and owners. On several corners, vendors featuring international foods found willing customers with no time to cook. Several entrepreneurs had set-up small kiosks filled with glittery watches, perfumes, and handbags. Most were knockoffs, but tourists were enticed by the bargains.

The community was rebuilding, and the small, low rent apartments were ideal for young men and women beginning careers after college. They worked long hours, had their own group of friends, and for the most part never made contact with each other. The apartment buildings had a quick turnover and renters moved on after a short period of time. It was only when a young man going door-to-door looking for his lost cat, that tenants living in the building next to him were brought to the attention of the local police. The cat owner had searched the alleys between the buildings, calling for the run-away, but the calico did not come forward. With no sign of his cat, he made his way to the apartments in the buildings closest to him. He knocked on the doors of people he had never met, asking if they had seen any sign of his lost pet.

There was something odd about the slender man who cracked open the door to answer the knock from the anxious cat owner. The neatly dressed man seemed nervous, and as the cat owner glanced past the open door, he noticed it was empty of furniture except for a long wooden table covered with stacks of paper. An open lap top sat next to an ash tray piled high with cigarette butts. A thin dark skinned man sitting on a crate next to the table locked eyes with him in a frightening stare.

"No," the man said in perfect English. "I haven't seen or heard a cat near our door."

"Okay, sorry to bother you. I've been going door-to-door looking for him."

The cat owner paused, and smiled as best he could. For a brief moment the hairs on the back of his neck stood up, and he felt a shiver run down his spine.

Quick on his feet, he added "If you see him would you let me know? I live in the building right next door on the first floor." His words felt hurried and he intuitively felt something was wrong. He pointed to the tall building and hoped the man at the door would not notice his nervousness as he felt beads of sweat begin to form on his forehead, and his heart begin to pound. Warning, Warning, Warning! Racing thoughts came billowing through his brain and a loud ringing began in his ears. He worked hard to compose himself, and he forced another smile. Somehow, a quick thank you came from his lips, and he was able to push back the urge to run as fast as he could. It took all of his self-control to walk leisurely down the stairs and head towards his apartment.

"Oh my God," he thought as he entered his building. "What just happened? Have I been watching too much TV? I feel like I've looked into the eyes of a terrorist!"

He hurriedly entered his apartment, bolted his door, and phoned the local police department to report his suspicions.

The police department immediately forwarded the man's concerns to Homeland Security. The agency interviewed the caller and stepped into action. They sent a task force to place the apartment and the men under surveillance; however, the men had already made a hasty decision to move quickly out of the neighborhood. They sensed the man looking for the cat had seen too much and they couldn't risk the chance of being detained or interrogated.

After seeing no one going in or out of the apartment, they broke down the door; guns raised, and found it empty. There were no visible signs of the men who had lived there and everything had been swept clean. Dry bread crumbs lightly littered a long wooden table and two broken chairs lay on a torn green shag carpet. Two tiny bedrooms were empty of furnishings except for a soiled mattress lying in a corner of one of the rooms. Cupboards were bare of food and there were no signs of habitation. The tenement, dingy and decrepit, looked like it had been used by homeless people, not the men who the cat owner described. They had left without a trace, and the only indication that someone had stayed there was the lingering smell of stale cigarettes.

A call was made to a terrorist task force, and a CSI team was sent to investigate. The team carefully and methodically searched every room, took apart kitchen and bathrooms drains, and searched all outdoor trash bins. Using the latest equipment and technology, they performed a careful sweep of every inch of living space. Nothing was left behind that could identify the men who had lived there, except for a tiny piece of wrinkled paper found when the baseboard heaters were removed. The penciled scribble of Arabic writing set-off red flags and an elite team of investigators who worked with biological threats was notified. Scientists, who specialized in bacteria considered dangerous and deadly, were brought in to join the team. The race was on to find the terrorists, and research on Botulism was now considered a high priority. Neither the building residents nor the man looking for his cat were informed about the dangerous men who had posed as their neighbors.

# Chapter 2

## Lyla's Farm

The sun was just coming up over the mountains when Lyla Bernhard turned her pickup onto the dirt driveway of her home. After her frantic trip from Vermont to her farm she called Meadow Brook, she was physically and emotionally exhausted. Relief flooded through her as she opened the passenger side door and carefully lifted her precious cargo from the seat of her truck. The Mini foal was still wrapped in a blanket and looked more alert. Lyla was dog-tired, and whispered a prayer of thanks that she had made it home in one piece. It had been a long trip and she had not stopped until she pulled into her driveway. She carried GiGi into her house and laid the wobbly foal on the stone floor of her sun room. After feeding the foal a bottle of mare's milk, Lyla went to the barn and returned with a bag of shavings. She dumped the shavings onto the floor and scattered them with her foot. This would be GiGi's home until she was strong enough to stable in a stall at the barn.

After the foal was settled in, Lyla went into the bathroom and took a long hot shower. She was still shaky but the hot water helped to relax her weary bones. Stepping out of the shower, she dried herself off and wrapped her body in an oversized fluffy blue bathrobe. For the first time in hours, she breathed in a big sigh of relief. As she towel dried her hair, she gazed at her reflection in the bathroom mirror. Her eyes scanned her face, looking for any telltale signs of the ordeal she had lived through. The lightly freckled nose, shoulder length wavy red hair and green eyes still looked the same. She squeezed her eyes tightly and opened them again.

Staring back at her was the face of an exhausted, teary eyed woman.

"I know it's me, but I feel different," she thought.

Her cheeks flushed with the memory of the scary night she had lived through.

Lyla turned her head away from the mirror and with arms that felt like limp rags, rubbed the towel over the back of her neck to wipe the trickle of water soaking her robe. Salty tears caused by exhaustion and fear, began to flow down her cheeks and she sniffled to stop the onset of something she couldn't control. Her eyes felt heavy and she yawned in an effort to stay awake. She knew she was too tired to finish drying her hair. She dropped the towel and headed to her bedroom. She would think about what to do later, but for now all she wanted to do was sleep.

# Chapter 3

It was early morning and Samantha Steele was enjoying a break from her morning chores. She closed her eyes and leaned her head back against the large white rocker, and sighed. Her quiet moment was broken from the loud noise of honking geese, flying high over her farmhouse. She quickly sat up to catch a glimpse of them before they moved out of site. As she turned her head to follow their flight path, she moved her hand up to shield her eyes from the bright sun.

"Yeah!" she thought. "How great! They're finally back." Sam counted the geese as her eyes followed the large V formation. They continued to call to each other as they glided over the top of the barn and were gone.

The sound of geese returning after a long cold winter was something Sam looked forward to. Now she was certain spring was here. She could feel it in the air. The daily temperatures reached sixty degrees and the snow from the relentless winter was gone. As usual, the melting snow and rains created mud that stuck to her muck boots and her dog's paws. Mud was everywhere. Fields were riddled with sucking puddles of it, and her Curly horses had dark patches spattered on their hooves and fetlocks. As the frost had melted, it pushed the ground up in dark cracked humps and jagged ruts pierced the landscape. Deep impressions left by horse's hooves traversed the fields and her driveway was a sloppy mess.

Life in New England always brought a surprise to the ever changing seasons. Some winters had been mild, but this past winter had been a bear. Heavy snow had taken down many of the older barns and several houses in her town were damaged by the seemingly endless snow storms. It had been a full-time job just keeping up with non-stop plowing. Her tractor had moved buckets of snow from her driveway and kept the path to the barn clear, but it had been a challenge. The Yellow Beast chugged and coughed from the work load, but surprisingly had kept on going. The snow piles on the side of the barn were so high; they almost reached its roof. Both the barn and house roof had required constant raking of snow to keep them from caving in. Several fence rails had been crushed by huge limbs laden with snow that fell down on them. Sam hoped to never see another winter like the one that had just passed.

None too soon the brutal winter ended, and Sam hosted her annual cousin party to welcome spring. It was a festive celebration and fourteen cousins gathered at her farm. They raised their wine glasses and toasted, "goodbye winter, hello spring!" Life was good. Another season had passed and the promise of warm summer days and gardens of flowers made the long, gloomy, cold winter, but a memory.

Finally, all was right in her world. The morning air was just cool enough for a light jacket, and the warm sun made it hard to imagine that only a short time ago she felt like a frozen Popsicle.

Sam reached over to a small wicker stand and picked up her favorite yellow mug. It was filled with hot coffee and she took in a long sip. This was the time of day she loved the most, and she soaked up the moment as she savored her second cup of the dark liquid.

"Ah," she sighed. "Hot nectar." A contented smile crossed her lips. "Dark, no sugar, just the way I like my morning brew."

She yawned and stretched her arms over her head in an attempt to focus on the day's list of things to do. Her eyes fixated on the upper field, beyond the barn, where her American Curly mares and their foals were pastured. The foal's whinnies could be heard as they ran the fence line chasing each other with joyful squeals. Mares, ever so watchful of their offspring, could be heard neighing as they called to youngsters who wandered too far from their sides.

Sam leaned back in her rocker and her thoughts drifted away from the sounds of horses. The warm sun felt soothing on her face and body, and she felt herself move into a sublime state of relaxation.

"I could fall asleep," she thought. She sighed and pulled her shoulders forward and backward in an attempt to get herself into a working mode.

"Just a few minutes more and then I need to get going. The ladies are always on time and I need to really get a move on."

Sam was rousted from her day dreaming by the bleats from her goats Rudy and Roger. They wanted out of their pen, and she quickly swallowed the last bit of coffee and headed towards the barn to finish her chores.

By noon, she had everything ready for her Wednesday ritual. The three ladies were coming for lunch. Minnie was Sam's maternal grandmother, and Doris and Dottie were Minnie's best friends. Elderly but not old, they acted and dressed much younger. Sam loved their company. The ladies never failed to amaze her with their funny stories, and their ultimate quest to stay young. Friends for years, they shared everything with each other including medications. Their attitude was, "What worked for one would surely work for all of them." Minnie and her friends were a huge part of Sam and her children's lives. Not only did her twins, Justin and Kristy, adore the ladies, but they had charmed their way into her fiancé Denver's heart. Who could not love the three most important women in her life?

The ladies were never late and she had one ear cocked towards the driveway as she sliced the rest of the tomatoes to add to the freshly made salad. She had filled soft rolls with chicken salad, and prepared a large bowl of Minnie's favorite potato salad. Not to forget Dottie, she had made her favorite dessert, vanilla pudding topped with fresh strawberries.

Her dogs, Sally, Jazz, and Ranger heard the sound of a car coming up the driveway well before she did.

Sam, followed by her three excited dogs, left the kitchen. Quickly walking towards the driveway, she was just in time to see Doris's car slowly wind its way up, splashing mud along the way. She knew that after greeting the ladies she would need to turn the car around so that it faced towards the road. Doris could neither turn her car around nor back it up, which accounted for the many dents on her car's bumpers.

The blue Honda came to a stop and three elderly ladies piled out. Each of the women stopped and patted the dogs.

"Alright, settle down," Sam tried her best to control the rambunctious dogs.

"Oh, they're so sweet," crooned Minnie. Minnie wore a long yellow and black striped shirt, belted over black tights and her sneakers of the day were yellow and black. Her curly grey hair was pulled back in a large black bow, and her smooth skinned face looked ageless. Dangling yellow earrings hung almost to her shoulder, and Sam had to stifle a laugh. Minnie looked like a bumble bee in her gaudy outfit. Sam believed that except for her crazy fashion style, Minnie could easily be a walking poster model for aging adults.

Dottie, short and cheerful, was bending down and rubbing Ranger's head. "You are getting so big," she said in a baby voice to the happy pup. The conservative of the three women, Dottie was dressed in jeans, white shirt, and white sneakers. Her wavy grey hair was pulled to one side with a large brown comb. The only makeup she wore was a touch of pink lipstick.

Doris, the driver of the entourage, was speaking to Sally. "How are you Sally?" She was being showered with wet kisses from the wiggly older dog. 'The princess,' as she was called by Minnie, was dressed in a matching pink shirt and pink pants. Pink was her favorite color. Her hair was always the same style. Puffed high on her head, it glistened with hair spray. Large pink button earrings donned her ears and a huge pink and white necklace graced her neck. As always, Doris wore pink sneakers to match her outfit of the day.

Fashion was everything to Doris, and she lived for Sunday church services, where her latest ensemble always drew compliments from astounded parishioners.

After being greeted by the ladies, the dogs settled down. In between all of the chatter, Sam hugged each one. Greetings complete, the gaggle of women headed to the house. But it was the matching sneakers that always grabbed Sam's attention. Sam could feel her eyes widen as she took in the whole picture. Sneakers were the ladies favorite shoes. They had reminded Sam during their last visit, that sneakers not only felt good on their feet, but made them look more youthful. That's what life was all about for the ladies. Live in the moment and keep up with the latest fashion trends.

Sam choked back a giggle waiting to erupt as she walked to the car, opened the door, and moved the driver's seat back. Doris, five foot two inches tall, so she claimed although Sam doubted it, sat on a cushion as close to the steering wheel as possible. But even with the cushion, Doris's head just about topped the steering wheel.

Sam got in and tossed the cushion onto the passenger's seat. She put the car in reverse and turned it to face the road.

"Gosh, I don't know how she drives," she thought as she stepped out of the car and closed the door.

The three dogs sat waiting for her. "Come on," she said as she walked towards the house.

By the time she and the dogs reached the porch she had pulled herself together. She paused for a moment and listened to sounds of the women's voices. Each one was over-talking the other.

She smiled, opened the screen door, and stepped inside.

# Chapter 4

After the wet cool spring the warm days of summer were a welcome relief to everyone. Saturday promised to be an especially warm day, but Sam was not complaining. The weather channel predicted severe storm warnings during the afternoon, but that was the last thing on her mind. She had other things to worry about and she was not in a good mood. She had started out early enough to complete all chores by noon, but now she was behind her schedule.

It was her fifth attempt to start the Yellow Beast so that she could move a large pile of manure down to the lower field. Yellow Beast, the name she had christened her old tractor, refused to start. In its usual beastly manner, it had turned stubborn and moody.

"Damn. I might have known." The engine turned over and gave a loud choking sound. She just knew that Yellow Beast was doing this on purpose. That wretched beast always picked the time when she was in a hurry to give her problems. Trouble with Yellow Beast meant that the "to do list" would get backed up, and nothing irritated her more.

A strand of hair had fallen loose from her ponytail. Unconsciously she pulled it behind her ear. The Yellow Beast sounded tired and winded. It couldn't be that it was out of gas because she had just filled the gas tank.

"Damn," she muttered again as she turned from the seat, jumped down onto the ground and moved to the side of the tractor to remove the bolts that held the hood to the frame.

As always, she found herself talking to the huge piece of metal that seemed to rule her daily life. Not that looking underneath the hood would help her much, but she felt she needed to do something rather than wait for Denver to arrive, and once again bail her out of her tractor dilemma.

"Look at you," she spoke angrily as she reached over to lift the tractor hood. "You seem to grow rustier each day. Pretty soon you'll be one total rust bucket."

The hood of the tractor, unlike an auto hood, was split into two sides. One side was so rusted that it was almost impossible to lift, but thankfully the side that needed to be opened was more forgiving and compliant. She lifted the hood and looked in.

"I'll check your air filter. With all that choking, you don't seem to be able to get enough air to start." She was still talking to the tractor whose front grill was bent and rusted into a perpetual smirk.

Sam worked to twist the cap off, but it resisted as she tried to turn it. It moved a click at a time and she finally gave up trying to turn it with her hands. She reached for her hammer and tapped lightly on the cap and then tried again. No luck. Her frustration grew as she slammed the hammer harder against the cap. Again she tried to turn the cap. This final bang with the hammer did it. She was able to loosen it enough to twist it off. She dropped the cap onto the torn seat and pulled out the old air filter.

"What's this?" Sam was amazed to see, wrapped around the filter, a large clump of shredded cloth and scraps of leaves.

"Now I see what the problem is. Those darn mice are building a nest. Where are my barn cats? They haven't been doing their job," she said in disgust.

Carefully she removed the nest from around the filter.

"I wonder where they dragged this mess of cloth from. What else can go wrong this morning?" she mumbled.

She placed the clean filter back in and twisted on the cap. "No need to look any further. I'm pretty sure I solved this problem."

It was already noon and her chores had taken longer than she thought.

"I think I need a break before I try to start the Yellow Beast again," she said to no one, as she pulled off one work glove and then the other. Where had the morning gone?

She shoved her gloves into her jean pockets and headed to the farmhouse. Rudy and Roger had been munching on grass in the paddock next to her. As soon as she turned to walk towards the house, they took it as their signal to follow. They were playful and trouble was their middle name.

Deep in thought she didn't hear Rudy running up behind her. His head hit her right at the back of the knee. The butt from Rudy caught her off guard and caused her to stumble. She almost fell, but caught herself as she lurched forward. As she turned around to catch the rogue goat, he took off like a shot and raced towards the upper field.

"Come back here Rudy so I can show you whose boss," she yelled. She knew there was no chance that Rudy would obey, but it felt good to shout at him.

Rudy and Roger were her resident goats. They were orphans she had rescued as babies and were too adorable to resist when she first saw them. But this sweet behavior hadn't lasted into adulthood. Although they were shy and respectful when they were younger, they now thought they were in charge of all the animals on the farm, and often pushed Sam's patience to the limit. They were very clever and sensed her moods. Just when she had enough of them, they would do something cute and all was forgiven. The dance between Sam and the goats went on and on.

Ranger was sitting on the ridge of the field and had been watching the whole scene. When the goats ran, he seized the opportunity to have his own entertainment and began to chase them.

"Oh, no you don't. Not today. I don't have time for this," Sam was finding herself more annoyed than ever. The goats loved to goad the playful dog, but today she was having none of it. She shouted for Ranger, and then gave a whistle. The Labradoodle pup turned on its heels and trotted back, wagging his tail, eagerly awaiting her approval.

"Well at least someone listens to me," she said as she ran her hands over the panting dog's head. "Good boy, let's go," she said firmly.

The happy youngster followed her to the farmhouse. Once on the porch, she stepped out of her mud covered Bogs and walked inside.

"Ahhh. Hot coffee and a blueberry muffin to go with it. That will work."

She dropped a K-cup into the coffeemaker and took a muffin from the basket that sat on the counter. After adding cream to the steaming cup of coffee, she carried the mug in one hand and the muffin in the other to the porch. She pushed the screen door open with her elbow, and stepped down. Carefully balancing the filled mug, she moved to her favorite rocking chair and sat down on its worn comfortable seat. The steam from the hot brew drifted up to her nose and she immediately felt content.

As she took another bite of the sweet muffin, she thought that if she didn't get a move on, she would lose all of her ambition.

Her mind raced over her list of 'to do' things. Still waiting for her attention was the piece half written, for one of the local horse journals. Sam not only cared for her farm but she held down two part-time jobs. She taught online courses for a local college, and also worked as a free-lance journalist.

"Someday," she thought, "I'll write the novel that's dancing around in my head. I just need the time and focus to do it. Hmmm, maybe a winter project."

Sam felt most alive when she came up with new ideas to work on, and loved to daydream about where her life would be in the next five years.

"Yes, that's it," she thought, excited to plan her next venture. "I'll start writing my novel this winter. Well, unless the snow hits us like this past winter, and then I'll have to make it part of my summer plan. She suddenly felt like there would never be a good time to take on a large project like writing a novel. She reminded herself to be more positive. Maybe she'd start by writing her thoughts down in a journal.

"That'll work," she mused. "Part of my five-year plan." Now she felt better.

As she wiped her mouth with a napkin, her mind ran through her latest project. The deadline for submission was the end of the month, and she wanted to complete it before Denver came home.

Denver, her fiancé, had been out of town on business for two days and during their last telephone conversation, he mentioned he had something important to talk over with her. He was planning to visit his folks in Texas at the end of the month, and she had a gut feeling it had something to do with his visit. She knew how much they wanted him to move back to Texas, but he always assured her that he had no intention of doing so, no matter how hard they tried to persuade him. Still, the phone call had unsettled her. Maybe that's why she was out of patience this morning. She felt something big was coming down the road.

"Enough!" she scolded herself. "Stop worrying about something that may be nothing. Give it up and get going." She drained her coffee and got up from the chair. It was time to clear her head, concentrate on the positive and not fill her mind with worry about things that may never come about. Minnie's words came to her. "Always live in the moment and don't get in a twit about things you have no control over, and may never happen."

She shook her head to chase away her unease, and although she still wondered about the call, she decided Minnie's advice was worth taking.

# Chapter 5

Lyla could not rid herself of the nightmares that haunted her since she made the treacherous trip back to her farm from Vermont. Many times in the middle of the night she found herself wide awake and drenched in sweat. The recurring nightmares had caused countless sleepless nights. Visions of the Mini farm, and the man called Doc, gave edginess to every part of her day.

She asked herself time and time again, "Do they know that I took GiGi? Are they looking for me?" These thoughts kept her constantly on guard. She was highly sensitive to any noise and was jumpy and fearful. No matter how much time she spent analyzing the situation, she didn't know what to do or how to solve her dilemma.

Logically, Lyla knew that by now someone would have contacted her about the Mini, but her fear was too deep-seated for common sense to rule. All of these thoughts ran through her head as she drained the last of her tea. She placed her spoon in the cereal bowl, left with remnants of granola swimming in milk at the bottom. Granola cereal, topped with bananas was her breakfast ritual; as such there was no thought of what to eat in the morning. Keep it simple was her philosophy.

Lyla picked up the cup and bowl, and carried them to the counter. After rinsing them and placing both in the dishwasher, she left the house and walked down to the barn to feed her pony Chip, and her Mini horse GiGi. This was her good morning kiss, and her favorite time of day.

She slid the barn door open and walked in to be greeted by her old barn cat Timmy. The scruffy thin tiger cat ran up to her and rubbed his body against her legs as she entered, leaving a swath of barn dust on her jeans. Lyla bent down and scratched behind his ears.

"How are ya old buddy? I know you're hungry. Wait a minute and I'll get your food for you." As she ran her hand down his back, Timmy arched it in typical cat response.

Chip, her black and white pony was leaning over the stall rail and greeted her with a low nicker. He was anticipating his morning grain, and knew that food was on the way. Lyla stopped for a moment and ran her fingers under his bushy mane.

"Good morning Chip," she said as the pony leaned into her hand.

"I know you want me to just keep on scratching, but I've got to get going."

Chip flicked his ears and moved his head closer and then raised it for her to scratch under his chin. "Ooh does that feel good?" she asked the contented pony as he reached his head higher for more scratching.

A small whinny, from the stall next to Chip drew Lyla's attention. It was followed by the impatient sound of a small hoof scraping the stall floor.

"Don't worry GiGi. I haven't forgotten you."

Lyla left Chip and walked to the next stall.

A small chocolate colored filly stood at the stall gate. On her forehead was a tiny white star. Her dark nose poked out through the slats. She was just tall enough for her eyes to peek through the open space.

"Hey there cutie. I see you," Lyla laughed. "Look at you. You're finally growing tall enough to reach the first board."

GiGi pushed her head in closer and Lyla reached down and ran her hand over the soft nose of the tiny filly.

"There you go my sweet girl, but you need to wait a minute."

Lyla quickly walked to the tack room and filled a pail with grain. Suddenly a loud crash came from the front of the barn. The noise startled her and she dropped the pail. The pail crashed, and all the grain dumped onto the floor. Lyla froze in place. "What was that? Oh my God!"

Timmy came running into the tack room. He rubbed his body against her leg again. Lyla caught her breath. The touch from the cat quieted her jangled nerves, but she was still so frightened, she hesitated to call out to see if anyone was there. She stealthily moved to the tack room door and peaked out. Nothing. Seeing no one there, she regained her composure and walked to the front of the barn. Timmy had knocked over a large can that had sat on the edge of the stall rail. It had hit a large metal storage can as it fell. It was as simple as that. Lyla picked up the can and set it back on the rail and hurriedly returned to the tack room to get more grain.

"I just can't shake the jitters," she thought as she scooped the grain into the pail. "I'm still afraid. When is this going to end?"

She reached for the broom and swept the grain from the floor onto a dust pan. "What am I going to do?"

For the next half hour Lyla worked on quieting her rattled nerves. She fed Chip and GiGi, and then brushed them down. Brushing them helped quiet her jangled nerves. The rhythmic movement of the brush on their warm bodies helped to regain her composure. It was a peaceful process and one she enjoyed. While she brushed, Lyla talked to them. They were her friends and solace in her lonely life.

After Chip and GiGi were meticulously brushed and curried, she led them to a small paddock next to the barn. She had already dropped a pile of hay in each corner of the paddock and she took a moment to watch them happily munch away.

"I love these moments," she thought as her eyes scanned the pasture and mountainside.

The mountains were filled with green, and for a brief moment she was content. "It looks like a picture perfect day. I could stand here for hours but I've got to get a move on. I still need to shower, and time is passing quickly."

With that thought in mind, she turned and walked back to the barn. She still had stalls to clean, and although her job at the bakery didn't start until ten, she felt an urgency to complete her chores before she left for the day.

Lyla poured some cat kibbles into a bowl for Timmy, picked up her manure fork, and walked the wheelbarrow to the first stall. She loved cleaning stalls. Most people who didn't own horses thought that it was too much work, but she found it helped her to relax and plan her day. To her, there was nothing like the smell of the barn. Music from the radio filled the air and this was her quiet time before she began her work at the bakery. It was also a time to think about GiGi and what would become of both of them.

While she worked, she thought about her job at the bakery. Thank goodness they didn't know her that well. If they did, they would have noticed changes in her behavior. She recognized that she was more jumpy and was also suspicious of new customers. When the bakery door opened and she didn't recognize the new person, her heart jumped and goosebumps ran down her arms.

It didn't help that she hadn't made any close friends at the bakery. She was naturally shy and growing up, her father always told her, "Work is work, and your personal life should never be shared there. Save yourself a lot of trouble, and keep your personal life to yourself."

Heeding her father's words, she did just that. Lyla made it a habit not to share her personal life with anyone at work, but the downside was that it made her seem mysterious and aloof to fellow employees. They would have been amazed to learn that when she wasn't baking, she loved to strum the guitar and sing old Arlo Guthrie songs. They did know that she had an elderly aunt who lived in Vermont who had fallen and broken a hip. She had to reveal that much, because she needed a leave from the bakery to care for her. Jennifer, the only person she had shared any of her personal life with at the Taste of Home bakery, also knew that Lyla's parents had died in an auto accident. And after settling their estate; she had moved to Mansville and bought a small farm on the outskirts of town.

Since moving to Mansville, Lyla had worked hard to build a new life. She was young and on her own, and although she could have stayed in the town she was born in, she felt compelled to move away from the sad memories and start over. She loved her farm and enjoyed her job at the bakery, but deep inside she knew it wasn't enough. Although she dated now and then, her shy nature made her seem unapproachable to most men. As content as she was, Lyla was smart enough to know that something was missing, and although she hated to admit it, that something was someone to share her life with.

One thing she knew for sure, she hadn't taken time to meet many people since relocating to Mansville. Her mother always said that if she wanted to have friends she needed to be a friend, and with that in mind she decided she would put in the effort and work on her social life.

An avid reader, Lyla had met Patty at the library and she enjoyed her easy laugh and endless chatter. They had met several times for coffee, and Patty had invited her to join her book club. The meeting was going to be at Patty's home on Tuesday evening, and she was eager to introduce Lyla to her friends. Lyla had finished reading the chosen book, and had promised Patty that she would bring the dessert. Chocolate cream filled cupcakes would be a hit, and Lyla was very excited to meet everyone. Most of all, she needed a distraction to help with her anxiety over GiGi.

Patty stopped at the bakery several times a week and knew that Lyla's forte was baked breads, muffins, and desserts of all varieties. The last time they met for coffee, Lyla brought her a jar filled with granola cereal. It was one of her new recipes and she asked Patty for her input. It was during these coffee hours that Patty discovered that Lyla made granola using her mother's recipe, and had a growing market for it. She poured the mixtures of dried fruits and grains into blue jars decorated with white flowers. Blue was Lyla's trademark color. Although Patty did not share Lyla's passion for baking, they both loved gardening and endlessly searched catalogs for new and interesting varieties of herbs, vegetables, and flowers.

Lyla confided in Patty that her dream was to open her own bakery, and she became her best cheerleader. Lyla's brain overflowed with designs for a small shop, and testing new varieties of savory desserts consumed most of her free time. Her best estimate was that it would take another two years to reach her goal. In the meantime, she sold her baked goods at the local farmer's market. She had developed a great following and her stand was always filled with eager customers. Sales were up and people were now asking to buy her products from her home. Patty, who never cooked or baked if she could help it, was fascinated with Lyla's culinary skills. She admired Lyla's spirit and her passion for baking, while Lyla admired Patty's easy going nature and upbeat attitude.

The sound of a dog barking snapped her back to reality.

"Darn," she thought. "My life was on the right track. Now I have trouble sleeping at night, agonizing over my secret." A flash of regret passed through her mind as she reflected on that dark night and how the impulse to save GiGi had changed her life.

Lyla pitched another fork full of manure into the wheelbarrow. She wished she could concentrate on her new recipe for granola, but again her mind kept reliving the night she ran with GiGi from the farm in Vermont.

"Oh my God," she thought. "I can't believe what I did!"

It still shocked her that she had done something so dangerous. In her wildest dreams she couldn't envision taking someone else's horse. Fear for GiGi's life had driven her to do something even she couldn't comprehend, and her suspicions about Doc and the Mini farm had forced her into action. It was all about what she read in the black binder that had put her in this situation, and now she found herself in a predicament where she could find no answers.

"What should I do now?" She was always left with this question and she had no answer.

Although it had been two months since she and GiGi had made the crazy ride back home, she still felt unsafe. Time and distance were not helping, and she believed that it was only a matter of time until someone would come looking for her. Then what? She was too afraid to go to the police, but she needed someone to help her figure out what to do. Her guilt was wearing her down, but fear kept her from going to the authorities. Trust was a big issue for her. Who could she take into her confidence?

# Chapter 6

## Pine Hollow Farm

A full moon illuminated the landscape, and tall trees cast ghostly shadows over the meadow and barns. It was two a.m. and all of the Mini horses had been loaded onto trailers and were on their way to another horse farm several states away. Carver watched as the last diesel truck, pulling a long horse trailer, slowly moved down the dark road that led from the barn.

In his usual abrupt manner, Doc had informed Bill and him a week ago that his project was complete and it was time to pack it up. The transport of horses, cleaning barns, and emptying the lab had begun when darkness fell, and by sunrise Doc expected the move to be complete. He had left the arrangements for the gigantic undertaking in Carver's hands. Carver scrambled to make it happen, and the caravan of moving trucks and vans with cleaning crews had arrived at sunset. Almost a year had passed since he was hired as the Security Manager for the farm, and although at the time he had no idea how long the job would last, it was his responsibility to plan for the dismantling of the farm on a moment's notice.

Large lights lit up the whole area and there was no wasted time as the movers worked quickly to complete the job. Carver was relieved that Doc had run such a tight ship, demanding the barns be kept immaculate and the lab pristine. It made everything easier. Empty trailers moved in and full trailers moved out in orderly fashion.

There were at least fifteen men loading trailers, cleaning out barns, and removing furniture from Doc's office and living quarters. As Carver stood watching, men dressed in white coveralls, masks, and head covers, were cleaning and sterilizing the lab. Thick white foam covered the lab walls and huge pieces of machinery made loud sucking noises as they extracted loose material and residue. Doc's lab equipment had been already loaded and trucked away and the suited men were an eerie site as they sanitized every part of the lab. The farm looked like it had been invaded by a task force of aliens.

Pine Hollow was returning to its original state, a farm with barns and fields and turnout areas. It would be left just the way Doc had found it when he moved in with his equipment and herd of Mini horses.

The farm had been carefully selected and it was accessed by an old road that wound around the side of a mountain. Most people driving by would not notice the private road that led to the farm, since it was nestled between trees and mostly hidden from view. Hanging haphazardly from a bent post and wrapped in tangled vines, the farm sign was barely visible to passing traffic. A long unkempt dirt road was the only way to and from the farm, and an iron gate blocked the entrance. Heavy and cumbersome, it had to be lifted and moved to the side of the trees to allow a vehicle to drive through, and then moved back to its resting place once it had passed. Nothing had been done to fill in the deep ruts that pummeled a car or truck, and drivers soon found that driving more than five miles an hour was a dangerous feat. After cautiously driving through deep ruts, at times filled with mud, the road ended abruptly and opened to large overgrown fields, broken fences, and several barns and paddocks. They were the remnants of a once productive farm, filled with cows and a few horses. Unfortunately, a fire had destroyed the farm house and only the stone foundation was left as the lone reminder of the family that had once lived there. After the fire, the farm had sat idle for several years, until Doc and his partner purchased it, and hired a contractor to refurbish the barns and paddocks.

The barns had been restored to fit the needs of the operation, and a large amount of money went into building and furnishing the state-of-the-art laboratory. A huge loft over the main barn was home to Doc's office and apartment. The sweet smell of hay lingered in the air and stray chaff could still be found in small corners of the loft. A recluse, and not a man concerned about where or how he lived, the apartment was sparse and small. His research was his priority, not his living accommodations. The narrow living room was furnished with a brown speckled sofa and a single table with a tall blue lamp plopped on it. A small flat screened TV hung from the wall, providing a respite when he felt the need to clear his mind from the magnitude of his work. An adjoining room held a single bed and narrow closet, and adjacent to that was a bathroom with a shower stall. A sliver of a galley kitchen was fitted with a sink and counter, coffeemaker, apartment sized refrigerator, and microwave. There was no need for a washer or dryer as Bill the farm's foreman, picked up Doc's duffel bag of dirty clothes and linens from his office once a week, and dropped them off at the Laundromat in town.

Although a portly man, Doc's diet was limited since he didn't cook. His meals were mostly TV dinners and whatever else he could microwave. His one vice was beer, and he enjoyed a cold one now and then. A six pack took up most of the space in his refrigerator and aside from the food brought in from the local deli; he filled himself with cupcakes and candy bars. Junk food was his obsession, and regardless of his plump paunchy body, he wasn't about to change his ways. Physical appearance was not something he cared about, and he was oblivious to anything except his research. A work fanatic and a man without the need of friends, Doc had not left the farm since the day he moved in.

Farm workers were hired with careful scrutiny and paid high wages to do their job and not ask questions. When hired, they were told the farm was owned by a pharmaceutical company working to develop a horse vaccine. Each job at the farm had its own set of rules and procedures, and everyone was expected to adhere to them. Large white signs listed the procedure for horse care, collecting mare's milk, and the disposal of foals. Insolence or bad behavior was not tolerated and there were no second warnings. Interestingly, only one employee, a woman from Massachusetts, had caused a serious problem, and Carver, Doc, and Bill had mulled over the situation for several days before they decided what action to take. In the end, they decided to do nothing. Chances were she would never go to the authorities and talk about the farm. After all, she had stolen the foal, and they were sure she didn't want any trouble. The whole incident was better left alone. Carver had grown fond of the pretty red haired woman, and convinced Doc that the matter wasn't worth pursuing. The sly man had reluctantly agreed, but only because he had completed his operation and it was time to pack up and leave Vermont. Carver and Bill were in the dark about this piece of information because Doc shared only what he deemed important. His modus operandi was to keep everyone in the dark until the last possible moment.

Bill had never been inside Doc's living quarters, and Carver avoided going there as much as possible. The apartment was untidy, and littered with pieces of paper. Overflowed trash poured out of waste baskets and it was a wonder he could find his bed. One thing for sure, living in the middle of a huge mess did not concern him. Stacks of computer printouts were piled high against the wall, and discarded clothes littered the floor.

The first time Carver had to enter Doc's apartment was when Bill called and asked if he had heard from the short-tempered man. He hadn't, and Doc didn't answer his cell phone when he called. Against his better judgment, he decided to check on him and headed up the stairs to the apartment. Passing through the office, he was disgusted with the messy small room and wondered why Doc couldn't at least pick up after himself. Cupcake and candy wrappers, along with empty Styrofoam cups were scattered on the floor. Kicking aside a crinkled empty cookie box, he knocked on the door located behind the cluttered oak desk, piled high with printouts and an open laptop. Doc opened the door on the fourth knock. His messy hair was standing up straight on his head and his sloppy untucked white T-shirt spilled out over baggy grey pants, held up by black suspenders. An unshaven face with bloodshot squinty brown eyes peered out at Carver. As usual he looked like he had slept in his clothes, and was in his typical disagreeable mood.

"What!" he demanded in a surly voice.

"Just checking on you. You didn't answer your cell phone."

"Don't worry about me. I'm fine. I worked through the night and didn't get to bed until the sun was coming up. As long as you're here, tell Bill I expect my reports ready and in my hands in five minutes."

"Will do," he replied as he closed the door. "Knew I shouldn't have bothered," he thought as he walked down the stairs, sorry he had listened to Bill.

"Next time you check on him," he told Bill when he gave him Doc's message. "He's not my problem."

Bill returned Carver's annoyance with a harrumph, and then rushed off to retrieve the paperwork before there was hell to pay. The routine for Doc was always the same. He worked until he could no longer concentrate, and got by on as little sleep as possible. His chronic bloodshot eyes said it all, and his short temper, lack of patience, and disdain for loud noise were all signs of sleep deprivation. He insisted on a quiet barn, and God help anyone if he happened to enter the barn and it wasn't. Even the horses' whinnies grated on his nerves and he barely tolerated the low playing radio. Everyone at the farm considered Doc a very strange man and did their best to stay out of his way. He kept to himself and there was never interaction between him and the farm hands. It was common knowledge that even after almost a year Doc didn't know any of the workers by name, and even his contact with Bill was cautious and limited.

Most of Doc's time was consumed with his research and he hurried to the barns only if Bill thought it was urgent. He had no interest in foals, and only the health of the mares was significant enough to draw his attention. Mares and their precious milk were the focus of his research. Although some mares died, and most foals never made it beyond the first few days of life, Doc believed the equines were expendable, and only the outcomes were relevant to his research. Behind his back, the workers called him the Grinch, but they never questioned his authority. High paying salaries kept them content and they learned to stay out of the bad-tempered man's way.

Having no medical background, Carver didn't understand the exhaustive study and testing required to develop a horse vaccine, so he was compelled to rely on Doc's justification. He felt really bad when a foal died, but it was made clear by Doc, that research was trial and error and in the end the results would be worth the sacrifice. Besides, losses were expected when developing new vaccines. Carver had his suspicions that Doc wasn't being truthful, but it wasn't his job to ask questions about the farm's operation. Research was not his field of expertise, and he was hired to provide a specific need. His job was to protect the farm from outside intrusion or inside theft. Highly-skilled with computers and surveillance cameras, he had been employed by many large corporations to guard against physical or computer threats. Doc hired him because of his notable background in Corporate Espionage and Intelligence Gathering.

Prior to this job, he had worked with several CEO's with difficult personalities, but Doc was in a league of his own. He was an enigma, and Carver viewed him as a man obsessed with research, but socially inept. After observing him for months, he had come to his own conclusions about the bad-tempered man. He believed Doc was a recluse with a brain that was filled with statistics and lab results. There was no room in his brain for anything else, since it was constantly on overdrive and pushed to the limits with what Carver called 'computer overload.'

Immediately after Doc purchased Pine Hollow, Carver began the work of setting up the intricate monitoring system that would become the eyes and ears of the farm. Out of view and hung on fine wires above the tree canopy, small security cameras captured every move. In a hidden room behind the wall of Doc's office, footage from the cameras streamed to a wall of flat screen monitors. The farm was impenetrable, except for the workers who swiped a card imbedded with a thumb print, each time they entered or left the farm. Electric fence lines, cameras, and alarms kept constant guard. His smart phone was with him at all times and he could access the streaming videos at any given moment. Cameras monitored and captured all movement throughout the property, barns, and the lab. Big Brother was watching and only Doc and Carver knew about the cameras and where they were located. Pine Hollow Farm was a mysterious, strange place.

Everyone had worked non-stop to remove the massive amount of equipment from the farm, however the workers were not allowed into Doc's office until he had removed his research papers, lap top, and precious black binder. A heavy duty shredder had been brought in, and Carver had been busy most of the evening feeding it piles of documents that were no longer needed. Only after Doc's office was empty of any remnants of files and paperwork, did he allow the cleaning crew and movers to enter the office and living quarters.

Doc loaded his personal items into a dark colored SUV and stopped for a moment to look around. Finally, he had what he came for and at last he was at ease. A subtle smile came to his lips. Everything was on schedule and he had one last thing to do. He called Carver and Bill on his cell phone, and asked them to meet him at the main barn to do a final walk through.

As he waited for the men to arrive, the short stocky man pulled a grey handkerchief from his pocket and wiped the sweat from his forehead. He shook his head in amazement. It was a marvel that the farm had been emptied and cleaned in one night, and if it had been his temperament, he would have done a dance and yelled hurray. He and his partner had succeeded with their secret initiative. No one knew the true story behind his research, and the havoc that the biological product they had been working on could cause. If they did, they would have been astounded. His thin lips curled ever so slightly in a smile, as he thought about what he had accomplished.

Carver had finished loading the last box of personal items into the back of his pickup when his phone rang. He slammed the tailgate closed and answered. It was Doc and he wanted to talk to him and Bill in his office. He ran his hand through his thick hair and rubbed his eyes. It had been a long night and he was ready to finish up. After drinking too much coffee, his nerves were on edge and his stomach growled with hunger. He was anxious to get through this last meeting. Towards the East he could see the beginning of a sunrise and if Doc wanted to be gone by then, they had all better get a move on. The sound of Doc's voice barking out orders, grated on his nerves and he was relieved that this job was done. It ended just in time as far as he was concerned. Fortunately, this was the last time he would have to listen to the voice of the irritable, annoying man. The idea of locking him in a closet and throwing away the key was sounding more and more appealing. Carver shuddered when he thought of working at the farm any longer. Thank God he enjoyed his life away from Pine Hollow, and when his work day was over he socialized with people he actually liked. Walking towards the office, his mind processed the information he had learned about Doc and the operation at the farm.

For sure, Doc had a partner, but he had never been introduced to him. That was odd, since the man kept him abreast about new employees or shipments of equipment that needed his security clearance. Another thing that caught his attention were the frequent phone calls that occurred at odd hours. When the phone rang, Doc moved away from ear shot to speak with whoever was on the other end. The strange calls always intrigued Carver, but it was none of his business. However, what did interest him were the visits from a man with a heavy foreign accent. Doc was in a twit when the visitor arrived in his black sedan and he hustled him to his office, all the while talking in a highly animated way. The mysterious man never made eye contact or spoke to anyone, but the foreigner appeared to be more than just a friend, and Carver assumed he was involved with the farm operation but how much he didn't know.

Doc's office and living quarters were the only places on the farm where surveillance cameras were not set-up. He had made that very clear when Carver was designing the plans to meet his security requirements.

Carver's mind was still puzzling over it all when he reached the door, gave a quick knock and opened it. Bill and Doc were deep in conversation but stopped talking when he walked in.

"Looks like we're all set but we need to take one more walk through all the barns before we give the okay for the last truck to leave," Doc said.

Bill held a clipboard with the list of everything that had been moved from the farm. His eyes showed the stress and exhaustion from the night's work, but Doc's eyes never looked sharper. The three men spoke briefly, left the office, and walked towards the barns and lab.

As they entered the first barn, Doc's eyes carefully scanned every corner of the stalls that had once housed horses and foals. Bill made a notation on the clipboard, and they continued to move to the next barn, and then the lab. It took a half hour to finish the final inspections, and satisfied that nothing had been left behind, they made their way to the last truck.

"You're good to go," Carver said to the driver. The driver, a large man with a scruffy beard, saluted, put the truck in gear, and turned the rig towards the dirt road that led from Pine Hollow.

The men watched the truck pull away. The sun was now peeking from behind the mountains, and the blackness of the night finally was giving way to the rapidly growing day light. They no longer needed flashlights or the large flood lights for vision, and the barns and barren fields were almost visible. For a moment no one said a word. The farm appeared ghost-like and strangely quiet. It was uncanny to see the empty barns and to hear nothing but the chirping of birds as they welcomed daylight. Pine Hollow, once a beehive of activity was still.

The silence was broken by the shrill ring of Doc's cell phone. He shuffled to the side of the barn to speak to whoever was on the other end. Carver heard him say something about 'he would see him soon.' He and Bill looked at each other knowingly. There was no question in their minds that the caller on the other end was the mysterious man Doc was in some way involved with. They stepped away from his conversation and began one of their own.

"So, what are your plans now that the job is done?" Carver asked Bill.

"I'll go back to Maine. I've got my farm there, and I've earned enough to be able to sit back for a while. And you?"

"Well, I've come to like Vermont, and I have a few months off before my next job begins, so I think I'll hang around for awhile."

Their conversation was cut short when Doc joined them.

Doc turned to Bill and gave his last orders. "Bill, you'll meet with the workers when they come in and give them their final pay checks along with a bonus, and I'll send your paycheck to you when I get your final report."

"Okay," Bill said. "I'll call you later today."

"Fine," said Doc. And for the first time since he had known him, Doc held out his hand to shake Bill's.

Next he turned to Carver. "Your job is done. I have everything I need from you," he said as he held his hand out. Carver shook Doc's hand and was mildly surprised by its firm grip. It wasn't what he expected from the short plump figure, but then there was a lot he didn't know about the man who had hired him.

"You'll both be hearing from me," he said." His steely eyes grew intense and his lips twisted in a half smile. "I know where to find you."

Before they could reply, he turned and walked away.

Bill stared at his former boss until he reached his vehicle, then turned to Carver and shook his head. "So, what the hell does that mean? I can't figure that man out."

"Me neither, but I guess it means something to him," Carver said.

It amused Carver to watch Bill puzzling over Doc's parting words. He wasn't the kind of man to be easily intimidated, but if he guessed right, Doc had done just that. The man standing next to him wasn't the sort of guy Carver would choose to hang out with. Carver studied the hard-handed man as he continued to glare at Doc's back.

Bill had been a stern taskmaster, ruling the farm and employees with his sharp voice and demanding requirements. But, he got the job done and Carver knew that's just why Doc had hired him. He was about fifty years old, medium height and had thinning grey hair, kept shortly cropped. His body was muscular from years of hard labor, and his brown eyes could turn mean in a minute. Bill had told Carver he had done a long stint in the Marines, and he looked every bit the part of a boot camp sergeant. Bill was a horseman, not a people person, which suited Doc just fine. A no-nonsense guy who was gruff and scary, he never had to give an order twice. Doc let him run the farm with a free hand and little interference. One look from Bill's flashing eyes was all it took to get the work done in the way he ordered and expected.

Any questions about the farm's purpose, or the foals that died were answered with a short, snarly retort, "It's none of your business. Just do the job you were hired for."

All employees were expected to be on time, work the hours required, and do what was necessary. If you couldn't do the job, so be it. Find another one was his attitude, and he had no problem making that clear to everyone.

"Not someone I could chug down a beer with," thought Carver as he watched Bill walk back to the barn carrying a briefcase filled with paper work and checks. "His job's not finished, but mine sure as hell is."

Carver yawned. It had been a long exhausting night, and he needed sleep. He couldn't wait to get home and hit the sack. When he first arrived to begin his security job, he had leased a comfortable farm house about five miles from Pine Hollow and he planned to take some time to unwind before his next job began. Plus, he needed some respite from the long hours at the farm and the constant barrage of demands from Doc and Bill. Unlike them, he had made a life in Barnsville, and was friendly with the people who worked at the farm. He often met a few of the guys for lunch at the Blue Cat Bakery and Deli and one in particular had become a friend. Jace and he met several nights a week to play a game of pool and enjoy a few cold beers. Jace owned two horses, and during their free time they rode out on some of the beautiful mountain trails. They had a lot in common. Both were single and marriage shy. Once in a while Carver had taken one of the waitresses from the Blue Cat out to dinner, but his work schedule didn't leave much time for a social life. Since he had lived in Barnsville, only one woman had interested him enough to make time for, and it was the one he had covered for. He thought she liked him, and just when he had decided to ask her out for dinner, she left without notice. She was not only pretty; she was sweet and kind hearted. Lyla was the type of woman a man could fall really hard for.

Although his job required travel, he had come to like the town of Barnsville and the people who lived there. His type of work required a lot of travel, but maybe it was time to put down some roots. As he rubbed his tired eyes, he thought about what was next for him. After living in Vermont for almost a year, he felt comfortable with the rural lifestyle. It was peaceful as well as beautiful, and it would be nice to settle down in one place. The house he was renting was for sale, and he was considering whether or not to buy it and make Vermont his base of operations. For an instant his mind wandered to the slim woman with the red hair. He smiled. Maybe it was time to phone her.

# Chapter 7

Sam felt a presence next to her bed before she was fully awake. She blinked her sleepy eyes open, and stared straight into the round dark eyes of Ranger. He was so close she could feel his breath on her face, as he waited patiently for her to stir. Once she opened her eyes, it was his signal that he had done his job. His tail rapidly wagged back and forth in anticipation of Sam getting out of bed, and it thumped loudly against her night stand. She had no choice but to get up and get going.

"What the heck are you doing?" Sam asked the apricot colored shaggy dog.

She stretched and then rubbed her eyes. Ranger continued to stare and wait for his best friend to sit up and pat his head. How long he had been sitting there, she had no idea. But it was becoming a habit to find him sitting by her bed in the morning. No need for an alarm clock when she left her bedroom door open. The Labradoodle had a keen sense of timing and was ready for morning chores long before Sam was. Ranger was proving to be a dog that loved being by her side and she knew he had developed a strong bond with her. Of course when Denver showed up, Ranger's true love was apparent to even the casual observer. Once Denver arrived, it was all about them. Denver could throw the ball over and over for the shaggy dog to catch, and Ranger never tired as his body hurdled into the air, flying over obstacles along the way. Playtime and the ball was what

Ranger lived for and it was as much fun for Denver as it was for the dog. When Denver was around he was the only person that mattered. Sam was the disciplinarian, and Denver was the playmate.

"Gosh when Addie said you'd be a loyal family dog I guess I didn't grasp the full meaning of her words," Sam said as she leaned over and patted Ranger's head. "You're such a good boy." Ranger licked her hand, stood up and did a circle, while waiting for her to put her feet into her slippers and follow him to the kitchen.

"Okay mister, let's go. Now that you woke me, I need a cup of coffee."

She reached over and pulled her robe on, and headed for the bathroom to brush her teeth. It was time to begin the day.

After showering and dressing, she made her way to the kitchen, opened the screen door and let all three dogs out. The dogs made a mad dash outdoors, jumping and running into each other. Returning to the kitchen, she dropped a bagel in the toaster, took her yellow mug from the cupboard and placed a K-Cup in the coffeemaker. This was her morning routine, and the one thing in her busy life that rarely changed. She never ate a large breakfast before nine in the morning. Coffee and a cinnamon bagel with cream cheese was all that it took to get her engine running. Reaching into the cupboard she took out the last of her Christmas paper plates. She always had an abundance of them left from her Christmas Eve party, and she used them 'till they were gone. Besides, they had a happy look about them, and reminded her of all the fun the family had at the annual celebration at her farm.

She paused to admire the decorations on the plate. Three snowmen smiled back at her.

"Hey mister snowman! Hate to hurt your feelings but goodbye winter, hello spring, and welcome summer! I don't miss the cold and dreariness of winter. I'm excited to feel the sun on my face. No heavy coats to wear and no snow to plow. Just as well you're the last of my snowman plates. Be gone with you!" she laughed as she dropped her toasted bagel onto the plate.

Reaching over the counter she pulled out a paper napkin adorned with a pine tree branch and two brightly colored cardinals. She never tired of these napkins and wished she had bought more. Cardinals were her favorite bird. Smiling, she slipped the napkin into her jeans pocket.

"I wonder if today will set a record for heat," she thought as she carefully balanced her bagel and mug of coffee while she pushed open the screen door of the porch with her elbow. Carefully, she placed her mug on the table, took a moment to stretch and looked out over her backyard. Many of the spring flowers were blooming and trays of white Impatiens sat under the magnolia tree ready for planting.

"I want to get all of the annuals in the ground this weekend," she thought as she bit into the sweet bagel and wiped the cream cheese from the sides of her mouth.

Last weekend, Memorial Day, her pickup had been loaded with trays filled with flowering plants, bought at the annual Garden Club sale. It was an event that she looked forward to every Memorial Day. Yes the parade was fun, and yes she enjoyed the pancake breakfast at the Federated Community Church, but the plant sale was her favorite part of the festivities. All self-control was lost when her eyes were drawn to row after row of plants, and each one beckoned to her. The result was an over-abundance of plants to set in the ground. Try as she might, she could not suppress her eagerness to buy new varieties of flowers, but she never had enough time to design and dig new beds. The problem was solved by randomly planting them here and there throughout her backyard. The result was each year flowers of different colors and heights grew haphazardly across the landscape. The sticks with the names of the perennials got lost, and each spring flowers peeked through the soil and made their way to the sun, but she couldn't remember their names. Surprise flowers, she called them.

Consequently, there was no rhyme or reason to her flower bed designs. This year she had repeated what she had vowed not to do. She had bought too many plants and now the task to get them in the ground loomed ahead. Her friends found the whole thing totally crazy, but she called it her flower addiction. Sam often wondered if her friends thought she needed a Garden Club flower intervention.

The only Memorial Day she had not gone to the plant sale was last year. Her riding club friends had talked her into riding her horse in the parade. They rode every year but Sam always begged out. That year was the first and last time she would ever ride in the parade. After that crazy experience, she vowed to never do it again. Just thinking about that day made her laugh out loud. It was a near disaster when her friend's horse bolted and ran down the road in the middle of the parade. Lucky for her, Wil was a steady, solid horse and fortunately he didn't bolt and humiliate her on her first parade ride.

"Now that was a day I'll never forget," she thought. "At least everything ended okay, but it sure brought a lot of embarrassment to the club riders.

Taking another sip of coffee, her eyes scanned the sky. The air was noticeably steamy and unnervingly still, but the sky was clear with no sign of rain.

"Maybe we won't get the storm that's being talked about," she thought still looking up. But she knew that was just wishful thinking, and her mind moved to her list of things to do before the rain came.

Sally broke her daydreaming when she ran up to the porch, gave a little bark, and circled in front of her. It was as if she was saying "I'm waiting, hurry up."

"Okay, let's go," Sam said as she scratched the back of the Border Collie's ears."

Draining the last of her coffee, she got up from the chair and returned the empty mug to the kitchen. Enough dillydallying, it was time to begin morning chores.

It was the first day of June, and the unusually warm morning reminded her of last July when she and her friends rode their horses through the mountainside searching for a small herd of runaway cows. The cows had been on the loose for several months after escaping from her friend Tom's farm. That was one crazy adventure they still talked about. What they thought would take only a few hours, kept them out on the trail for the whole day. Between Caryn getting dumped in the brook, and her own horse Wil's leg breaking through the old wooden bridge, everyone wondered why they had decided to search for the cows on one of the hottest days of the year. Of course, each of them knew that if Tom asked for help, he would never be turned down. It was that simple.

The dogs were extra frisky, and took turns chasing each other as she made her way to Rudy and Roger's pen. Rudy and Roger bounded out of the goat house and followed the dogs and her to the barn. After settling the mares and foals in the paddock, she returned to the barn to clean stalls and feed the barn cats. The radio was turned up, and country music filled the air as Sam mucked out the stalls, but the unsettling interruption of weather reports kept her moving more quickly than usual.

Barn chores completed, she had one other task. A pile of manure waited to be moved with her tractor to the lower field. Sam jumped up onto the tractor and turned the key. Much to her surprise, the yellow tractor fired right up. Yellow Beast was having a good day and even though it growled and back fired in its usual nasty form, at least it didn't die. But although the tractor was raring to go, a sudden impulse to wait until tomorrow made her turn off the key. The urge to hurry before the storm came was foremost on her mind.

Worried, she climbed down off the tractor and whistled to the dogs. They followed as she climbed the ridge and hurriedly walked to the lower fields to check on the rest of the horses. They were grazing contentedly, and to her relief everything was okay.

By noon she had finished morning chores, and her stomach was growling. Hungry, she brushed her jeans off and headed to the house. All she could think about was a glass of cold lemonade and a grilled tomato and cheese sandwich.

The past couple of weeks had been unusually quiet for her. Denver was away on a business trip and wasn't expected home until early evening. The twins were on summer break from college, but they were staying with their dad and weren't due back until the end of the month. Life had changed immeasurably since last year. Once the twins were born, they and the farm had been her focus. Now grown and in college, Sam finally had more time to devote to herself, Denver, and her horses.

Sam's mind drifted to Denver and she thought about how resistant she was to be in a romantic relationship with him, or any man for that matter. Denver was patient and waited until she was ready. What began as a strong friendship grew into a romance and then an engagement. That Texan truly made her happy. He made her feel safe, loved, and cherished. The twins adored him and were anxious for their fall marriage. She looked down at her engagement ring and smiled. Sitting on the finger of her left hand was a green emerald, surrounded by small diamonds. For some reason, although his business required some travel, this time she missed him more than ever. Something about his phone calls, the sound of worry in his voice, made her uneasy.

Yesterday he had phoned and said he would love a dinner of spaghetti and meatballs when he returned. Denver would be content to eat pasta and sauce every day of the week. But Sam, accustomed to serving healthy food to the twins, kept the pasta request down to every few weeks. This time she agreed, and yesterday had made the homemade sauce and baked a pan of brownies, one of his favorite desserts. Now all that was needed to complete the menu was a loaf of Italian bread and vanilla ice cream to go with the brownies. Although there was plenty of time to go to the market, she felt she needed to hurry. She couldn't kick the feeling of unease.

After a quick lunch, she turned on the television to watch the weather report. A severe storm warning was still in effect. It seemed that the unusual warm day would be interrupted by a fast moving cold front. Heavy downpours and lightening were predicted. The reporter said to stay tuned throughout the day for more weather alerts.

As Sam finished the last of her lemonade, she felt a growing concern about the storm and picked up the phone to check on Minnie. The phone rang several times before it was answered by her cheery voice.

"Hello Sam. How are you honey?"

"Hi Minnie. I'm watching the weather report. Just thought I'd check in on you. Do you have your television on?"

"No I don't, but Doris called and said that a powerful storm is coming in around three this afternoon, and I was just going to phone you. Don't worry. I'll stay on top of it. I told Doris to pick up Dottie and come to my house. You know how Dottie hates thunderstorms."

Sam laughed when Minnie mentioned Dottie and thunderstorms. Dottie was deathly afraid of them. If she was by herself during a storm, she ran to her bedroom and covered her head with blankets. Loud thunder frightened her to the quick, and Dottie would never choose to stay alone if she could help it.

"That's good. Looks like you have time to get ready. Do you have fresh batteries in your flashlights in case you lose power?"

"Yes, everything's all set, and I have a blueberry pie in the oven and a deck of cards on the table. We'll play a game of Rummy to keep Dottie's mind off the storm."

Sam chuckled again. "Sounds like a plan. If you need anything, call me. I think everything will be okay, but I'll keep my cell phone close by."

"What time will Denver be home?" asked Minnie.

"He said late afternoon. I'm going to run my errands now and get everything I need. I'm so glad we put in the generator. If we lose power, everything will still work."

"Okay, I'll let you get going." replied Minnie. "Kiss, Kiss." Minnie made a kissing noise into the phone.

"Kiss, Kiss back at ya," replied Sam. "Don't forget to call me if you need anything."

Sam was relieved that everything was all set for the storm and that Denver would be home soon. But try as she might, she couldn't shake the unsettled feeling the constant weather reports were causing.

"Those weather reports always alarm us for nothing," she thought. "How many times had they frightened us with a bad weather forecast, and it ended up being nothing. At least the ladies will be safe at Minnie's, and they can ride out the storm together."

She smiled as she pictured the three ladies playing cards and eating pie. It sounded like they were ready for their storm party and they were planning on making it fun. Maybe she was worrying for nothing. She was beginning to feel like a Nervous Nellie.

Minnie's upbeat voice calmed any apprehension she had about the storm and as she walked to her truck she brushed away any lingering concern. As the truck left the driveway, the voice of Willie Nelson filled the cab with 'Always on my mind.' Sam sang along with her favorite vocalist and as always his voice brought her good friend, Chet Granger, to mind.

"I need to give him a call," she thought as she steered her truck around a corner. She vaguely remembered him telling her that in June he was trailering two Curly horses from his home in Virginia to New Hampshire.

"On my list," she thought as Willie crooned out his last note.

The market was packed and it took longer than expected to pay for the few items she bought. Everyone was concerned about the storm warnings. As usual when a storm is in the forecast, people swarm to the market to buy last minute items, and lots of comfort foods. Losing power because of downed trees and dangling electric wires was the topic of conversation. Having gone through several bad storms, the impending one bearing down on them was rattling everyone.

"Have you heard the latest weather update? Did you buy a generator after the last storm? Which one did you buy? Is it gasoline powered or propane?"

After listening to so much talk about power outages, Sam gave a sigh of relief. If the power went out, the well would work and the refrigerator would keep on running. She was all set.

"One less thing to worry about," she thought as she loaded her groceries onto the backseat of her truck.

Winter and summer storms had knocked her power out on several occasions, and her well was a priority. Sam's horses and other farm animals needed to have access to water. She couldn't afford to be without her well for more than a couple of days. Although a quick flowing brook ran through her property at the bottom of the mountain, it was a long way to carry water to the barn.

By the time she had put away her groceries, it was after two o'clock. She opened the fridge and found a place for the bowl of salad, and took out the tall pitcher of lemonade. The glass filled, she carried it to the family room, set it on a small table, and turned the television on to watch the latest weather report. The phone had been ringing non-stop since she arrived home. Everyone was worried about the same thing, being without power for an extended period of time.

A female reporter gave the latest update. "Severe storms will be passing through as a cold front moves in. Large hail and lightening should be expected. Be prepared to take cover. Stay tuned for the latest news as this fast moving storm hits our area."

Sam set her glass on the counter and walked to the screen door. The day was growing darker. There was no sound of thunder but she was keenly aware of the change in the temperature.

The sudden urge to bring in the mares and foals moved her quickly out of the house, and she jogged to the barn with the dogs scampering close behind.

After leading the mares and foals back in the barn, she walked up the ridge and looked down at the field below. Dark thunder clouds were quickly filling the sky. They were moving in from the West.

"Wow, this looks like it will be a huge storm. I think I got everyone in just in time."

The horses in the fields below the ridge were still grazing, unconcerned about weather reports or the ominous dark thunder clouds floating in. They turned their heads towards where she was standing, and then went right back to munching on the grass. When the rumble of thunder began, they would instinctively make their way towards their large run in sheds. Many times during heavy downpours, they stayed in the open fields and didn't bother to seek shelter.

Sam called those times "nature's baths." Horses knew when to take refuge without anyone coaxing them.

"If only humans had that sixth sense," she thought as she trotted to the goat shed with Rudy and Roger hot on her heels.

She had just closed the door to Rudy and Roger's shed when her cell phone rang. It was Denver.

"Sam where are you?" Denver's voice sounded frantic.

"I'm just going back to the house. There's a storm coming in so I brought the mares and foals in and closed up the chicken's coop and the goat's shed."

"Well, take the dogs and get in the house now! Get down in the cellar. There's a tornado coming your way." Denver was shouting into the phone.

"What? We don't get tornados here!" She was trying to make sense out of what he was saying.

"It's moving fast and heading in your direction. I tried the house phone and when you didn't answer, I left a message on the answering machine. Then I tried your cell phone and you still didn't answer."

"Oh my God! I left it on the rail and I never heard it ring," she yelled into the phone as she ran towards the house.

"Hurry up, and keep talking to me. Let me know when you're in the cellar. I'm about two hours away."

"You're breaking up. I can't hear you," she shouted into the phone. "I'm losing the signal. I love you," her cell phone went dead.

Sam slammed into the house. The three dogs were right behind her. She threw open the cellar door, flipped on the lights, grabbed a flashlight from the shelf, and ran down the stairs.

"Oh my God. I hope Minnie and the ladies are okay." she yelled aloud.

Even with the light on, it was dark in the far corners of the 'old dungeon,' the name she had christened her cellar. A hundred years ago, the cellar hole had been dynamited in order to break through boulders and ledge. It was the only way a foundation could be built. This was the first time Sam was happy that the cellar hole was deep in the ground and surrounded by huge boulders. She shined her light on an old wooden chair and dragged it to the corner wall. Then she sat down and waited. The dogs huddled around her.

The wind suddenly picked up and next came the sound of hail hitting the windows. The loud banging was deafening. Suddenly there was a piercing clap of thunder, and the lights went out. Only the light from the flashlight kept the dungeon from becoming totally black.

Now Sam was really scared, and she could feel her heart beating. The dogs were whimpering and Ranger had his head on her leg. If he could have, he would have climbed right up onto her lap. He was shaking. Sally and Jazz sat so close that they were sitting on her feet.

"It's okay," she said as much to reassure the dogs as herself. She ran her hands over each of the dog's head to quiet them. "We'll be fine."

71

The sound of hail died, but the rain was now beating on the windows. A tremendous clap of thunder seemed to shake the house. Lightning flashes, only seconds apart, danced outside the cellar window. Each time a flash came, a loud cracking noise came from the opposite side of the cellar wall where a copper grounding cable ran through the stone foundation. The storm seemed to be right over head, and the deafening sound of thunder exploded with such force that she held her hands over her ears. It was the most violent thunder she had ever experienced. Then quiet, but only for a moment. Just when she thought the worst was over, the sound of screaming wind whipped past the windows. Now she, as well as the dogs, was shaking.

"What about the barn and horses in there? Are Rudy and Roger okay? What about the horses in the fields?" She felt tears come to the corners of her eyes as scary thoughts ran through her mind.

Her thoughts raced to her twins. "Thank God they're visiting their dad. At least they're safe."

Denver came to mind and she forgot about herself and focused on the man she loved. "Where is he and is he okay? When will it end and what's happening outside?"

Tears welled up in her eyes and small streams of saltwater flowed down her cheeks. There was nothing to do but pray and as she did, she hugged Ranger tighter and waited for the storm to pass.

# Chapter 8

It had been a horrible ordeal for Sam, alone and frightened in the dark cellar, her dogs shaking as they huddled by her chair. When all was quiet, she made her way out of the cellar and was shocked at the power of the tornado. The first thing she saw when she opened her door was the tree in her backyard, split down the middle by lightening, and still smoking. Never in her lifetime did she think this would happen in New England, and never had she seen such destruction except on television.

The tornado touched down and roared up and down the mountain range felling trees and everything in its path. Its vortex cleared a jagged path through dense forest and small towns. The large swath of downed trees looked like piles of tangled matchsticks. The tornado left more than 39 miles of destruction as it traveled from one town to another and it leveled many homes and businesses. Some homes were blown from their foundations, and cars and trucks were crushed like paper bags.

Electric poles were snapped in half, trees were uprooted, and a direct lightening strike had split many trees along the road. Five towns, including hers, had been in the eye of the vicious tornado. The landscape was changed, power was out, trees and homes destroyed, and animals displaced.

Denver had made it to Sam's farm but only after parking his truck and walking the last mile. All roads into town were blocked by downed trees and power lines. For the most part,

Denver and Sam's homes had been spared, but trees torn up by the roots lay on fence rails, and a huge oak tree, broken at its trunk, blocked the driveway.

Sam's farm had sustained more damage than Denver's, and they worked until sunset cutting up felled trees and dragging huge branches into piles. As darkness fell, the generator was running and the house lights were on. Sam had phoned Minnie and the ladies. They were safe and more worried about her than themselves. To her relief, their town had been spared and their power was never lost.

The next day Sam and Denver were awake before the sun came up over the mountains. The early morning air was warm and it promised to be another hot day. After a quick breakfast of coffee and bagel, Sam and Denver went straight to work. In no time at all, the animals had been fed and foals and mares had been turned out. The arduous task of cleaning up the monstrous mess of fallen trees and broken branches began. Sam was grateful that none of her horses had been injured, and although fence rails lay crumpled by heavy tree limbs that had dropped on them; Rudy and Roger's shed was still standing. Even the chicken coop was in one piece, although she didn't think there would be any eggs for some time. The tornado had rattled everyone, including animals.

Sam and Denver spent the muggy morning dragging tree limbs and repairing fences. The air was filled with the sound of gas generators and chain saws. Cleaning up the mess was only a part of the toll that the tornado had caused. Trees that had survived the horrific wind were still standing, but huge limbs were ripped from their strong trunks and now lay in tangled piles on the ground. A large tree was pulled up from its roots, and leaned across the top of the barn, its branches and leaves covering the roof. The gambrel roof didn't show damage, but Denver was now working the chain saw, cutting the smaller trees surrounding it and slowly making his way to its large trunk. Justin and Kristy were flying home on Friday to help, but for now it was up to Sam and Denver to try and clean-up as much as they could. Their neighbors had their hands full, and it would be days before all of the damage could be assessed.

It was exhausting work. Fallen trees had to be moved with the tractor, and huge pine branches littered the open fields. Yellow Beast proved its worth. Denver had hitched a huge chain to the tractor and wrapped it around trees and branches that were strewn across the backyard and driveway. The tractor puffed and groaned as it dragged the heavy load behind its rusty body. Much to their relief, the old tractor didn't stall and had shown once again that it was a strong, tough machine. Sam was more amazed than Denver at the power of the tractor. Denver had already made several trips to the lower field, and Yellow Beast just kept on going. Its huge mouth, as Sam called the bucket, had been filled to capacity with broken branches. They hung out from each side of the bucket, and Sam was amazed that Denver was able to drive to the lower field without losing any of the debris. Yellow Beast took on a life of its own, and if she didn't know better, she thought it relished the act of doing something good. But then, she always thought of Yellow

Beast as a machine with human characteristics. It was stubborn, cantankerous, and annoying. Just when she was ready to junk it, the engine turned over like a charm, and although it gave its usual harrumph backfire, it coughed its way forward. Its crooked headlights and bent grill gave it a comical appearance, and its perpetual smile was frozen on its rusted front end. Beast's front tires were toed inward and its back tires didn't match. No wonder, Beast lumbered along swaying back and forth and was testy to drive. It was amazing that it moved at all. Denver loved to hear Sam talk to the tractor as if it was a person, but to Sam it didn't sound strange at all. The golden tractor she had fallen in love with years ago was not only a part of her farm, it was also a part of her life, and she was keenly aware that it had developed into a love-hate relationship. Love when it did the job, and hate when it would not start.

Sam watched as another load left the yard. The bucket was filled with the remains of the White Birch, which had toppled onto her backyard. The White Birch was one of her favorites, but the tall thin tree was no match for the fierce wind that had knocked it over. The driveway was now clear and things were looking somewhat better. Damage to her farm wasn't as terrible as her unfortunate neighbors, and looking around Sam now understood how tornadoes were selective in their path of destruction. Her property was on the edge of its path but neighbors up the road were not that lucky. Their damage was significant.

The cleanup work was hot and tedious. Sam was exhausted. After dragging a huge limb from an oak tree, she stopped for a moment to quench her thirst. Perspiration dripped from her forehead and trickled down into her eyes. Both eyes burned from the salty sweat, and she squeezed them tightly as she reached into her pocket to retrieve a tissue. Her neck ached and she tipped her head back and forth to relieve the pain, and then stretched her back sideways lifting her shoulders to get the kinks out. She took in a deep breath and looked around. It was going to be a long day. There was still so much work to be done, and she was tired and thirsty. She reached over and picked up a bottle of water that sat on top of a huge stump left from one of the toppled trees. The water felt good on her dry lips and she gulped down a large mouthful, and then drank more. The distant sound of the tractor faded just in time for her to hear her cell phone ring. She placed the bottle back on the stump and picked up the phone.

"Hello."

"Hi Sam."

"Hi Patty. How ya doing?"

"We're okay here. Still digging out but it could have been worse. We're a lot better off than some of our neighbors."

"I know," said Sam. "I can't complain. We're so lucky. It's a disaster just up the road. I know your town's in much worse shape than ours."

"It's terrible here," Patty said with a sigh. "I still can't wrap my head around it. Is Denver there?"

"Denver made it home yesterday. I was never so happy to see him. The twins are coming home on Friday to help."

77

"That's good," said Patty. "Your horses and goats okay?"

"Well, we've had damage to our fences, lots of trees down, and a large one lying on the barn roof, but thankfully no animal injuries."

"Thank goodness for that. Sam, I've a favor to ask. I've a friend whose barn was severely damaged. Roof ripped off and trees laying all over her property. She's in desperate need for a place to keep her pony and Mini horse until she can get her barn repaired. And she needs a Vet to check out their injuries. They both have cuts and gashes from fallen roof pieces. Would you have any room at your barn to keep them until she can get this done?"

"Oh my gosh! My heart goes out to her. Of course I'll take them. Tell her it'll be fine. I'm glad to help," Sam replied.

Sam had heard that many barns and fences had been damaged or destroyed. Volunteers were searching for lost pets, and many animals were in need of temporary shelters. Several horses had been killed and others injured. It seemed everyone knew someone who lived in the path of the tornado.

"I'll let her know you have room for her horses," said Patty. "Can we bring them to your farm this afternoon? They're in a temporary enclosure but need to be moved as soon as possible."

"Sure. We'll be here. Denver and I are still putting fences back together and cleaning up fallen trees. I'll get everything ready, and look for you sometime later. By the way, what's your friend's name?"

"Lyla Bernhart."

"Okay. I'll look for you and Lyla this afternoon," Sam said.

"Thanks Sam. I'll see you later." Patty clicked her phone off.

# Chapter 9

It was late afternoon, and Sam was working down at the barn when she heard the sound of a diesel truck. She put down her manure fork and walked to the top of the driveway. A dark blue pickup, with a blue horse trailer attached was slowly rounding the bend. Always on the alert for anyone coming up the long dirt driveway, the three dogs took off towards the sound. After three whistles and a loud yell from Sam, they quickly returned to her side and waited for the vehicle to come to a stop.

As the truck pulled up, Sam pointed to a turnaround spot. The driver slowly maneuvered the truck and trailer so that it faced towards the road, and then carefully backed the rig in the direction of the barn.

At the barn, the pickup truck braked and came to a full stop. The driver, a pretty red haired woman smiled at Sam as she opened the cab door and stepped down. The passenger door opened and Patty got out. She walked around the truck to greet Sam. Lyla and Sam were already introducing themselves.

"Hi Lyla, I'm Sam," she said as she held out her hand. "I'm so sorry to hear about all of the damage at your place. I'm glad you took my offer to bring your horses here. I've plenty of room in my barn and I'm glad to help you out."

"I can't thank you enough," said Lyla as she gratefully shook Sam's hand. "I'm so happy that Patty helped me out, and that you said yes. So many people in our town are looking for places for their animals. This whole thing has been a nightmare."

"For gosh sakes, Lyla. That's the least I can do for you, and by the way, that's what friends are for," Patty said.

Patty walked over to Sam and gave her a hug.

"Who's helping with your barn, and how is your house?" Sam asked as she studied the pretty young woman with the curly hair drawn back and tucked under a white baseball cap. There was something sweet and honest about her and Sam immediately liked her.

"My house had some damage, but not as much as my barn. I can't tell you how touched I am that people I have never met have come to help me. They showed up with ladders, chain saws, and large blue tarps. They covered my barn roof, and cut down the huge tree that fell on it. That should save some of the hay I've stored up there. I can't thank them enough and I don't know how I would have done this on my own."

"We're so lucky," Sam said as she looked around. "Fences down and toppled trees, but it just nicked us. I still can't believe the extent of damage just two houses up the road."

Sam's horses, Kai and Hope, heard the truck pull into the area in front of the barn and ran from the upper field to greet the new arrivals. The two horses were very inquisitive and they trotted along the fence line, whinnying and tossing their heads in excitement. The Mini and pony returned their calls, and voiced their impatience to leave the confines of the trailer by stomping the floor with their hooves.

"Time to unload, they want out," Sam said as she walked to the back of the trailer with Patty and Lyla.

"How do your horses know when a new horse arrives?" Patty asked.

"Horses have a strong sense of smell and also have an acute sense of hearing. They can be at the bottom of the field and know a new horse is at the barn. The older horses may whinny but continue grazing; however, the younger horses are more curious and will run up to see who's here. I think they're 'watch horses.' Even if someone is walking by their field they look up and call out. Those two are especially curious," she said as she pointed to Kai and Hope.

"They are so pretty," said Patty as she glanced at the black Curly and the sorrel Quarter Horse standing next to her.

While they were talking, Lyla lifted the pin out of the doors and pulled them open.

Sam watched as Lyla opened the doors, and was immediately captivated by the Mini horse standing next to a black and white pony. Although she had seen lots of Mini horses, this was by far the smallest one she had ever set eyes on. Lyla stepped up and into the trailer. She spoke softly to the horses but the Mini continued to paw the floor with her tiny hoof, while Lyla attached the lead line to her halter. Sam's eyes were drawn to the gaping laceration that began at the Mini's poll and ended down and onto the side of her neck. She glanced at the pony, and from what she could see his injuries didn't look quite as bad. A large gash ran across his rump, and several long gashes zigzagged down the side of his round body. Her eyes welled up with tears, and she squeezed them tight to stop their flow down her cheeks. A small shudder ran through her as she thought of the terror the horses must have gone through when the barn crashed down around them.

Lyla carefully backed the Mini out of the trailer, handed Patty the lead line and went back to unload the pony.

Once on the ground, both horses looked scared and Sam's eyes quickly scanned their bodies looking for other wounds. She noticed deep cuts and scrapes on each of the equines that weren't apparent in the trailer. The sound from the tornado and its unimaginable ferocity as it collapsed the barn must have been deafening. It alone would have been enough to spook any horse, but the wood and debris flying through the air must have frightened them beyond belief.

Patty glanced at Sam and knew she was surprised to see the injuries and concerned about the mental anguish that the horses had lived through.

"Half the roof of her barn was blown away and all of the windows were shattered," Patty said to Sam. "She's lucky her pony and Mini survived."

"God, I remember how traumatized I was when a coyote almost killed Kai. I know how it feels to almost lose a horse," Sam said as she reached out and touched Lyla's arm.

Lyla turned to Sam, still visibly shaking from the ordeal. "I'm still in shock, and I think it will take some time to get over this," she said with tears in her eyes.

"So, what are their names? " Sam asked as she stroked the pony.

"This is Chip," Lyla said with a smile, and this is my little princess GiGi."

"I've never seen anything so darn cute," said Sam.

GiGi, showing her nervousness, began dancing in place and Lyla spoke softly to quiet her as she ran her hand down the side of her neck.

"It's okay GiGi," she said. Her voice had a sing song tone, and the filly sensing her calm manner settled down and leaned her head against Lyla's leg.

"Well, she sure loves you," said Sam as she walked closer to GiGi and scratched under her chin. "Let's get them in the barn. I'll show you which stalls I have ready for them. We'll give them a leaf of hay and let them settle in." Sam took the pony's lead line from Patty and led the way.

After settling the horses in the barn, Sam asked Patty and Lyla back to the house for something to drink. The closer to the house they got, the louder the generator sounded.

"Does the loud sound bother you?" asked Patty.

"No, I'm used to it. I know it's noisy, but it's the one sound I'm happy to hear," Sam said as they entered the kitchen.

She opened the refrigerator and took out a pitcher of ice tea.

"The hum of gasoline generators is all I hear now," said Lyla as Sam handed her a glass filled with the cold drink. "It used to be so quiet, and now the air is filled with the jumbled sound of generators, chain saws, trucks, and tractors. We passed utility vans with license plates from so many different states we lost count. It's amazing to see how fast everything is being cut up, and power lines restrung. Nearly all of our electric poles were knocked down and lines were laying everywhere. It was very scary. Most people are still in shock, but helping others makes it easier. Since this happened I've met so many people I would never have known. I guess tragedy brings a community together, and that is the only good thing I can say about this disaster."

"You're right about that. I'm going to volunteer as soon as we finish-up here. That reminds me. I'm calling my vet right now to see if he can get here and take a look at your horses. By the way Lyla, do you need a place to stay?"

"No, I'm all set. But thanks for asking. My house is fine and except for no power, I'm okay. I can't thank you enough, Sam, for taking care of my horses and asking your vet to check them out. I cleaned the wounds as best as I could, but I know they need to be examined. I hope they don't need stitches, but some of the gashes are pretty deep."

"No problem. I know Doc Mike will be glad to come by." She picked up her cell phone and tapped in his number from her contact list. His phone answered with, "Leave a message and I'll get back to you as soon as possible."

Sam left a brief description of the horse's injuries and asked Mike to call her back.

"I sure dodged a bullet," said Patty as she took a sip of cold drink. "Nothing on my road was touched. My kids are fine and Ken is out helping with the clean-up. He's been

85

working with our chain saw all day. I've been helping at the church to distribute food and clothing and we're serving meals all day."

"We should be all set with our clean-up by tomorrow or the next day," Sam said. "I'll come by and see what I can do to help. I need to do something and I'm sure Denver will also be able to help. The twins will be home by the end of the week and I know they'll want to volunteer.

"Thanks Sam. I'll be there all week. Just ask for me. We can use everyone. There's so much to do. Already we're accepting truckloads of water and food and so many donations are pouring in that we're opening another church hall to manage everything. It's a huge undertaking to organize all the donations and get them to the neediest people."

"Well, if anything," Sam said with a smile, "I'm good at organizing."

An hour later, and after one more check on the horses, Patty and Lyla left to return to Mansville. Lyla's eyes showed the stress from exhaustion and worry, and Patty was bringing her home for a warm shower and badly needed rest.

For Sam the respite was over, and it was time to get back to work. Denver was still down in the lower field and she knew he must be thirsty and hungry. She filled a bottle with ice tea, and packed a tuna sandwich along with a few cookies in a tote bag and made her way out the door. After latching the gate to the dog's pen, she headed in the direction of lower field. The distant sound of the chain saw became clearer as she made her way past the piles of brush and tree limbs. There was still a lot of cleaning up to do, and the day was going by much too fast.

Although she felt compelled to hurry, she stopped at the barn to check on GiGi and Chip. GiGi was lying down and immediately got up when Sam reached her stall. Sam held her hand and GiGi nuzzled her fingers. Sam's hand caressed the filly's soft nose and she spoke to her. "How are you little one? You'll be okay now. Don't worry."

Chip nickered for Sam's attention and she reached over the rail and ran her hand down his forehead. "And yes, Chip, you'll be fine too, you pretty boy." She stood for a moment gazing at the horses that had miraculously survived the tornado, when others didn't.

"I wonder where Lyla found such a precious filly," she thought as she stared at GiGi. Something in her gut told her that this tiny horse was very special.

# Chapter 10

Doc Mike never answered his cell phone except for emergencies. He was usually busy on another farm call, working in his office or performing a surgical procedure. Mike picked up his messages and returned calls after he had completed whatever he was working on. Sam's voicemail explained what had happened to Lyla's horses, and asked him to phone her. Sure enough, Mike returned her call within twenty minutes, and said that he would be at her farm within the next hour or so. He was finishing up with two horses also injured in the tornado.

Sam really liked Mike. She had great faith in his skills as a vet and his ability to think ahead of the problem at hand. And she would always be grateful to him for the care he provided when her filly was attacked by a coyote and almost died. It was one of Sam's scariest moments. Although it had been a year since the terrible ordeal, she remembered that day as if it were yesterday. She had come home from a shopping trip to find Kai, her precious black filly, stretched out on the ground and bleeding profusely. A large coyote lay dead in the corner of the paddock. Kai's mom had saved her foal from the coyotes grip as it tried to pull the wounded filly under the fence. The mare had landed a well-placed kick to its head and had killed the large animal before it could drag Kai away.

Mike had come immediately, and after treating Kai's injuries onsite, he had taken the filly back to his clinic where he sutured up her deep ragged tears, placed an IV in her leg, and filled her with antibiotics. Kai's condition was grave, and he gave Sam and Denver the bad news. "Plan for the worst and hope for the best."

It was touch and go for Kai, and Sam and Denver sat by her side all evening, waiting for the critically injured filly to respond.

"If Kai makes it through the night, she'll be okay," Mike told them with a tired look in his eyes and a grim expression on his face.

For Sam, two life changing events happened that long stressful evening. Kai survived, and because Sam almost lost her, she became her forever horse. She knew she could never part with Kai, and the amazing filly would always hold a special place in her heart. The near tragedy also worked as an epiphany for Sam. Suddenly, the light went on and she acknowledged how important Denver was to her. At last she admitted to him, and to herself, how much she loved him. Denver had been in her life for several years, and she always considered him a best friend. She struggled to control her feelings for the attractive man, and although tempted more than once to open the door to more than friendship, she always held back. Years ago, when the children were young, she had made the firm decision to not allow any man in her life until they were grown and on their own. And although he often accompanied her and the twins on ski trips, and became an important part of their lives, she shied away from anything more than friendship. Kai's near death experience solidified their love, and the twins were thrilled that Sam had agreed to marry the man they had long wished she would. The fall wedding promised to be a huge celebration for friends and family. Surely, the tornado would not interfere with all of the plans they had made.

Patty and Lyla had been gone for almost an hour by the time Doc Mike arrived at the farm. As usual, the dogs heard his truck before she did and ran helter-skelter to meet him at the barn. They were overjoyed to see the vet, and began their typical unrelenting jumping and circling just as he got out of the truck and turned to close the door.

He paused for a minute to speak to Jazz and Sally, and then picked up a stick and threw it towards the field for Ranger to chase. The shaggy dog immediately took off after it, with Sally hot on his heels. Jazz was too tired to jump anymore, so she was happy to sit and watch.

Next he leaned down and scratched the lab's head. "Hi girl, how are you doing?" Jazz looked up and cocked her head, happy for the attention.

Sam studied the easy going vet as he took time to speak to each of the dogs. Mike was slender in stature, and his light brown hair was always cut short. Although he was in his late forties, he looked much younger. Today he was dressed in his usual farm call clothes; a brown shirt over dark jeans and well-worn brown boots that had seen better days. His upbeat personality was only one part of his charismatic charm. She admired his ability to multi-task in a nonchalant way, and his analytical style made it seem so easy. During his visits he listened to her concerns while at the same time gathering the medical supplies he would need to take care of the problem.

It was fun to watch him as he assessed the situation, and at the same time processed the information. He had an uncanny way of talking through all of the options for treating the horse, before he decided on a course of action. It was amazing to watch as he pondered the options and then suddenly, whala! Without skipping a beat he would begin dictating to his attentive assistant his clinical observations and plan for treatment.

Horses sensed his calm demeanor, and they allowed him to examine them in some of the worse situations. Sometimes it was an injury and other times the horse was 'just off', as Sam would say. She thought of him as the original horse whisperer because the horses seemed to sense he was there to help them, while at the same time respected his space.

During his barn calls they bantered back and forth, and it didn't matter if the talk was politics or horses, it was always interesting. But most of all Sam valued Mike's knowledge of equine medicine and his deep concern for his patients.

At his clinic in Connecticut, his specialty was rehabilitation of injured horses and conditioning of race or endurance horses. Using the buoyancy of water, his patients were exercised and rehabbed in a large equine swimming pool, and it was a thrill for Sam and Denver to watch as they swam with ease and comfort. More important, the horses seemed to enjoy the low impact exercise as they moved their huge bodies seemingly weightless through the water. Mike was a modern vet with big ideas, who understood the advantages of hydrotherapy and its physical and psychological benefits for his horse patients. Rehabilitation was a large part of his practice, and Sam was grateful that he continued to make barn calls to her farm and always came when she needed his expertise.

As usual, all it took for the three dogs to quiet down was his attention. He walked over to Sam, a big grin on his face and gave her with a hug.

"Hi Sam. I guess I needn't ask how you are. It was a mess just getting here and the calls have been coming in non-stop."

"I can imagine how busy you are," she said. "Sorry I didn't get to you before the dogs did. Where's your assistant, Grace?" she asked as she stepped back.

"I started out real early and she had a lot to do at the office. Hey, don't worry about the dogs, I enjoy their rowdy greetings. Makes me feel wanted," he laughed.

"So what's the problem, as if it's not bad enough you had a tornado come through?" he asked as he opened the tailgate of his SUV and picked up his container of supplies. "Looks like you have one huge mess to clean-up," he said as he looked around.

"Well, it's a mess here but it could have been much worse. I must have thanked God a thousand times for sparing us. We weren't in the direct path of it like our neighbors. Our barn and home are still standing and our generator is running. Lots of people who lost barns and fences are looking for places for their animals, which is why I called you. I'm taking care of a pony and a Mini horse that were injured when their barn roof fell in. They have some nasty looking abrasions and cuts. We've cleaned their wounds as best we could, but I think they may need some antibiotics. The main thing is for you to look at them and see what you think."

"Let's see what you've got. Been treating lots of horses injured from flying debris," he said as he closed the tailgate.

After a thorough exam of both horses; Doc swabbed the wounds with ointment and gave each a tetanus shot. To Sam's relief, neither animal needed sutures. He left her with enough antibiotics for a week's treatment, and gave her extra tubes of ointment to cover the wounds after cleaning.

"I'm surprised they weren't injured more seriously, with the barn falling in on them. They look better than I thought they would," Doc said as he washed his hands at the barn faucet. "That is one sweet Mini, and the name GiGi seems to fit her. She was excellent when I cleaned her wounds. I can see she's been handled a lot and I've got to say, she's the smallest I've taken care of. Great conformation and super disposition. Where did she come from?"

"I'm not quite sure. I just met her owner. From what Lyla said, she came from a farm in Vermont. She told me the filly was sickly at birth, and the owners didn't want to put time and money into her, so they gave the Mini to her. Lyla brought her home, and nursed her back to health. I can see she's very attached to GiGi and I think she's lucky both horses survived. Sure they have injuries, but it could have been so much worse. I told her they're fine here until she gets her barn back together, and I'm more than happy to help her out."

Doc picked up his supplies while Sam cleaned up the soiled materials. They continued their idle chatter about the tornado as they walked towards the truck, and their conversation moved from horses to small talk.

"So, Mike how've you been these past months? We haven't seen much of each other, which I hate to say, has been a good thing," she laughed. "Not that I don't enjoy your company, but I usually see you when I have a horse problem. Denver was just asking about you. He was hoping he would be here when you arrived but he had to drive to the next town and get some gas for the generator and chain saw."

"I've been busy, but busy is good." Mike stopped walking and turned to Sam. "Hey, I do want to ask you about something that came to my attention last week. I was going to call you about it, but you got to me first. Have you heard anything about horses around here, or in neighboring towns, dying unexpectedly?"

"No, I haven't heard anything about that. Why do you ask?"

"Well, I had an interesting visit by someone from Homeland Security and he asked some intriguing questions. He wanted to know if any horses in my area of practice had died without warning. Not sick or injured, just dropped."

"What?" Sam's brows furrowed in surprise. "That's crazy. Why would someone from a government agency ask you that?"

"You got me," Mike answered. "I told him I haven't had any in my practice, and I asked him if this was happening anywhere else in our state. He said they were just beginning to visit local vets and they were trying to find out if it was a problem, but so far no sudden deaths were reported." Mike could see the worried look on Sam's face.

"No doubt they have a reason for the interest, but I haven't heard anything on the news about it, have you?" she asked. "I wonder if it's some virus coming in from other states. A lot of horses are trailered from different parts of the country and many are imported Warm Bloods. What about any of the other vets? Have they had any sudden deaths in their practice?"

"None of my friends ever mentioned any sudden equine deaths to me or said they had been visited by the Feds," Mike paused for a minute as he thought about the visit. "So, of course I asked the agent why Homeland Security was involved in something like this, and he just danced around the question and said something about they were just following up on a problem reported to them and he couldn't share anything else with me," Mike's eyes narrowed as he thought back to the agent's reply.

"So," Sam asked with concern, "he never hinted at why it was a problem or if it could be?" Now she was really confused.

"No," Mike replied, "and he wouldn't answer any other questions, which made me even more suspicious. He was short and to the point. You know, the whole interview reminded me of a James Bond movie," he grinned.

"So, where did that leave you?" Sam asked as they reached the truck and continued talking.

"Can't imagine what this is about. The agent left a business card and asked me to keep this on my radar. So, that's about it. Only interesting thing that's happened since I last saw you. I've been busy since he showed up, and put it in the back of my mind until I got here."

"Now that's what I call strange," Sam said. Then with a slight smile she looked at Mike and held her hand to her chin as if in deep contemplation. "Sounds like we've got the makings of a CSI episode," she said with an exaggerated deep voice.

Mike laughed. "Well they say that lots of real facts go into any mystery but it's probably nothing. Anyway, I think you have enough to concern yourself with right here. Just thought I'd pass this one on to you, but if you hear anything about this sort of thing, give me a call."

"Well, I've never heard of a government agency interested in horse deaths but I'll ask around and spread the word to my horse friends in the area," she replied frowning as she mulled over the idea of equine deaths.

"Do that, and let me know if you hear anything," Mike said kicking a small stone with his boot.

He opened the tailgate and placed his container of supplies in the back, slammed it shut, and turned to Sam. "Guess we'll never know what the Feds are looking for. But it sure makes me wonder."

Sam nodded in agreement. "That was an interesting visit. Kind of scary. I'm still thinking that maybe there's a rare equine disease they're worried about, but you're right. We'll probably never know. They always fall back on the reasoning that they don't want to alarm the public," Sam shrugged her shoulders. Right now she had other things to think about. This was something that usually made her mind run wild with theory and conjecture, but she decided she would tuck it away and think about it tomorrow. She reminded herself of Minnie's pearls of wisdom, 'Don't worry about the small stuff, there's enough to just getting through life as it is.'

Mike opened his truck door and slid behind the wheel. "If I hear anything more from them, I'll call you and do the same for me," he winked.

"I will for sure, and thanks for coming so quickly. Lyla will be relieved to know her horses are okay. One less thing for her to worry about." Sam's mind had already shifted to the problems at hand.

"If she has any other concerns, have her give me a call," he said as he started the truck. "By the way, how is my favorite filly Kai doing? If I had more time I'd check her out, but I've got another call to make before I head home."

"She's fine, thanks to you. Don't forget, you and Ellen are invited to our wedding."

"That's right. You can count on us. Say hi to Denver for me and I'll talk to you soon."

Mike put his truck in gear and slowly pulled away. Hearing the truck start up, the dogs ran to Sam's side to watch as it slowly moved down the driveway.

"Sudden equine deaths," she thought as she turned to walk back to the house. "Hope that's not something I'll ever hear about or see."

# Chapter 11

The early morning air felt just right on Sam's tired body. She sat in her chair, coffee mug in hand, and surveyed her backyard. It had been a grueling two weeks cleaning up the tree limbs, and she and Denver had finally finished setting the last of the new fence posts to replace the broken ones. She had slept little since the tornado, and what sleep she did have was restless. Justin and Kristy had arrived on Sunday and pitched right in to help clean-up the rest of the mess left from the high winds and lightning strikes. Sam and Denver felt they were now in good shape, and could turn their attention to other needs.

At last, the loud noise from the gasoline generators was stilled. Most people had power back on and the only sounds breaking the quiet were from chain saws still at work. Sam finally felt that things were beginning to come together.

The twins had left to spend the day volunteering in Lyla's town where the damage was much worse. Mansville had been directly in the path of the tornado, and had suffered terrible damage to countless homes and businesses. Many homes were beyond repair and trees uprooted from the mountains lay toppled like pick-up sticks. The mountainsides lay bare. Main Street was a disaster zone and the First Church, which suffered damage to its exterior and the loss of its beautiful steeple, was now the center for volunteers. Donations of food, clothing, and water continued to pour in and everyone worked to clean-up the rubble.

Luckily the bakery where Lyla worked was not one of the buildings in the path of destruction, since just as in Sam's town the tornado had spared some businesses while leveling others.

Although Lyla was grateful for the twins help, she missed her horses and couldn't wait to get them back in their own barn. Her barn roof was almost completely repaired by volunteers, and Justin had finished nailing the last boards to the posts of her corral.

For Sam, it was time to sit back and rest. So much had changed in the past weeks. The tornado had altered, not only the look of the landscape but the natural order of things in her life. As with others in the surrounding towns, it had been a rude awakening. Everyone knew that snowstorms could be treacherous, and even hurricanes and nor'easters were dangerous and did occur, but a tornado? That changed everything. The weather patterns were not the same, and the preconceived notion that tornados did not occur in the northeast was shattered. It was difficult to return to the everyday rhythm of life, and she was one of the lucky ones. Her heart went out to those less fortunate, who had felt the force of nature and the loss of treasured belongings. They were still trying to put their lives back together.

She reached over, picked up her empty plate and glass, and got up from the chair. It was time to get herself moving and begin her day's work. The house phone rang and she quickly walked to the kitchen to answer it.

"Hello," she said.

"Hello, this is Anna Brooks from the 'Times'. How are you today?"

"Fine thanks and how can I help you?" asked Sam.

"Well," replied the cheerful voice, "one of your neighbors told us that you have two horses from Mansville at your farm. She said the owner's barn was badly damaged and the horses suffered some injuries, but survived. I'd like to write an article and take some photos of them for our next issue. Sounds like these are two lucky horses and it would be a great story to share in the midst of so much destruction. And we understand that one of the horses is a Mini and very cute."

Sam felt her heart quicken. "Yes, I'm taking care of them while the owner repairs her barn. They are, as you said, lucky to have survived in a barn that crashed down around them. But, I'll have to ask the owner if she'd want to do an interview with you. She'll be here this afternoon and I'll give her the message."

"Sure, here's my number and you can have her call me." Anna gave her number, and Sam promised to pass it on to Lyla.

As she hung up the phone her mind was racing. "What great news," she thought. "This is so exciting. Not only will Lyla have a photo of GiGi in the paper, but she could also mention that she works at a bakery. And of course she could slide in the interview, that she sells her own baked goods at the farmer's market. She'll get some free advertisement. I can't wait to tell her about this. Maybe something good will come out of this after all. "

Sam had grown fond of Lyla and her precious Mini horse. More than once, she had fought the compulsion to pick GiGi up and give her a big hug. Even Mike was smitten with GiGi. Last night he had phoned to check on the horses, and had said for the zillionth time, that GiGi was the cutest Mini in his practice. And Chip was so sweet and easy to work around, that adding Curly ponies to her long range breeding program was taking on a life of its own.

Visions of Curly ponies swirled through her head. Now she had a new plan and if she wasn't in a hurry, she would have phoned Denver and shared her vision with him. But this could wait. For now it was about Lyla and her horses.

The screen door slammed behind her as she hurried to finish chores. "I can't wait to see the expression on Lyla's face when I tell her about having a photo of GiGi and Chip on the front page of the Times. She will be so excited."

After all of the tense moments and all of the worry, finally something good was going to happen for Lyla, and Sam couldn't wait to share the news.

It was late in the afternoon by the time Lyla arrived at Sam's farm. She was working with Kai when she heard Lyla's pickup drive up. Luckily, she had the dogs in their pen or they would have met Lyla before she did. Sam could hardly contain her excitement about the phone call from the reporter. She was at the pickup before Lyla could open her door.

"Hi Sam, how's it going?" Lyla asked as she opened the truck door and stepped out. Her curly red hair was wrapped in a tie and her long bangs were pulled back and held in place by a black hair comb, sprinkled with colored crystals. With her hair tied back away from her face and the smattering of freckles across her nose she looked like an innocent school girl. Sam studied Lyla's face and immediately thought how pretty she was. She had a fresh scrubbed look that made her appear years younger, and her voice was soft spoken, denoting shyness and vulnerability. Sam thought of Lyla as a gentle young woman, who had suffered loss, but had survived and grown stronger because of it. She felt a kinship with her, and the longer she knew her the more she liked her.

Lyla opened the rear door and reached onto the back seat and took out a green tote bag. "I've brought something for you," she said as she handed the bag to Sam.

"What another loaf of your delicious bread? You're spoiling me."

Lyla smiled. "It's the least I can do for you. But it's not bread this time. It's some ginger cookies. I made them from a recipe I found in my grandmother's old cookbook and I want you to try them and give me your opinion. Please let me do this for you. I enjoy baking and love sharing desserts with you. It's my way of saying thank you. You and Denver and the twins have been a God send, and besides baking is therapy for me. It makes me feel useful and I value your input on my desserts. If you and your family like them, I'm sure my customers will."

"Lyla you're the best, and by now you know my darkest secret. I admit I am a junk food addict. I love my desserts, and some days I could settle for a hot fudge sundae or a piece of chocolate cake and skip dinner altogether."

Lyla laughed at Sam's admission about junk food, but gulped when she thought about her own dark secret. She wished it was as easy as a junk food addiction.

Sam peaked into the bag and sniffed the mouthwatering aroma of freshly baked ginger cookies. A slender woman, she looked like she could eat a dozen cookies and a quart of ice cream every day, and never gain a pound. Work on the farm kept her trim and she was physically strong for her stature. Her mind was always filled with some new project or business plan and her friends found humor in her many ideas, some of which worked and others that didn't. Although many would call her a dreamer, she preferred to think of herself as a 'visionary' and even though she admitted her fondness for desserts, she was a woman who ate healthy foods most of the time. To quote Minnie, 'everything in moderation is the way to live a healthy life.' And if that philosophy kept the peppy grandmother physically active and young at heart, it was good enough for Sam.

Baking was Lyla's way of giving back to the woman she had grown to admire, and think of as a friend. "By the way," she said. "I would love your recipe for Welsh cookies. They were delicious and I'd like to add them to my book of favorite recipes."

"Will do," said Sam as she walked with Lyla towards the house. "And I know I promised you the recipe for my sticky buns. But that can wait. I had a phone call this morning and

I think you'll be so excited to hear about it. Before we see GiGi and Chip, let's have coffee and cookies. This is important and I can't wait to tell you all about it."

"Okay," said Lyla. "I can use a cup of coffee after the day I just had, and in case you didn't notice, I also put some chocolate chip cookies in the bag. I know they're Denver's favorite."

"My mouth is watering," Sam said as she opened the door to the kitchen.

She placed the bag of goodies on the counter and dropped a K-cup in the coffeemaker. While the coffee was dripping into the mugs she took paper plates, decorated with a holly wreath, from the cupboard and set them on the table.

They carried the mugs of steaming coffee and plates of cookies out to the porch. Lyla was now accustomed to Sam's use of leftover holiday plates. Waste not want not was Sam's motto. Who cared that they were now into summer, 'Christmas is forever' was her mantra.

"Let's toast to this Christmas and better days ahead," said Sam as she clunked her mug to Lyla's.

"Here's to the end of a crazy summer," said Lyla as she took a sip of coffee. "And by the way, I love Christmas in June," she said as she reached for a ginger cookie. "So, tell me about the phone call. I can't wait to hear about it."

"Well," said Sam as she took a bite of a soft chocolate chip cookie. For a moment she paused, as the rich chocolate licked the back of her tongue. She wiped her mouth with a napkin and began. "I had a phone call from a reporter for the 'Times.' Her name is Anna Brooks and she wants to do a story about GiGi and Chip."

"What? A reporter?" Lyla almost choked on her coffee. "Definitely not! There are so many other people who have suffered more than me. They should do a story about them." Lyla's face was flushed and she could feel her heart beating.

"Lyla, don't get upset. This will be a story about horses. Everyone has heard about animals injured, displaced or killed in the tornado. Now, they want to read about something good that happened. People love to read about animals that have beaten the odds, and GiGi is so sweet and pretty. Everyone would love to see a photo of her. Why not give the interview? And plus I was thinking that it would be good publicity for your bakery business."

Lyla was visibly shaking. She got up from the table and turned away from Sam so she wouldn't see the tears coming from the corners of her eyes.

"I'm sorry Sam. I can't do it."

"Lyla what's the matter? I'll help you with the interview. You know if Anna doesn't write the story someone else will want to. People are curious."

Lyla turned and faced Sam. "Sam I just can't do it. I don't want the publicity and please don't ask me why."

Sam could see the worry in Lyla's tear filled eyes, and noticed her hands were trembling. Something was terribly wrong.

# Chapter 12

Sam got up from the table and put her arms around Lyla. Her tears were flowing uncontrollably. It was as if a dam had burst.

"What's wrong? I didn't mean to upset you. I know it's been difficult with the tornado aftermath and all the worry you've had about your horses. But things are getting better. Your horses will be home this week and power is back on everywhere." Sam didn't know how to comfort the sobbing woman.

Lyla stepped back from Sam and sniffled. She took a napkin from the table, wiped her eyes and blew her nose then sat down on the chair. "Sam, I can't have the newspaper do a story on GiGi. You know I'm new in this area and I just started making friends. I'm basically shy and it's difficult for me to meet people. What's more I don't have anyone I can really talk to."

Lyla's mind was racing. "How can I explain what I did without Sam thinking I'm a horse thief? If I tell her the real reason I can't have GiGi's photo in the paper, what then? She'll probably hate me and feel I've betrayed her and took advantage of my situation. How can I explain that I saved GiGi, not stole her? She'll never trust me again if I tell her the truth."

What little check she had over her emotions was now gone. She could not stop the flow of tears streaming down her cheeks and she tried to stifle a sob, but it didn't work. Nothing could stop the flow of tears.

"Oh my God, Lyla. What is it? What can I do?" Sam was totally taken aback watching Lyla, now overcome with racking sobs. She was falling apart right in front of her and Sam felt completely helpless.

Lyla couldn't answer. She was paralyzed in thought and uncontrollable sobbing. She had to make a decision and it had to be right now. The weightiness of her worry was too heavy, and the piling on of events broke her resolve to keep her secret. Now a reporter wanted to interview her? It was the final straw, and she couldn't do this anymore. Should she take Sam into her confidence? Would Sam understand and keep her secret? Meeting Sam had opened the door to a new friendship. Patty was Sam's friend, and through their conversations; she believed Sam was a woman who, if she promised to keep a secret, would do so. She had to take the risk, and tell her the truth.

Lyla leaned on the table and held her head in her hands. She was still trying to stop crying, but she couldn't quell the tears or catch her breath.

Sam went into the bathroom and brought out a box of tissues. She put the box in front of Lyla. "Tell me what's wrong? You're not alone with whatever it is. You have Patty as a friend, and now you have me. We care about you and I'm choosy about my friends," she said as she tried to break through Lyla's meltdown.

Lyla reached for a tissue and took in a deep breath as she tried to regain her composure. She wiped her eyes again and looked over the table at Sam.

She cleared her throat. "Sam, I have something I need to tell you, but if I do you'll have to promise me that you will tell no one including Patty. I know I'm asking a lot from you, but you deserve to know why I can't have anything in the paper about GiGi. I need to trust someone and I don't know why, but I believe it's you. Maybe you can help me find a solution to my predicament. Or maybe you can help me see something I've missed. I just don't know what to do, but I need to do something," she said slowly with a shaky voice.

Sam studied the woman sitting across from her. Lyla's eyes were red from crying and her heart went out to her. She reached out her hand and placed it on Lyla's. She went still for a moment as she considered what Lyla asked of her. Should she promise to keep a secret that was so serious it caused her to fall apart? Sam's gut instinct cried out yes, while she ran through everything she knew about Lyla.

Lyla knew that Sam was thinking about what she asked, and she sat quietly waiting for her response as she wiped away the last of her tears.

Sam looked directly into Lyla's eyes. "Well, Lyla, unless you committed a murder or some atrocity, your secret is safe with me, and when I give my word to someone, I keep it."

Lyla didn't say anything as she tried to pull herself together. "Where to begin?" she thought. "You'd better fill our mugs with more coffee. This will take some time to tell you the whole story." She paused again and drew in a long breath. "First of all I need to tell you the owner of GiGi didn't give her to me. I took her."

Sam's eyes grew wide as saucers. "You what? Are you saying you stole GiGi?"

Hearing Sam's accusations opened the faucet once more, and tears cascaded down Lyla's cheeks. She had never been accused of stealing anything. Again, she choked back a sob and tried to regain her composure. "Please Sam; let me explain what happened and why I did it. I want you to understand that I didn't steal her, I saved her."

For the next hour, Sam sat spell bound while Lyla told her about the farm in Vermont and her fear for GiGi's life. Lyla talked and talked, and Sam only interrupted when she had a question. The flood gates opened and Lyla hesitated only long enough to take sips from the coffee mug that Sam kept filled. She began her story with measured words and only stopped for a sip of coffee or to answer Sam. She had to make Sam understand what she had done, and more importantly why.

# Chapter 13

Lyla had sniffled back the last of her tears and didn't leave anything out. "I had gone to Vermont to take care of my only living relative, Aunt Mamie. She had fallen and broken her hip. Her only companions were her cat, a dog, and an old horse named Goldie. I took a leave from the bakery and sent my pony to a stable in town, and my cat to a woman I knew through work at the bakery. I wasn't sure how long I'd be there, but I knew it would be for at least a month or so."

Sam leaned forward in her chair, anxious to hear Lyla's entire saga. Her eyes never left Lyla's, and she was relieved that she had stopped crying.

"At first caring for my aunt took up most of my time, but after a few weeks Aunt Mamie was doing much better and I decided to take Goldie out on a trail ride. That was when I first saw the farm where GiGi was born. I had ridden Goldie for quite a long way on a trail that began at the back of Aunt Mamie's house. At the end of the trail I came to a hard pack road, which soon turned into a main road. I decided to follow it a little way to see where it went," she said as she drew in a quick breath.

Sam was becoming more and more engrossed in Lyla's story. She was glued to the chair and could hardly contain her impatience to hear more.

"There was no traffic except for the occasional pickup truck that passed by. Just about the time I decided to turn around and head back to Aunt Mamie's, my eyes caught a glimpse of a sign sticking out from some bushes on the side of the road. I was curious, and I rode up to take a look at what had grabbed my attention. Sure enough there was a tall crooked post with a wooden plaque hanging from it. Although the letters were faded, it read 'Pine Hollow Farm,' and hanging underneath was a big yellow metal sign with 'No Trespassing' printed in large black letters."

Lyla paused for a moment and murmured, "I wonder if it was my destiny that brought me to that road."

Although it was a question, it was something Lyla had pondered over before, and it gave her comfort to believe that it was fate that brought her to the farm, and the reason she had acted so irrationally.

Sam had been so engrossed in the story, she had lost track of time, and leaned back to stretch her shoulders while she thought about what Lyla had just said. Her back ached from leaning forward in the chair and she could see that Lyla was searching for any reason to help her understand how she got to the point where she stole a horse.

Sam thought for a moment and said, "Well, some people believe that our life's journey is planned before we are born. It's an interesting concept, and I say anything is possible. Who knows? But I do believe we have some control over our own destiny, if not the world would be even more chaotic than it is." She caught herself before she added, "And everyone would be stealing and committing crimes."

Lyla didn't need to hear the word thief. Her guilt was painful enough. She leaned forward again and urged Lyla to continue. "So, what happened next?"

"Just as I was getting ready to turn Goldie around to head back to Aunt Mamie's a pickup truck came out of the driveway and stopped. The driver asked if he could help me. I said no, I was just taking a ride on my horse and I stopped to read the sign. He was friendly and we talked a while longer, and then he asked if I was interested in working a few hours a day at the farm. I told him I was caring for my aunt but I was getting a little bored since she didn't need me as much, and a part-time job working with horses sounded appealing. He explained it was a Mini horse farm and that it was used as a research facility, and if I wanted a job to fill in my spare time, to call the number on the card he gave me.

Sam could see that Lyla was tired, and asked if she wanted to take a break.

"No, I need to keep going. I'll be all right." She hesitated to collect her thoughts. "By the next week Aunt Mamie was even more improved, but I knew she would need me for at least another month, so I phoned the number to see if they had any part-time hours. I was hired for three days a week, which fit my schedule perfectly. Mostly I cleaned stalls and fed the horses. I had never worked around Mini horses and I fell in love with them. They were so sweet which is why I had a hard time watching foals die."

"What? The foals died? That is horrible," Sam was aghast.

"Yes, and some mares as well. I couldn't understand it, and when I asked why, I was told they were testing a vaccine that would help all horses and it was an expected outcome for any research facility. I was told there were always sacrifices made in the name of medicine. Have you ever heard of horses being used for research?"

"Yes, I've read numerous articles about the use of horses in research," Sam frowned. "They still use pregnant mare's urine to make hormone replacement medication for women. The foals are disposable, and the mares are kept pregnant until they can no longer conceive. After that, they are also disposable. It broke my heart when I read about it. It's a terrible life for the mares and their foals and it still goes on, but luckily some are saved through horse rescue organizations. They are called PMU mares, which stands for pregnant mare urine."

"Oh my God, Sam, even I didn't know this. Why don't more women know how the drug is made?" Lyla asked in astonishment.

"Let's say animal sacrifice isn't a priority. But many women do know about it, and in this country the use of this particular drug has declined. However, it is still prescribed to millions of women for menopause, specifically hot flashes." Sam shrugged her shoulders as she thought about Lyla's question. "Who knows what goes on in these labs? I know I would never work at a place where animals are sacrificed in the name of research." She grimaced at the thought.

"That's exactly what happened to me," Lyla said. "I knew I couldn't continue working there even if losing foals

113

saved other horses. It made me too sad. Mares in foal either miscarried or the foals died within the first few days. I hated to watch those tiny babies die, but most of all I disliked the vet who owned the farm." Lyla scowled as she thought about the man she despised.

"Who was that?" Sam leaned forward in her chair with anticipation.

"Everyone called him Doc," Lyla's face showed her contempt. "And he was the reason I took GiGi."

"So he wasn't the man who hired you?" Sam was getting confused.

"No, Carver was the man who hired me." Lyla's voice was almost a whisper as she said his name. Truth be told, she had a crush on him but it was too late now. He must hate her for what she had done. And she never said goodbye to him, she just ran.

"Tell me about him," said Sam as she walked to the counter to pour some lemonade into tall glasses. They were both coffeed out and she knew that Lyla needed a moment to pull her thoughts together before she began again. She had been talking non-stop, but Sam knew she was compelled to go on until she had emptied herself of the whole story. Sam sat the glass on the table next to her.

Lyla leaned back to regain her thoughts, and then lifted the glass of cold drink to her lips. Her mouth felt like cotton and the lemonade felt good on her dry throat.

The glass was half empty when she sat it back on the table and began to talk about Carver.

"I really liked Carver, and I felt he liked me. He was the only one at the farm I had a chance to talk to. Of course, I was only there a few hours a day so I didn't really get to know anyone else, and I'm a shy person to begin with. I enjoyed taking my breaks with him. He genuinely cared about the horses and constantly reminded me that Doc had his reasons for running the farm the way he did. When I questioned him about Doc, he told me to stay out of his way and that he paid everyone very well, and never bothered anyone as long as the work was done to his satisfaction."

Now Sam was really curious about the man who hired Lyla. "What does Carver look like?" she asked as she studied Lyla.

For the first time since she began the story, Lyla smiled. "He has thick light brown hair that always looks disheveled in a very sexy way. At times it dropped onto his forehead and I often had the urge to reach over and push it back off his face. He's tall and lean and his body had a gracefulness about it and his eyes are a dreamy light blue." Lyla sighed as a picture of Carver filled her head. "I loved to watch him walk through the aisles of the barn."

"Wow, from your description, he's a very attractive man and sounds to me you more than liked him."

Lyla's eyes lit up at Sam's suggestion, but then she shrugged her shoulders and sighed. "I did, but I'm sure he hates me now."

"I doubt it. You're a very pretty woman and I bet if you had worked longer at the farm, he would have asked you out."

Lyla's eyes lit up at the thought. "Maybe so, but I'll never know. Anyway, he was very handsome, but serious about his work. He told me he had worked at the farm since it opened, and that he had a good relationship with everyone who worked there. I could see that myself. Everyone liked him. I never asked exactly what his job was. I took it for granted he was the manager, after all he hired me."

"That's true," said Sam as she got up and walked to the end of the porch to see why one of the dogs was barking. It was nothing, and she sat back down to hear more about the man named Carver.

"One day I asked Carver the names of the horses, and he told me none of them had names, only numbers. I said I hated to think of them as numbers but he told me that most people get emotionally involved with an animal that has a name. He said that neither Doc nor Bill would allow anyone to get attached to the horses, and naming one was the first step. I took his words to heart, that is until GiGi was born."

"I think Carver was right in telling you that," said Sam. "The same goes for beef cattle. It's never good to name an animal you may eventually use for food. Still, that farm must have been a bizarre place. What was it like to work there?" she asked. She could tell by Lyla's demeanor it was time to change the subject.

Lyla closed her eyes as she remembered the farm. After a moment she opened them and continued. "It was weird and kind of eerie. There was no laughter while we worked, and no idle chatter was allowed. The barns were all business. The radio played Bluegrass music throughout the day, and

116

except for the sound of a horse's whinny, or the clunk of a manure fork when it hit the side of a wheelbarrow, it was very quiet. When workers did speak to each other, it was in low voices."

"Just get the job done," Bill the barn boss ordered in his snarly way. "Doc's not paying you to have fun at work. Do it on your own time. And don't ask any questions you won't like the answers to."

"I don't like him at all," said Sam as she pictured the man Lyla described. "He sounds really creepy."

"It wasn't that he was outwardly cruel," replied Lyla. "It was the way he gave orders. Kind of like a boot camp commander. He was very demanding, and no one ever questioned what he asked. I once heard him tell someone that he wasn't there to make friends, he was there to do a job."

"Even so, I don't think I could work for anyone like that, no matter how much they paid me," said Sam. "I don't have tolerance for bullies but I can understand the lure of money if jobs are scarce. You certainly had no idea what you were getting into when you took the job."

"You're right. It was all new to me, but I knew I couldn't last there."

"So, tell me about GiGi. You were there when she was born?"

"Yes, I was there at the exact moment of her birth. I was on foal watch and GiGi was one of several foals born. Each birth excited me and left me with the hope that the new foal would beat the odds and live. In the brief time I worked at the barn, most foals succumbed within the first twenty four hours. I remember stroking her mom's belly as she moaned and pushed with each contraction. And at last, with one huge push the smallest foal slipped out and onto the bed of straw. I immediately began rubbing her with a dry towel. Her wet coat was dark brown and she had a tiny white star on her forehead. I fell in love with her that very minute."

"I know how you felt." Sam thought back to Kai's birth. "There's nothing more that I love than being in the barn when a foal is born and watching it take its first shaky steps. They're the moments I'll always save in my memory bank. GiGi must have been so tiny. She's still a very small filly, even for a Mini."

Lyla stretched her arms over her head and her voice became animated as she described GiGi. "Yes, she was so tiny I couldn't believe it, and from the moment she was born she had such a strong spirit. She was so feisty she surprised everyone. I thought the name Spirit was perfect, but then the name 'God's Gift' came to me, and I believe that is what she is," she said with determination.

"What a great name. It fits her," Sam smiled as she pictured the special Mini she had come to love.

"I knew it was her name the minute I looked at her. Of course I had done something I was told never to do." Lyla's eyes grew big. "But I never told anyone what the letters 'GG' stood for. It was my secret. Some of the workers thought I was silly for naming a foal that would probably die, but when I told Carver that I named her, he just shrugged and grinned."

Sam could see the pleasure in Lyla's eyes as she talked about GiGi. She thought about the birth of the foal and Lyla's excitement in naming her GiGi. "So, unlike the other foals, she seemed healthy?"

"Yes, she grew stronger each day and I became hopeful that she had beaten the odds. She showed none of the shakiness the other foals had before they dropped to the stall floor and drew in their last breath." Lyla squeezed her eyes and shook her head in an attempt to push the vision of the dead foals from her mind.

"I spent all of my free time with her, and when she was two weeks old, I made the impulsive decision to take her from the farm and bring her home. Honest Sam, I want you to understand that it was only fear for her life, after I read Doc's notes which drove me to do something like that, but now..."

Lyla's body shuddered when she thought back to what she had done. She wondered what gave her the courage to act so out of character. She had never done anything so reckless in her whole life. That evening she had felt like a woman possessed, and it was a feeling she hoped she'd never have again. Tears burned her eyes and she squeezed them tight to stop the inevitable flow.

"Wait a minute!" Sam said bewildered by what Lyla said. "What does Doc and his notes have to do with your decision to take GiGi?"

"That's what I'm getting to," Lyla said as she leaned back in the chair. "This is the part where I felt the only way to save GiGi was to take her back to my farm.

# Chapter 14

Sam sat forward in her chair in eager anticipation for the rest of the story. Lyla stared ahead, deep in thought as Sam waited for her to pull herself together and begin once more. Something told her to give Lyla a moment. She knew patience was what Lyla needed most. This story was going to take time, and come out in bits and pieces. Sam leaned back in the chair and studied Lyla as she worked to pull herself together.

Lyla rubbed her eyes as she tried to concentrate on Doc, but all she could see was Carver's face. Her emotions ran wild as her mind flicked from Doc to Carver. Everything was mixed up, and she frantically tried to separate what was evil from what was good. She had worked hard to keep all memories of the farm out of her mind. It was the only way that fear didn't consume her every waking moment. But now, she was once again experiencing panic creeping in and taking over. Pushing things to the back of her mind and not thinking about them was a survival skill she had used to cope with the tragic loss of her parents. Don't think about it. It's too painful. Get on with your life. This is how she managed to put one foot in front of the other and keep on going. Now, all self-control was dwindling, as she shared the story with Sam and faced what she had done and what drove her to it. She dropped her head down and tried to control her emotions to make Sam understand the mess she had got herself into.

Sam watched the woman sitting across from her. Her head was bent down and tears were flowing down her cheeks. Lyla sniffled, and leaned over to take another tissue from the box. Her hands were shaky as she wiped her eyes and blew her nose.

"Lyla, are you okay?" Sam asked as she got up from the chair and went to her. She placed a hand on her shoulder and asked again, "Are you okay?"

Lyla looked up and her voice trembled as she said, "I wonder what Carver thought when he found GiGi missing, and I didn't show up for work?"

"Don't worry, Lyla. It'll be alright," she said to reassure her. "Sounds like he's a smart man. He knew you cared about GiGi, and one less foal that would likely die wasn't worth chasing after," she said gently.

Sam sat down and drank the last of her lemonade while she gave Lyla a moment to collect her thoughts. Now her curiosity was killing her. How did this man Doc fit into the picture?

"I still don't understand how Doc played into your decision to run with GiGi and was he the only person you were afraid of?" she asked.

Lyla went still for a moment. "Other than Doc, the only other man I tried to avoid was Bill. He took orders directly from Doc. One day he heard me talking to GiGi and he warned me not to get attached to her."

Lyla mimicked his gruff voice. "No sense in getting too fond of her. I ain't seen any foal last longer than a few days. That's the way it is and you knew it when you took the job.

Remember what Doc says, it's for the good of all horses." She drew in a short breath and dabbed her eyes, "Although he scared me when he said that, I couldn't understand why or what was going on at the barn, but it just didn't seem right."

Sam was on the edge of her seat. "What then?"

"I asked him, what if he's lying to everyone. That was the wrong question to ask Bill, and I was immediately sorry that the words had spilled out of my mouth. When Bill got his angry look, everyone stepped back and got out of his way. He looked at me and his mouth curled down and his voice took on a low growl and he said, 'It's none of your business. It's what he does and we're lucky to have a job. Don't start questioning everything you see and hear. It's not healthy for you or for the rest of us.'"

"It was more the look in his eyes then the sound of his voice that scared me, and I knew I would never bring the subject up again. As far as the other workers, they seemed nice but as I said, I didn't really get to know any of them."

"Wow, Bill sounds like someone I wouldn't want to cross," Sam said.

"That's for sure, but he's not what pushed me over the edge and frightened me enough to take GiGi. There's more. Even though Carver assured me that foal deaths were not in vain, he never told me what the vaccine was for that they were working on. When I asked, he said it was too complicated to explain and besides that, it was top secret. So, I took him at his word until one day I was called into Doc's office."

Lyla took another drink of lemonade. Her mouth was becoming dry once again. She drew in a long breath and spoke softly. Sam leaned forward, the suspense was intense. She could hear the raw emotion in Lyla's voice.

"I was really scared because I thought someone told him I was paying too much attention to GiGi. Doc always scared me. He was always rushing to see a mare that had given birth, and he never spoke to anyone except to bark out orders, and I wasn't the only one afraid of him. All of the men stayed out of his way. Well, except for Carver. He spoke to Doc routinely and so did Bill."

"Oh my God, I can't wait to hear about your encounter with him. You must have been so nervous wondering what he wanted." Sam took another cookie from the bag and bit into it, as she waited with bated breath for Lyla to continue.

"You can't imagine how nervous I was, and Carver wasn't there to tell me what it was all about. He was gone for the day to run an errand." Lyla's eyebrows furrowed as she thought back to that day. "I reluctantly went to Doc's office located in the main barn. I was climbing the stairs when he rushed past me and almost knocked me over."

"He what?" Sam almost choked on the cookie. "What was his hurry?"

"I don't know but something excited him. He careened down the stairs and yelled as he ran, 'Got an emergency at one of the lower barns. Go and sit down and don't touch anything or move from the chair until I get back.'"

"And I had no doubt that it was an order that I knew I had to follow," she said as she looked directly into Sam's eyes.

"Did he hurt you?"

"Not that much, but I was shocked to be shoved against the rail. Before I could even reply, he was at the bottom of the stairs and out the door. I shook my head in disbelief, climbed the rest of the stairs, walked inside the open door, and sat down on a broken one armed chair."

Lyla got up from the chair and walked to the window. "I checked my arm where it hit the wall, and it had a large welt down the side. While I rubbed it, my mind ran through a list of things, I either said or did that might have brought me to his attention. I didn't even think he knew my name and although it was the first time I was in his office, I hoped it would be my last."

Lyla returned to the chair and sat down. Sam was glued to her chair in anticipation of what happened next.

"I sat there worried and scared. The minutes ticked away and I finally pulled myself together and looked around his office. Since I had never been there before, I had no idea what to expect. It was very dusty, and the only light, except for the one over his desk, came through a cobweb covered window." Lyla's eyes grew dreamy as she pictured the room where she had sat waiting for Doc to return.

"It sounds like the office was made to fit his needs but not a place easy to work in. Was it an area separate from the rest of the barn?" Sam was trying to envision its location.

"Well from what Carver had told me, the barn loft had been made into his office when the farm was first bought and his living quarters were also up there. But it was a mess. A shabby green light fixture hung over his desk and the room smelled like an old messy house that was never open to air. Stacks of files and papers sat on the floor and there was barely any room to walk. The only modern thing in the seedy room was a laptop computer sitting on his cluttered desk," Lyla said as she cleared her throat.

"Looks like he had more things on his mind than a clean office," Sam said in an effort to lighten the mood.

Lyla was staring at her hands, lost in the moment. She looked up at Sam and a faint smile crossed her lips as she continued. "Discarded candy wrappers were scattered around the laptop, and a wastebasket sitting by his desk was overflowing with trash and cupcake wrappers. For a moment I lost my fear of why I was there, and I started to laugh. Now I knew his secret. He lived on cupcakes." She stopped talking as visions of Doc filled her head.

"What does he look like?" asked Sam in an attempt to break the trance Lyla seemed to be in. The expression on her face revealed how frightened she was as she thought about Doc and that day in his office.

"He's a short, heavy man who's always sweating and he carries a large handkerchief he's forever wiping his brow with. His shirt always looks rumpled and soiled, and it doesn't matter which one he wears or which day of the week it is. He isn't a man who cares about his appearance, that's for sure."

She smiled as she described Doc to Sam. "His huge belly hangs low, and his pants show his butt when he bends over. No one dared to ask him why he didn't wear suspenders for fear of a quick tongue lashing. What's more, no one seemed to know his first or last name and he was called Doc by everyone who worked there. The only time he spoke to anyone was when he wanted something done, and then he said it in a demanding flat voice."

"I can see why he frightened you. I'm nervous and I've never met him." The description of Doc was clear, and he wasn't someone she would have wanted to meet.

Lyla got up from the chair and walked to the window. "It was his eyes that were scary. Those small beady brown eyes pierced right through you and they flashed when any questions were asked. I soon figured out that he ruled by intimidation and money. He paid all of us generously, and in return he expected blind obedience and he got it. Doc never had to ask twice for something to be done. It was an order that was quick to be filled since he tolerated no excuses. Most of the time he spent in his office or the lab, since the daily care of horses and chores were not his concern." She sat down on the chair and went still for a moment.

"My God, Lyla, the man sounds evil," exclaimed Sam.

Lyla squeezed the bridge of her nose and then ran her fingers through her hair. She pushed a loose curl off her face and waited as she tried to gauge Sam's reaction to her story. "What does she think of me now?" she thought as she stared into Sam's narrowed blue eyes.

Sam could see the exhaustion on Lyla and knew instinctively it was time to stop. "Let's take a break and have something to eat. Although I'm dying to hear the rest of this, I can see we're both ready for a time out. What do you think about switching from lemonade to a Margarita, and how 'bout a chicken salad sandwich?"

She didn't admit it to Lyla, but she also needed a time out. This story was too much to comprehend. It was like something out of a suspense novel. Her mind swirled with questions, and although she was anxious to hear more, it could wait.

"I'd like that," said Lyla. At this point I could use a Margarita, and then I'll tell you what finally pushed me to take GiGi."

"Say no more," Sam said. "It can wait even though my imagination is running wild."

Sam got up from the chair, pulled her shoulders back and walked to the kitchen. So many questions ran through her mind. "What was Lyla most afraid of? Doc, the farm, or the fact that she had brazenly taken a horse that wasn't hers and now didn't know what to do about it?"

# Chapter 15

After a quick sandwich, Sam and Lyla carried their Margaritas to the porch and placed then on the tables next to their chairs. Neither woman had spoken much while they ate their lunch. There was nothing to say that couldn't wait until they were both refreshed and ready to pick up where Lyla left off.

"Okay Lyla. I'm ready to hear what happened next. I can't stand the suspense. Go on." Sam lifted her glass and took a sip. She licked the salt from her lips and placed the glass back on the table.

Lyla cleared her throat and began again, her voice vibrating with intensity. "It seemed the emergency was taking longer than expected and I didn't know whether to leave the office or stay put. But then, Doc's stern voice when he told me to wait for him, took away any impulse I had to get up and go back to work. The longer I waited for Doc, the more curious I became as I looked around his repulsive office. There was a stack of papers on his desk, and I noticed a large black binder sticking out from under it. Maybe I had sat there too long and I was bored, but my curiosity got the best of me and I took a quick look at the door, and when I didn't hear anyone coming up the stairs, I got up from the chair and walked behind the desk to take a look. I carefully slid it out from under the pile of papers and opened it."

Lyla's eyes teared up again with the realization at what she had done. "Oh my God! Sitting here, and listening to myself talk, I'm even amazed at my audacity, and I can't begin to fathom why I did such a thing," she said with shock in her voice.

"Wow, and I can't believe you were so daring. Weren't you afraid you would get caught?" Sam's eyes were bright with excitement.

"I guess I wasn't thinking clearly, and curiosity overcame common sense," Lyla murmured.

Sam leaned forward and touched Lyla's arm. "Listen Lyla, you were afraid but curious. You had too many questions that no one wanted to answer. I would have done the same thing. You felt something wasn't right about the farm and didn't know for sure what was going on. Think about it. He left you alone in the office for a long time, and you took the chance to sneak a look at something that might provide some answers. It took a lot of chutzpah for you to do that," Sam said in a reassuring voice.

"Thanks for not thinking badly of me," Lyla said with a weak smile. "I just felt that there was something wrong at that farm, and maybe I could find out what it was."

"Wow," said Sam. "So what did you see?" She reached over and took another drink from her glass. "What was in the binder that frightened you enough to run away with GiGi?"

Lyla's voice dropped to almost a whisper. She could feel her heart beating faster. "It was filled with spreadsheets and records of all of the farm's horses and their offspring. Next to each number were marks and notations about equine deaths, and the name of the vaccine introduced to each mare. In the next column were doses, dates the mares were given the vaccine, foal births, deaths and results. Now I knew why the horses weren't named. They each had a number! Then I saw a column titled Autopsies and underneath it was a word I couldn't quite make out, but it looked like it began with the letter 'B'. The whole thing gave me shivers," she said as a sudden chill made her body tremble.

Sam was spellbound, as she listened intently to Lyla's every word. Her eyes grew wide and she felt a chill run down her spine. The thought flashed through her mind that this was something bigger than anything she could have imagined.

"And then what," Sam asked almost afraid to hear the answer.

"I heard a noise and the sound of footsteps coming up the stairs. I quickly closed the binder, slid it back under the pile of papers and ran back to the chair and sat down. My heart was racing and I felt my face flushing. I heard his wheezy, labored breathing before I saw him barge through the open door."

"Oh my God, did he catch you?"

"No, but I was petrified, and I thought for sure he could see right through me. He went behind his desk and looked straight into my eyes and said, "Good you obeyed my orders not to leave 'till I got back. I've got some questions for you and I want the answers now," he ordered.

"How could you even answer?" Sam gulped.

Lyla drew in a short breath. "I was frozen in place and felt so guilty. I thought for sure he could read the guilt on my face. I felt like a deer caught in headlights and I was ready to bolt out of there. Just then his phone rang. He covered the mouthpiece and said, 'You can go. I don't have time to talk now. I'll see you tomorrow.' He waved his hand toward the door, and I had to stop the urge to run out of there."

"How could you even speak?"

"I somehow found the words that were stuck in my throat and said okay, and got up and left the office. My legs were shaking and I couldn't get out of there fast enough. I didn't know what to do, or who to tell about what I read. I knew I did something I shouldn't have. It was sneaky and dishonest. I couldn't tell Carver. I was embarrassed and scared. I wanted to go back to my aunt's house and think about it. I went downstairs and told Bill that I had to leave to take my aunt to a doctor's appointment and I all but ran out of the barn."

The memory of her last encounter with Doc jolted Lyla with stabbing fear. She shuddered and took another sip of her Margarita.

Sam was speechless. Lyla was drained. For what seemed like forever, they both sat in silence. It had been a long afternoon.

Lyla stared at Sam waiting for her to say something. Sam got up from the chair, walked over to Lyla and gave her a hug. "I'm still in shock by your story, and I don't know how you've managed to keep this secret for so long. Now, I understand why you can't have anything in the newspaper about GiGi and I don't blame you," she said.

They continued talking for a while longer, Lyla wiping away tears and Sam consoling her as best she could. Sam still couldn't fathom how Lyla had kept the whole story to herself. Now that Lyla had taken her into her confidence she realized her secret was more than she had bargained for.

"Let's call it a day and let me think about how I can help you. And don't worry; your secret's safe with me. You have my word," she said as she carried the empty glasses back to the kitchen.

"Thank you Sam. I'm exhausted," Lyla said. "But I feel a big weight off my shoulders, and I'd appreciate any ideas you may have. I'm tired of being on guard and scared all the time."

"I don't mind saying that I'm also wiped out, but more spellbound than anything else. There's got to be a solution, but now I'm as worried as you are. I think you read something you were never supposed to have access to and I don't know what you should do about it. There's too much we don't know and can't understand. I don't have any answers for you right now. I understand why you're reluctant to go to the authorities. If it's nothing, you can be accused of stealing and if it is something, it's bigger than both of us."

It was now late afternoon. Lyla's eyes were red from crying and Sam was still in a state of disbelief. Both were quiet as they walked to Lyla's truck.

As she turned to say goodbye, Sam gave her another hug. "I'm going to think about this tonight. But for now, all I can say is we need a plan."

A thought flashed through her mind as she watched Lyla's truck drive away. She recalled her conversation with Mike and his visit from Homeland Security. Could there be a connection? "Now that's a stretch," she thought as she walked back to the house.

# Chapter 16

Sam tossed and turned all night. At one point she got out of bed and went downstairs for a glass of water. There was so much to think about and so many unanswered questions. Lyla's story stunned her, and at the same time left her wondering about the mysterious farm she had run away from. Before she heard the whole story, Lyla had asked her to keep a secret about something Sam thought only happened in mystery novels. And now she was involved and worried, but what could she do? She had promised that she wouldn't share their conversation with anyone and once she made a promise to keep a confidence, she never broke it. However, after the sleepless night she had, she decided to ask Lyla if she could talk everything over with Denver. He was a smart, rational man and he could provide another point of view and clearer insight to help with the quandary Lyla was in. This was just too big, and involved for her and Lyla to try and unravel without help. There must be options. Three heads were better than two, and Sam thought the more trustworthy people involved with this sticky situation, the better.

She reached down and slid her grey scruffy slippers onto her feet and made her way to the kitchen, tying her robe as she walked. What to do was the question she kept coming back to. One thing for sure, they could not unravel this mystery without help.

Even though she had promised Lyla she wouldn't tell anyone her secret, the promise was made before she had any idea how crazy and scary this whole story was. Plus, it was filled with characters she had never met and never wanted to. It was all so mysterious and out of her realm of expertise. What Lyla told her changed everything. If Lyla said she couldn't share her secret with Denver, she would still keep it, but she would step back and admit she had no advice or ideas. Lyla's story was very complicated, and even though she believed that something sinister was going on at Pine Hollow Farm it was too far out of her life experience for her to be of much help.

So, many questions ran through her head. Why hadn't anyone made contact with Lyla when she didn't show up for work? More important, the foal was gone in the morning. Now that was too coincidental. Could it be that they thought the foal had died that evening, and Lyla was so distraught that she couldn't return to work? Lyla didn't have time to read the whole binder but the word that frightened her most was Autopsies and next to the list, were abbreviations foreign to her. And what did all of this have to do with GiGi?

Sam shook her head. Try as she might, she couldn't connect all of the pieces to the puzzle. Her mind was a jumble of theories and conjecture, and none of them made sense. Lyla's portrayal of the farm, and the events that led up to her sudden impulse to take GiGi, left her perplexed. And most of all, there was a quagmire of suppositions on Lyla's part. Sam was a logical woman, and there was no logic in what Lyla had told her.

Sam stared out the window but her eyes saw nothing. She was deep in thought. There was too much that she couldn't wrap her head around. A strand of hair had loosened from its tie and dropped over one eye, and she unconsciously reached her hand up and pulled it behind her ear. She had barely been able to eat breakfast, and the quick mug of coffee she had gulped down felt sour in her stomach. Her eyes burned from lack of sleep and they picked and itched. Even though she had splashed cold water on her face and used the last of the eye drops, nothing helped. Without thinking, she rubbed her eyes again which only irritated them more. She yawned and stretched, trying to clear her head. Lack of sleep was catching up to her. She had so much to do, but she felt immobile. Her mind was racing.

She walked to the sitting room still thinking. Her tired body dropped onto the tufted blue rocking chair, and she leaned her head back in an effort to understand everything Lyla had told her.

"I'm amazed that Lyla has been able to live with this worry for so long," she thought as she closed her eyes and tried to concentrate.

It was all about the black binder and Doc. Why did he call her to his office in the first place? When he came back, could he tell by the look in her eyes, or her flushed face that she was guilty of something? And why did the phone call distract him so much that he dismissed her so easily?

She had so many questions, and Lyla had no answers. The only thing for certain in her story was that she truly believed GiGi was special and in danger. After all, she had lived longer than the other foals. Central to the mystery was why did Lyla think that 'Autopsy' meant that GiGi would be sacrificed in the name of science? For sure she panicked and stole the tiny foal, but if the horse had been so important to Doc, why didn't he contact her? Maybe he didn't care, but then again what if someone was watching her and knew the Mini was thriving. Now that was a scary thought. Sam felt herself shudder as she pictured some sinister person spying on Lyla, just waiting for the chance to steal the filly and take it back to the research farm.

"Maybe it's my lack of sleep, but nothing is making sense to me." Sam felt overwhelmed with concern. She had to concentrate on one thing at a time, but she always came back to the same question. What was really going on at Pine Hollow Farm?

# Chapter 17

Denver Chase Maxwell ended the phone call from his mother with, "I'll be there as soon as I can book a flight. I love you mom, and tell dad I'll see him soon." He knew what he had to do. First, he would go on-line and book reservations to fly to Texas, and next he would phone Sam.

Just when he thought life was moving along smoothly, he was faced with a family crisis. The phone call from his mother changed everything. His father was in the coronary unit at a hospital in Dallas. He was doing well, and the doctors had assured his mother that a coronary stent and medication, would keep him healthy for a long time. Now, mom's biggest concern was having him stick to a required change in his eating habits. He would be on a low fat diet and need to eat more vegetables and fruits. The worst part for dad would be to cut back on red meat and fried foods. That would be the most difficult challenge for him and mom. Meat, desserts, and fried food were a part of his parent's lifestyle, and although his mom had introduced more fish and chicken into their diets, it had been difficult for his dad to wean himself from foods he was accustomed to. Denver smiled when he thought about his dad eating healthier. He knew his mom had her work cut out for her. Dad could be a stubborn man.

As he rubbed his forehead, he realized what a jolt this news was to his orderly life. Now he knew what his friends meant when they talked about their aging parents. It was easy to listen to their concerns, but his parents were young and healthy. The call hit him like a ton of bricks, and he finally understood their worry. Denver thought his parents were ageless, and never expected either would have serious health issues this soon in life. To him, they would live forever.

"Several of our friends have stents," his mom had said. "And they're doing fabulous."

He knew his mother well enough to know that these words were meant to reassure him, but the tone of her voice conveyed concern. She didn't need to ask him to come; he told her he would be on a plane as soon as he could book a flight.

He ran his hand through his tousled hair. It was an unconscious habit he had when he was deep in thought. He was still shocked by the news. His sixty-two year old dad, Earl, was a strong man and never sick. He, and Denver's mother Louise, lived the good life. Earl was the CEO of Downing Software Corporation. His ranch had been in the family for several generations, and he planned to keep it that way. The fields were hayed every summer, but most was sold to other ranchers. He kept enough for his herd of Angus cattle and seven Quarter Horses. The family was avid riders, and now the grandchildren were asking for ponies. Just this past year, Earl had added two American Curly horses to his ranch. Sam's enthusiasm for the breed had rubbed off on him. He and Louise rode several times a week and vacationed frequently. Denver's siblings lived close by, and although his parents didn't press Denver, they made it clear they hoped one day he would return to Texas for good.

Now that he and Sam were engaged, this was the topic of many of their family dinners. Denver however, was his own man, and although his parents were careful not to pressure him, it was usually a part of their conversations when he visited without Sam.

His mother's favorite way to entice him was to remind him that with all the land they owned, Sam could increase her Curly herd to a much larger size. "Wouldn't that be so much fun for her," she would say in her sweet southern voice.

To not worry Sam, he kept as far away from the Texas moving subject as possible. Some things were better left unsaid, and Denver was a smart man.

Still deep in thought, he remembered he would need to cancel the flight to Texas he had already booked. He had ordered tickets for a flight home for next month, and he hadn't been looking forward to it. He knew his parents would work on him to at least think about moving back to the ranch after he and Sam were married. Today he had planned to reassure her that he had no intention of returning to Texas for good. When they had first met, Sam had told him she would never move away from New England, and he could understand why. It had everything they both loved. There were mountains to ski on and oceans to swim in. He had made a life here and he knew that Sam would never leave her grandmother and the ladies. Not only that, she had friends, family, and her farm. She had roots here, and it was her children's home. Even though they were now in college, this was the place they loved to come back to.

Denver leaned back in his chair. This news changed everything. Although he was anxious to see his dad, he hated to leave Sam after just getting everything cleaned up from the tornado. The twins were returning to their dad's home in Colorado and would not be back until the beginning of fall semester, so she would be on her own once again. He had no doubt that she was perfectly capable of taking care of herself and her farm, but he wasn't eager to be away from her for too long. Denver, a slim, blue eyed, dark haired man loved that woman. Nothing made him happier than to spend time with her. She charmed him with her easy going way, and loved to tease him about his southern drawl. His standard retort, "I don't have the accent, you do," always made her laugh.

He'd been married once, but since he left Texas he had shied away from any serious relationship. That is, until Sam came into his life.

"Moving to New England was one of the best decisions I made," he thought. "My business is growing, and I have a small farm, a horse, and a dog. What more could any man want? And now I have Sam and her son and daughter. It's what I've always wanted, my own family."

His mind traveled from his life in Texas to how he met Sam. After his marriage fell apart, he traveled to Massachusetts to stay with a former frat buddy. He fell in love with New England and decided he needed a fresh start, and began to earnestly look for a small farm. It just so happened that the farm he bought, was located in same town where Sam lived. Once settled, he bought a horse and adopted a large brown Lab mix dog. His consulting company was thriving, and except for short business trips, he worked out of the large office he had added onto one wing of the home. His business kept him busy, but once in a while he trailered someone's horse a short distance, just because he loved doing it. That's how he met Sam. He had trailered one of her horses, and they became immediate friends. However, as much as he hoped for more than friendship, it took a couple years for them to become more than that. It wasn't until a near tragedy occurred that Sam opened her heart to him.

Denver leaned his head back in the chair. He loved to recall the day that Sam finally admitted how much she cared for him. Her Curly filly was attacked by a coyote, and almost died. The near disaster broke down all the barriers for commitment that she had built. He had loved her since the day they first met. Although it was love at first sight for him, she had two teenagers and wasn't ready for a serious relationship.

"Funny how life is," he thought. "Sometimes out of tragedy come new beginnings." He smiled. He couldn't wait for them to become an official family.

Denver stretched and stood up. He poured a fresh cup of coffee, walked back to the chair and sat down, then picked up the phone and called Sam. He had a lot of planning to do and needed to see her right away. This couldn't wait. Since he had no idea how long he would be gone, he would bring his horse and dog to stay at Sam's farm.

Sam answered, with her usual "hello cowboy." He smiled when he heard her voice, but he had a nagging feeling that life for him and Sam was going to change.

# Chapter 18

Denver pulled into Sam's driveway within the hour of their phone conversation. The anxious call from his mother troubled him in several ways. Not only was he concerned about his father, but he felt she would pressure him, more than ever, to move back to Texas.

The tornado, and the fear he experienced when he lost the connection to Sam's phone, made him reluctant to leave her. Returning that evening to find her amidst all the destruction in town still tugged at his heart. Wrapping his arms around her and holding her in those moments, reenergized his commitment to her and the twins.

He parked the truck and paused for a moment before he opened the door and looked towards the ridge beyond the barn. From a distance he could hear the whinny of a horse and a gentle breeze carried the scent of summer in the air, a promised reminder of the long warm days ahead. There was no doubt that he had grown to love the village of Algonquin, where he had settled and met Sam. Sam's family and friends were a significant part of his life and he was happy. His business was flourishing and he had a marriage to look forward to. He truly believed that although his path in life had taken him a long way from Texas, it was a destiny that was meant to be.

Much as he tried to avoid the subject, the day after the tornado he had a serious talk with Sam about his parents and their wish to have him move back home to help with his

Dad's business. He had reassured her that his heart belonged to her and this town and he would never consider moving back. She had hugged him extra tight after their conversation. Sam was relieved that he was so decisive about the issue and admitted how anxious she was when he said that he had something to talk to her about when he got home from his business trip. Her mind ran wild from one possibility to another, and although he didn't talk often about the draw from his parents, she knew it was always sitting there, like an unspoken nagging potential. Now, everything was settled. They went about cleaning up her fields, and talked about their coming marriage and what he would do with his farm. There were lots of decisions to be made and Sam was happy that the Texas option wasn't in the mix.

For a brief moment he thought about the town he now called home. He remembered how he had researched several rural towns in Western Massachusetts to help him decide where he wanted to live. After a drive through Algonquin he immediately made up his mind. For some reason, or as Sam often said "it was karma," he knew this was where he would begin a new life.

Algonquin was nestled between two mountain ranges. The picturesque Main Street was dotted with old trees and vintage homes, and displayed an ambiance very different from Texas. Its rolling valleys and green mountain views imparted a feeling of serenity, and artists loved to set-up their easels during the fall season to paint the magnificent colors of stately oak and maple trees. The narrow Seantuk River flowed lazily down one side of Main Street, and charming old homes lined its banks as it made its way to the larger Connecticut River. The town boasted a population of around five thousand residents, and its claim to fame was that there were no stop lights or numbered highways on any of its roads. This fact alone, made him smile. He was happy in Algonquin, and as much as his mother wanted him to return to Texas for good, his boots were now firmly planted here.

So many thoughts about his last conversation with Sam ran through his mind as he walked to the house.

Sam greeted him at the door with a huge hug and kiss. "So, what's so important that it can't wait until tomorrow?" she asked taking his hand and leading him to the kitchen.

"Well, darlin get the coffee ready. I need one and you will too." Denver's voice had a serious tone and Sam felt herself take in a quick breath.

"What's wrong?" she asked as she reached into the cupboard and took out two mugs. She placed the half-and-half cream on the table while he fixed their coffee. There were still cookies left from the box that Lyla had brought and she filled a plate with them and set it on the table next to his chair.

"I'm thinking it's a chocolate chip cookie conversation," she said with a weak smile.

"These yours or Lyla's?" he asked with a wink. As always, the wink made her face pink up.

"Darn now, aren't you so pretty with that extra color on your cheeks," he teased.

"Stop it," she said. "I'm trying to explain. Lyla brought these by today. She said you'd like them. It's another tweak to her standard recipe. She added a little mint to the batter. She's spoiling me with her desserts, but I don't mind being her official taste tester. Of course she knows these are your favorite cookies. So, there, as usual it's all about you and the women who adore you," she said as she walked over to him.

He tilted her head back and brushed her nose with his lips. "That may be true, but I'm all yours," he grinned.

Sam took a sip of coffee and reached for a cookie. For the first time, she caught the worried look on his face. His deep blue eyes met hers, and she was suddenly apprehensive about what he was going to tell her.

"My dad had a heart attack," he said with concern in his voice. Before he could go any further Sam left her chair and went over and wrapped her arms around his neck.

"Oh my God. Is he okay?"

"Yes, he's going to be fine, so my mother says. I phoned you right after talking to her, but I wanted to tell you this in person. I've booked a flight for tomorrow evening, and don't know how long I'll be gone."

Now he had her full attention. "You had tickets to leave at the end of the month for a visit anyway," she said reassuringly. "So, you just bumped up the date sooner. The most important thing is for you to be with them, not how long you will need to stay."

"You know I hate to leave you so soon after the tornado, and the twins are going back to their dad's the end of the week. But at least the hay is in the barn and you don't have

147

to worry about that," he said as he took another swallow of coffee.

Sam placed her hand on his, and looked into his eyes. "I don't want you worrying about me. I'm fine and you know I've lived on my own for years. I love having you here, but for now you need to be with your parents. This can't wait. I wish I could go with you but there's still a lot of work to be done around here."

"I want you to leave all of the heavy work until I get back. Promise me you will."

"I will," she sighed. "I have a lot of work to catch up on while you're gone. My piece for the magazine is only half written, and I'm prepping for a new course to teach this fall. I have plenty to keep me busy. You just take care of the things you need to," she said with a reassuring grin.

"Okay, I'll bring Jet and Fletcher over tomorrow morning and get them settled in," he said as he leaned back in the chair.

"Sally will love that," she said.

All their dogs got along and Jet, Denver's horse, was easy to work around. "Slow and mellow, just like his owner," Sam always said.

"So, are the twins back tonight?" he asked with a mischievous grin.

"No, they're staying with their friends in Somers. They want to spend time with them, before they go back to their dad's."

"Well," he said as he moved the chair away from the table and got up. "I guess I know where I'm staying tonight."

He leaned over and kissed her. She felt her heart quicken and thoughts of the long night together, pushed the feeling that she already missed him to the back of her mind. For sure she wasn't ready for him to leave again, but she would never tell him. It was his place to be with his family, and after all they had a lifetime together to look forward to.

# Chapter 19

What Denver didn't know was that after another sleepless night, Sam had asked Lyla if it was okay to bring him into their circle of confidence. This was too big for them to figure out. They needed another perspective to help come up with a plan, or at least some new ideas on what to do. She phoned Lyla and explained why they needed to confide in him and after a short pause, Lyla agreed. Sam knew without a doubt that Denver would be a great sounding board, and that he would be more than willing to help Lyla.

At last, Lyla believed she was one step closer to finding a resolution for the predicament she was in. Although still frightened, now that she had confided in Sam, she was less anxious about sharing her secret with Denver.

Lyla really liked Denver, and got to see a lot of him during the weeks that GiGi and Chip were at Sam's farm. He loved all of her desserts; but his favorite was cookies and she made sure she always brought a bag for him when she came to visit her horses. She found herself as excited as everyone else about their coming marriage. They were a great couple, and Denver was now Lyla's gold standard for any future man in her life. In some ways he reminded her of Carver. Both men had a great sense of humor, were charming and strong. And being handsome didn't hurt. They had an honest sincerity, that women found attractive, and Lyla knew immediately when she met Denver that a woman could depend on him.

Unfortunately, Sam never had an opportunity to disclose Lyla's secret to Denver. The subject was on the tip of her tongue when he told her about his dad, but she knew he had enough on his plate to worry about. She decided to wait until he had everything straightened out with his parents. Not confiding in Denver made her uneasy and she found it difficult not to divulge what Lyla had told her. However, to Sam everything in life was timing, and this certainly was not the right time to burden Denver with Lyla's saga.

The next evening Sam drove Denver to the airport and kissed him goodbye. On Friday, she watched the twins board a plane to complete their visit with their dad. They would return home the week before the college semester began.

The house was empty once more, and Sam eased herself back into the rhythm of daily life. Gone were the distractions from the twins and the commotion from their friends coming in and out of the house. It was peaceful without their music blaring from the family room, and now she could enjoy the melodic voices of Willie Nelson and Elton John as she went about her chores. She worked on her magazine pieces, finished her chores with new resolve, and still had plenty of time to mull over Lyla's predicament.

Denver phoned her every day. His father was well, his mom enduring and his brother and sister were happy he was there. It took some of the pressure off of them. His mom wanted his dad to work less, and his brother and sister wanted him to retire. Denver didn't think either was an option for his father. At family meetings, they pressured him to move back to Texas but he didn't want to worry Sam so he left that part out of their conversations.

Lyla's saga continued, and she and Sam spent countless hours talking about Pine Hollow Farm and the events that led up to her fleeing with GiGi. They discussed options, drank too much coffee, and ate more desserts than they needed, but they could not find any resolution to the problem. There were still too many unanswered questions. All of their conversations ended with 'what to do?' Sam reassured Lyla that when Denver came home she would tell him all about GiGi, and she was certain that he would be able to give her some solid advice.

A week after Denver and the twins left, Sam received a phone call from her friend Addie Andris. Addie, her best friend, lived in Vermont. They had many things in common; most important was that they both raised American Curly horses. Curly horses were their passion and they usually hosted a booth at the Equine Fall Expo, an annual horse show that spanned three days. Aside from breeding horses, Addie had established a therapeutic riding program, and last year Sam had donated one of her Curly mares to Addie with the hope that she would have the temperament to become a part of it.

Dancer was born on Sam's farm, and sold to a woman named Lisa. After a difficult divorce, she could no longer afford to board Dancer and gave her to the woman who owned the facility. The new owner contacted Sam to see if she wanted to buy the mare back, and Sam brought Dancer home to her farm. Although Dancer did not work out at her farm, to Sam's delight she fit right into Addie's riding program. And her 'kids', the name she called her students, loved the steady steed with the Alpha personality.

As always, Sam and Addie were connected by their love of horses, and came to each other's rescue on many occasions. In the horse community close bonds are made, friendships are formed, and horses are always the main ingredient.

Although Sam and Addie were best friends, it was difficult to find time for visits, but they did try and squeeze a few in here and there. With her large herd of horses and her riding program, Addie could not stay away from her farm for very long.

"So, with my boyfriend in Texas, and the twins back at their dad's home, how about coming here for a visit?" Addie asked towards the end of their phone conversation.

Addie had fun referring to Denver as 'her boyfriend,' and Sam knew they had a mutual admiration society going on. Addie had been after Sam to make Denver more than a best friend for as long as she could remember, and Addie could never understand her hesitation. It was clear to everyone how deeply they cared for each other. Addie and Denver plotted constantly about how to break down Sam's wall and open her heart, but as with all things in life, love had its own timetable.

When Sam and Denver made the decision to marry, Addie jumped at the chance to be the wedding planner. "No more dragging your feet," she told Sam. "You and Denver are made for one another, and that's that. Get the calendar out. We're setting a date."

Sam was more than happy to turn the whole extravaganza over to her and they were on the phone weekly to talk about the wedding. Some of Addie's ideas fell on deaf ears, and others were offered just to hear Sam's reaction. One in particular, was to have Minnie, Doris, and Dottie wear matching pink dresses. Sam laughed 'till she cried, as she pictured the ladies in their outrageous getups and pink sneakers.

Last year was filled with changes and new ventures. It had started out peaceful, no big problems, the twins settled in college and a wedding to look forward to. Things were good. Now everything was turned upside down, and it seemed there was so much to worry about. There was the tornado, Denver's dad's heart attack, and Lyla's tangled web of intrigue. Sam was feeling a bit overwhelmed, and a visit with Addie sounded just fine with her.

"What a great idea. I would really love to see you, and I could use some R and R. We could talk about the wedding and go riding on some of the new trails that you've been posting on your blog." The urge to see Addie came to her during the phone call, and it seemed Addie had intuitively picked up on it. "Let me see who I can get to stay at the farm while I'm gone. I'll work on it as soon as I hang up."

"Okay, call me back when you're all set. I'm ready any time you are." She hung up the phone and yelled "yeah!" She missed Sam and she had a feeling that Sam had more on her mind than she let on.

Sam hung up the phone and ran through a list of friends who she could ask to help out while she was gone. Her cell phone rang and interrupted her thoughts. It was Lyla and she wanted to know if she would like company for dinner.

"Hey, what a great idea. I'd love some company," she replied.

"Don't worry about cooking. I made a casserole and will bring dessert. If you want, you can make a salad but that's plenty for the two of us," Lyla said.

Lyla had saved the day. Sam couldn't begin to think about what to eat with so many thoughts running through her mind.

As she left the house to finish chores, an idea popped up. "I wonder what Lyla's doing next week?"

Six o'clock came quickly, and Sam had just finished topping the salad with raisins and cheese, when she heard the dogs barking. She wiped her hands on a paper towel and went to the door just in time to see Lyla backing her pickup into the parking spot by the side of the shed. Sally, Jazz, and Ranger raced to meet her but Ranger was the first to reach her truck.

Sam walked briskly to grab the dogs before they knocked her over. The dogs were jumping and circling the truck and she grabbed Sally by the collar so Lyla could open the truck door.

"Sit! Stay!" she said in a stern voice. Sally and Jazz immediately sat, and after much circling, Ranger sat and stared at Sam. Each dog was waiting for the 'okay' to race each other to the house. Sam was having none of it, and made them sit until Lyla was out of the truck and walked to the passenger seat to remove the food.

"Wow," said Lyla. "Ranger is finally paying attention to commands. He's not moving."

Sam laughed. "That's the way it is when Denver or the twins aren't home. But when they are, Ranger gets away with too much." Ranger sat and waited for the release command, but Sam was in no hurry.

"I love dogs and hope I can own one someday," Lyla said as she picked up the food carrier. "For now, with my schedule, it's just me and Timmy. Cats are simple."

"On that I agree," said Sam looking at the panting dogs, waiting for her to give the okay. "Okay," she said and before she could utter another word they raced towards the house, each one trying to out run the other.

Lyla laughed as she watched the dogs scamper across the driveway, Jazz was trying her best to keep up with the other two, but being the oldest she was always left behind.

They continued chatting as they walked toward the house. Sam carried the casserole and Lyla the dessert. Everything smelled delicious. The aroma of chicken and broccoli wafted from the carrier, and Sam could almost taste the sweetness of the ginger cookies that peeked out of the blue Tin Tie cookie bag. She loved the design of Lyla's dessert bags and pastry boxes, and told her so when she first met her. Printed on Lyla's blue bags were two white flowers that had special meaning. She had confided to Sam they represented her mom and dad, which at the time, brought tears to Sam's eyes. Lyla still hadn't decided on a logo, so for now the bags said, 'Lyla's Cookies.'

Although not ready for her own bakery, blue bags and jars were Lyla's trademark. She was a smart, artistic woman, and Sam had great confidence in her culinary skills. She knew that when the time was right, Lyla would open a business that would thrive, and that she and Denver would be faithful customers.

They entered the kitchen and set the bag on the counter. The table was set for two, and the salad bowls were ready to be filled. Sam thought about how much she enjoyed Lyla's company and how close a friend she was becoming. They had a lot in common. Now, if they could only find a way to resolve the dilemma Lyla was in, and figure out if Pine Hollow Farm was a real threat or something she could let go.

After dinner Lyla helped Sam clean-up. Sam was not going to mention Pine Hollow, or ask Lyla if she had any more insight until they were ready for dessert. Lyla made the coffee and they retreated to the porch to enjoy the cookies.

"Umm," Sam said as she bit into one of the soft ginger cookies. "These are delicious. What's in them?"

"Well if you'd like, I'll give you the recipe," Lyla said as she took a sip of her coffee.

"No, I'm not about to bake cookies. I'll eat them all," said Sam. "I'm trying to go to the gym three times a week and I barely make that. If I keep eating your pastries and breads, I'll have to go seven times a week. Denver can eat and eat, and he doesn't gain an ounce, and I have a feeling its always going to be easier for him."

"Stop it Sam," Lyla said smiling. "You look great, and actually if you gained a few pounds you would never show it. You work out just taking care of your farm, never mind the gym."

"And what if I didn't go to the gym or have the farm and eat like I do. What then? Believe me Lyla; if desserts are in the house, I will eat them until they're gone. I have no will power when it comes to sweets. I take after Minnie."

The women continued bantering back and forth, but they both knew it was an excuse not to have to talk about the problem at hand.

"So, Lyla I've been thinking," Sam said as she leaned forward in her chair. "Even though you said I could talk to Denver about GiGi, you know I couldn't worry him at this time. I'll talk to him about it when he comes home, but for now I'd like your okay to share your story with my friend Addie. She lives in Vermont and has asked me to visit while Denver is in Texas. I really want to go, and maybe if I take her into our confidence, we can brainstorm and come up with some new strategies. She's a very loyal, honest friend, and if she gives her word about keeping a secret you can be sure she will. I trust her completely. What do you think?"

Lyla nodded her head in agreement. "I've complete trust in you and your judgment. If you think she can help, I'd like you to tell her my story. I know I've given you a lot to think about, and I feel bad that I've even brought you into my mess. Go ahead and tell her. Maybe she can give us a new perspective. See what she says. At this point, I know I need help and whatever you think is fine with me. It's a sticky situation."

"Okay, then. I'll talk to her when I see her."

"So, who's going to take care of your farm while you're gone?"

"Funny you should ask. I was just going through my list of friends."

"Sam, I'd really like to do this for you." Lyla reached over and touched Sam's hand. "You've done so much for me. Please let me help, it will make me feel useful. I can trailer my horses here, and take care of everything. I know the drill. I can stop by my house and feed Timmy every day after work. See what I mean about cats? Easy keepers." Lyla picked up her empty mug and walked to the kitchen. "I'm so tired of thinking and worrying about what I did, and to tell the truth, I still haven't a clue about what to do. So, go and talk to Addie. Another point of view is all I can hope for." Lyla reached over and gave Sam a hug.

Sam placed her empty mug in the dishwasher and turned to Lyla. "Look, I know it's not enough to say, don't worry, but I'm sure we'll think of something. Thanks for offering to take care of the farm. I really appreciate your help. Addie's a very smart woman. If there's a way out of this, she'll think of it. Maybe she'll think of something we haven't even considered."

As she listened to Sam's words, Lyla felt somewhat relieved if only for the moment, but she couldn't stop the nagging feeling in the pit of her stomach. She wanted the whole thing to be over. Maybe she should go to the authorities and confess.

Sam walked Lyla to her truck and she could see that although she had tried to put her mind to rest, Lyla was wearing down. It had been a heavy weight for the young woman to carry. Secrets are never easy to keep, and Sam knew how much a toll this had taken on her new friend. After meeting Lyla and watching her with her horses, she knew she was a gentle, thoughtful woman but somehow she got caught up in something that scared her. And it had caused her do something impulsive that changed her life. To be truthful, she didn't know what she would have done if she had found herself in the same situation. Maybe what Lyla had read in the black binder was only a small part of what was going on at Pine Hollow and there were other postings that Lyla either didn't understand or didn't have time to read.

# Chapter 20

Early Friday morning, Lyla pulled into the driveway just in time to watch Sam load Kahasi onto her trailer. They needed to go over the 'to do' list one more time before Sam left for Vermont.

Sam had already filled the back seat of the truck with horse tack, her saddle, and a suitcase packed with enough clothes for the week. She was eager to be on her way. Kahasi's hay bag hung from the corner of the trailer, and Sam knew he would be content to munch away during the long drive.

Sam was a worry wart when it came to her farm and animals. Although it didn't stop her from vacationing now and then, she double checked everything before she left. Long ago Minnie had impressed on her how important it was for her to enjoy time away from the farm. "Take time for yourself, or the joy you get from your farm and animals will become drudgery, and that's never a good thing," Minnie had reminded her many times.

She was confident her farm was in good hands with Lyla and she had given her names of friends for any backup help she might need. Lyla also had Denver's horse and dog to care for, but she relished the thought of giving back to her new friends who had done so much for her. Patty had volunteered to come by and help Lyla, and there were always Sam's friends, John and Alice Goodrock, who lived

161

close by. John said that he would stop in and check on the dogs during the hours that Lyla worked at the bakery.

She had phoned Minnie and told her she was going to Addie's for a week and that Lyla was staying at the farm. Minnie was happy to hear that she was taking time for herself, and said she would check in with Lyla and see if she needed a hand with chores. As she hung up the phone, she burst out laughing. She could picture Minnie in her pink tights helping Lyla tend the goats and chickens. Sam had no doubt that Minnie would be driving out to the farm to visit Lyla. Minnie was fussy about making new friends, but she immediately took a liking to Lyla. And after hearing she was on her own without family, Minnie made it her mission to become her surrogate grandmother. Of course Lyla's desserts and special attention to Minnie's fashion statements helped seal the friendship. Minnie passed on some of her old family recipes to Lyla and she was eager for her to take the plunge and open her own bakery. She even tossed out the idea that she would be a silent partner in Lyla's business, or help out behind the counter. Now that would be something to see, Sam had thought when Lyla told her about Minnie's offer. But there was no stopping the eccentric lady when she took hold of a new scheme. It soon became her focus and everyone had better get out of her way. Pearls of wisdom sat on the tip of her tongue and she was willing to offer them up to anyone who was even slightly interested. Sam had learned long ago to either take her advice or just smile and reply, 'Thanks, I'll think about that one.'

Lyla was enthralled with Minnie and had a special affection for the elderly woman. Minnie never failed to amaze her with her interesting notions and fashion getups, but Sam knew that eventually she would learn that her unconventional grandmother had her own spin on life and that she was a risk taker to the ninth degree. Minnie kept her friends and Sam laughing with her stylish wardrobe and flirtatious ways. Most elderly men were fascinated by her charm and wit and she had a steady following of eligible suitors. Young in spirit and young at heart ruled where she was concerned, and Sam believed that's what made her fun to be around. There wasn't a subject she couldn't talk about, and if she didn't know the answers, she did a Google search. Minnie was a computer fanatic, and took lessons at the senior center to enhance her skills. She had become so proficient on the computer that the director asked if she would assist in some of the classes. Doris and Dottie knew that Minnie was a wild, sometimes outrageous friend, but she was their fearless leader and they were her loyal followers.

"Don't forget Minnie will be coming by to help," Sam said as she rolled her eyes.

"I know," Lyla chuckled. "It will be fun. Don't worry, I can handle everything here. You just enjoy and have a safe trip," she said as she handed Sam a basket filled with desserts and bread.

"Lyla, you're spoiling me," said Sam as she placed the basket on the passenger seat of the truck.

"Just a little something to share with your friend. I think you'll both need some comfort food once you begin telling her my story," she said with a slight smile. "I'm anxious to hear what she says."

"Don't worry. I'll call you, and if Addie has any questions or thoughts about what to do, you'll hear from me right away."

Lyla closed the driver's door and Sam turned the key to start the truck. "I'll see you next week," said Sam as she put the truck in gear.

"Bye, Sam. Have a good time and enjoy. You deserve it," Lyla said as she stepped back from the truck.

Sam slowly drove the truck down the long driveway and headed to Vermont. "What will Addie say when she hears this crazy story," she thought as she turned the CD player on and Willie's voice filled the cab of the truck.

# Chapter 21

Sam was glad she was on the road before the mid-morning traffic filled the highway. Traffic was light, just the way she liked it, when she was pulling a horse trailer. An early start was perfect, since she felt no urgency to rush and now she could relax and enjoy the ride. Willie's music kept her company and 'City of New Orleans' filled the cab. She joined in without worrying about who was listening to her somewhat out of tune voice.

The sound of Willie never failed to remind her of Chet Granger, a Willie look-a-like, and she immediately thought about the first time she met him. He had trailered Wil, her first Curly colt, from his farm in Virginia and their friendship had grown, bonded through their love of Curly horses.

She would never forget the moment; she heard the sound of a truck pulling a long horse trailer, coming up the driveway. The truck stopped, and the driver opened his door and jumped down. For a brief moment she just stared, at a loss for words. Before she could say anything, he reached out his hand to shake hers. He was grinning as she shook his hand and she knew, that he knew, just what she was thinking. He was the spitting image of Willie Nelson. Everything about him screamed 'Willie,' from the grey braid hanging from the back of his black cowboy hat, to his worn jeans and boots and his slim stature. For sure he was Willie's double. His slow southern drawl was Willie, and although she heard his name when he introduced himself, "Hi, I'm

Chet Granger," she had to stop herself from replying, "Hi Willie, I'm Samantha Steele."

Thinking back to that time made her smile. She couldn't look at him without seeing Willie, and she remembered a silly idea had flashed through her mind. She'd ask him if she could take a picture of him and post it on Facebook to fool her friends. Of course, she never did ask him, but later as their friendship grew, she did post photos of her and Chet, and always titled them WN and Me.

Chet had taken her up on her offer for coffee and a bite to eat before he started back to Virginia. They sat at her kitchen table and ate Sam's homemade sticky buns, and drank more cups of coffee than they could count. Time flew by because of their mutual interest in American Curly horses and Sam's tales about her crazy tractor. Although she didn't buy Wil from Chet, she learned he owned a farm in Virginia, and had a large herd of Curly horses.

Finally, after an hour of talking about horses, she couldn't hold back any longer and commented on his resemblance to Willie Nelson. She confessed that Willie was her favorite country singer and she couldn't stop staring at him without seeing his face. Chet was amused by her admission and said he got that a lot, but he couldn't sing a note. Even in his small town, people chuckled about his resemblance to Willie and they nicknamed him CW, short for Chet Willie. He told her he kind of liked the name, and Sam did too. By the end of the visit, Sam realized Chet was much more than a Willie look-a-like. He was a proficient horseman, and that alone meant much more to Sam than the Willie resemblance. By the end of their visit, it didn't take long for her to realize that Chet was a real cowboy and she felt an immediate kinship with him. While listening to him talk, the thought flashed through her mind that through Curly horses she had met a man who could become a lifelong friend, and she was right.

That evening she phoned Addie to tell her all about Chet, and sometime later, he became not only her friend but Denver and Addie's as well. Sam looked forward to his visits and phone calls. He always answered her calls with 'Willie here.' It was their private joke and it always made her laugh.

Throughout the next few years, Chet trailered horses up and down the East coast, and always made a stop to visit Sam and the twins. Last year she had bought a gorgeous Curly mare from him. On his way through Vermont, he often stopped to visit Addie, and they had traded several Curly horses to change their blood lines.

"I need to phone Chet," she thought as she flipped her truck signal on for a right hand exit.

The song ended and another favorite, 'Always on My Mind' filled the air. Remembering Chet, she thought about the day S. Woodrow Wilson, aka Wil, arrived on her farm. After the shock of meeting Willie's double, she opened the trailer doors and saw Wil, her Curly colt, for the first time. He turned his head and looked at her with interest; his liquid brown eyes staring intently at her. She was in awe. His sturdy body was covered with a thick brown wavy coat, and a black ringlet mane hung down the side of his neck. As she walked up to him, she spoke quietly to reassure him that he

167

was okay and safe. She gently ran her hand along his side and continued speaking as she attached the lead line to his halter and backed him out of the trailer. His inquisitive eyes, draped by long, curled eyelashes were soft and trusting. It was love at first sight.

The spell was broken when 'On the Road Again,' began. She straightened her back against the seat and watched as a tractor trailer pulled in behind her. "So many large trucks on the road," she thought. "I wonder where they're all going." She remembered, as a young girl, counting state license plates on the many trips her family made to Pennsylvania. That's where she was born and where Minnie still had family. It was a fleeting thought and her mind quickly drifted back to Curly horses and her obsession to introduce them to the world of established breeds.

She was smitten with the breed from the time she had seen a photo of a beautiful black Curly in one of her equine magazines. The article told how American Curly horses, also known as the American Bashkir Curly, were a rare breed that ran with the wild mustangs on the North American Plains. Also noted was that they were the favored steeds of the Sioux and Crow Native Americans. She was totally enthralled with the rare horse, seeped in American history and different from any she had owned or seen. Now, five years later, she was involved with breeding, selling, and showing Curly horses. All of her hard work was now paying off and along the way she had met many horse enthusiasts and made treasured friends.

Sam believed that life had its own rhythm and purpose, and people were linked together by an invisible thread. The article about Curly horses piqued her interest enough to follow her dream to own a horse farm, and through that passion she had met Chet, her best friend Addie, and the man in her life, Denver. Now, through horses and a tornado, there was Lyla. The circle of friends was growing larger and more intricate. It was an amusing way to view life. Everything has a purpose and every purpose opens more possibilities. She smiled and shrugged her shoulders. She liked that thought.

"There it goes again, the invisible thread connecting all of us," she mused.

As if on cue, Willie's music ended and Jason Aldean's voice kicked in with 'Big Green Tractor' and her mind quickly filled with thoughts of Denver.

"I wonder how things are going with his parents," she thought as she listened to his favorite song. It seemed his time in Texas was going to be longer than he had planned. She was worried about him and although he said everything was under control, she could tell by his voice that he wasn't ready to talk about what was really bothering him. When she asked if everything was okay, he hesitated a little. This wasn't like him. He said that when she got back from Addie's, he would explain some of the issues he was having with his parents and siblings. He wanted her to have a great time at Addie's and told her to give Addie a big hug from him. Cheerful as his voice was when he said that, an uneasy feeling came over her, but she quickly brushed it off.

Before she knew it, she was almost at Addie's. Day dreaming and music had made the time pass quickly and the miles seemed to melt away. Fleeting thoughts about the twins and their next year of college swirled through her mind, but nothing at the moment concerned her more than Lyla. She was anxious to share her story with Addie, and maybe they could brainstorm and come up with something she had missed.

"What will Addie have to say, and will she have some great solution that I haven't thought of?" she wondered as she rounded the last bend in the road before the farm.

A few minutes later, she reached the bottom of Addie's driveway. It could be tricky to maneuver during winter or summer storms. Sam put her truck in low gear, and slowly maneuvered up the dirt and stone surface. The last rain storm had carved in new ruts, and puddles still filled some of the lower spots. Addie's large white farm house sat at the top of the hill and several horses raced the fence lines that ran along both sides of the drive. Kahasi whinnied to them from the trailer and they whinnied back a welcoming call. This was the first time he had returned to the place he was born, and she knew he was anxious to unload, and she needed to stretch her legs. Although it had been a quiet, pleasant drive, she missed Denver and the fun it was to make the trip with him.

Addie reached the truck before Sam could open the door. Her dogs were circling the trailer, curious about the horse, now impatiently scraping the floor with his front hoof.

Sam opened the truck door and stepped down. Addie's dogs turned their attention to her and began leaping in front of her trying to plant big sloppy kisses on her face.

"Okay," she said. "I see you." She reached out and gave each of the poodles a pat on the head.

"Off," Addie said sternly, and the dogs stopped their giddiness and sat waiting for her next command.

"Wow, I'm impressed," said Sam. "How do you get them to be so obedient?"

"It's taken some time," the dark haired pretty woman said as she shooed the dogs away. "But I had to do something with all of the kids that come here. I couldn't have the dogs scaring them."

"Nice work," Sam said as she reached over to give her friend a hug.

"So, how are you and how was the trip?" Addie asked as she walked to the back of the trailer with Sam to unload Kahasi.

"The trip was fine but I missed having Denver ride with me."

"I don't blame you, and how is my favorite cowboy doing, and how's his dad?"

"His dad has recovered and is back to the office, but I can't say as much for Denver. He seems concerned about something. I hear it in his voice, but I think everything will work out. I can't wait 'till he comes home."

They continued talking while Sam backed Kahasi out of the trailer and onto the ground. The white Curly horse stood with his head held high, nostrils wide, as his eyes watched

171

the horses along the fence line. They whinnied to him as he unloaded from the trailer, and if not well behaved and held tightly by his lead line, he would have bolted.

Sam and Addie watched his excitement as his muscles twitched. Then he let out a loud whinny, calling back to the horses. Again, they returned the greeting, but Sam knew he needed to focus on her, not the horses calling to him.

"Behave Kahasi," she said and then turned him in small circles several times to draw his attention back to her. She brought him to a halt, when his eye caught hers and his body showed he was calm and his mind was on her.

"He's so handsome," Addie remarked as she ran her hands down his side. "I'd love to ride him while you're here," she said as they walked towards the paddock that would be his home for the week.

"I'd love to have you ride him, and that's one of the reasons I brought him instead of Wil. I thought it was time Kahasi came back to the place where he was born and I also want to put some miles on him. This will be a perfect place to do it."

Sam led Kahasi to the paddock and Addie held the gate open. She unclipped the lead rope and in a flash, Kahasi kicked up his heels and ran the rail. Every now and then he stopped and whinnied, then with mane flying and tail out straight, he again galloped along the paddock rail.

"My God, he looks magnificent when he drops his head. He's muscled out and he looks so powerful. He's gorgeous."

"You should be proud of yourself and your breeding program," Sam said as they leaned on the rail and watched

Kahasi. Denver had bought Kahasi from Addie as a surprise for Sam.

"He still reminds me of a unicorn with his white body," said Sam. "His large head, long curled eyelashes and thick wavy mane are like something out of a fairy tale."

"He sure does," Addie replied as she studied the colt she never thought she would part with.

"I've had so many photographers ask to take photos of him. There is something magical about him," Sam said as Kahasi walked towards her and stopped, nuzzling her hand for treats.

"So, are you done with this?" she asked the gelding as she ran her hand down his neck. Finding no treats, he turned and walked to the water bucket. He wasn't accustomed to expending all that energy. Life was easy on his farm. His excitement gone, he walked over to the pile of hay, dropped his head and picked up a mouthful. His eyes met Sam's and he held the stare for a moment. If Sam didn't know better she could almost imagine him saying, "Thanks mom."

# Chapter 22

After watching Kahasi a bit longer, the women headed to the house, dogs jogging behind them.

Sam carried the basket of desserts, and they entered the large country kitchen of Addie's farm house. She set the basket on the counter and breathed in the familiar fragrance of Addie's' kitchen. The kitchen exuded a rich bouquet of intermingled scents and Sam could only hope that her own provided the same type of warm pleasant ambiance. She never tired of inhaling the blended smell of leather and lavender that was imbedded in Addie's home. The aroma from bubbling Mac and Cheese drifted from the oven, and her mouth began to water. It was her favorite comfort food, and Addie made it special for her whenever she visited.

Even though winter had long passed, the kitchen still held the pleasing smell of leftover chunks of semi-burned apple wood. A variety of herbs and green plants set in colorful pots stained red and blue, sat on the long counter that separated the family room from the kitchen. Looking over the counter and into the family room she could see the black wood stove sitting on a large stone hearth. During the cold Vermont winters, it was kept chock full of wood, and its cozy warmth filled the large downstairs open area. An old iron tea kettle sat empty on top of the stove, and the delightful fragrance of sassafras still lingered in the air, a reminder of frigid days of winter.

The sun streamed through the long window over the sink, casting shadows on the terracotta granite counter-tops, enveloping the kitchen with warmth.

Sam walked to the window and looked out. The view was beautiful and serene. Large climbing yellow roses brushed the window, and in front of the fence, raised beds were filled with vegetable plants. A wooden fence separated the small garden, and four Curly mares and foals were leisurely grazing in the sloped field. She leaned against the counter and soaked up the beautiful scenery. Her eyes focused on the hills and mountain wood line some distance away. Across the mountain she could see a narrow road as it snaked its way up and out of sight. She had often told Addie that if this were her kitchen she wouldn't get any work done, since she would spend most of her day gazing out the window.

While Sam was lost in thought, Addie busied herself setting the wooden harvest table with food. She placed a bowl filled with salad near their plates and removed a pitcher of ice tea from the refrigerator. As she took two glasses from the cupboard, the clink from them snapped Sam out of her daydreaming, and she turned from the window and asked what she could do to help.

"Take the oven mitts from under the cupboard, and you can get the Mac and Cheese from the oven," she said as she reached into the drawer for the forks and knives.

Sam removed the steaming casserole and placed it on the table. "Gosh, this smells so delicious. I'm starving."

"So, let's eat," Addie said as she placed a large spoon in the casserole.

Sam filled each of their plates with the Mac and Cheese and Addie filled the bowls with salad.

"So, how's Big Orange doing?" Sam asked.

'Big Orange' was the name Addie had christened her tractor.

"Well, he's still the only man in my life," Addie said as she reached for a napkin. "And he never disappoints," she laughed.

"Bet you can't wait for Denver to move in and bring his green tractor to your farm?"

"You bet I can't," said Sam as she reached for the salad dressing. "And that's not the only benefit I can think of." The words spilled from her mouth before she could think, and she could feel herself blushing.

"And what would that be?" teased Addie.

"Time to eat," replied Sam in her usual way of changing the subject to one she would rather talk about. She picked up her fork, and said, "We have a lot to talk about and my main subject, for once, is not Denver."

# Chapter 23

An hour later they finished eating, cleared up the table, and stacked the dishes in the dishwasher. Lunch was over and it had been filled with conversation about Sam's twins, Minnie, and Addie's daughter Eden. Addie brought Sam up-to-date about her riding program. Sales of Curly horses were up, and Addie was going to host the annual meeting of the International Curly Horse Organization in September. It would be a four day affair, and owners from as far away as Sweden were expected. Sam and Denver planned to stay overnight for the gala, which included a pig roast and a band from Addie's town. Addie talked about her plans for the event, and Sam reminded her that she was going to contribute a beautiful piece of jewelry, designed and made by her friend Caryn, for the auction. The proceeds would provide scholarships for children in Addie's program, which was always in need of contributions.

Addie got up from the table and removed two red coffee mugs from the cupboard. Sam stood beside her as they filled the mugs with steaming coffee. There was a pause in their chitchat, and Addie turned to Sam and said, "So, I'm ready. What is the huge dilemma you want to share with me and what does this woman Lyla have to do with it?"

"Let's take our coffee and basket of goodies out onto your porch. This is going to take time, and lots of coffee and cookies to get through this whole story. And when I'm done with it, I hope you can come up with something I haven't thought of."

"Now I'm really curious. I can't wait. Let's go." Addie picked up her coffee mug, and Sam followed mug in one hand and basket in the other.

The screened porch faced the distant mountains. A sloping green metal roof protected it from sun and rain. Now and then, calls from horses broke the quiet, and a light breeze trickled through the tops of leaf filled trees. The porch was lined with old rockers, interspersed with small side tables just the right size for coffee mugs. An old butcher block table stood stoically against the wall, and a mishmash of books were piled here and there in a haphazard way. Addie was an avid reader and when she wasn't working, she always had a novel going. Hanging from the ceiling, a large fan whirled lazily, its low hum intermingling with the sounds from farm animals and calls from birds resting in the trees outside the porch.

Red pottery jug lamps, with yellowed shades sat on tables next to a few of the rockers. Bright colored floor cloths painted by Addie, lay scattered, their multicolored patterns breaking up the dark colored wood floor. Sam admired each floor cloth as she placed her mug of coffee on a table next to a soft green pillowed rocker. Here and there Addie had added new floor cloths and they provided a warm, country ambiance to every room in her home.

As she walked onto the porch, she stopped to admire one of Addie's latest designs. The love of floor cloths was another thing they had in common.

"I really like this one," she said as she stopped and looked down at a colorful cloth, with two black cats staring up at her.

"Thanks," Addie replied. "I'm trying different colors and I have a few new ideas in mind."

With Addie's tutelage, Sam had made several floor cloths and she could see why Addie loved them so much. Her porch like the rest of her home, oozed with inviting comfort. It was Addie's retreat, a place to kick back and relax after a hard day's work.

Sam admired Addie. She was a strong, self-made woman, and once she made up her mind to do something she never wavered. A widow with a teenage daughter, she dreamed big and made things happen. To Sam, she was fearless.

Addie's husband had died in an auto accident when Eden was a baby and she hadn't found any other man to fill the empty space left in her heart. She had loved Andy with a passion, and no other man could begin to live up to the image she held on to. This is probably why, Addie, a pretty and smart young woman, always found fault with any man who showed interest in her. She was always waiting for her prince to come knocking on her door and her expectations were high. Addie had a way of choosing relationships that she knew would fail. It was her wall of protection, and Sam understood it very well. She had once been in the same place as Addie. But, as she often told her, once she opened her heart and gave love a chance, her world became more complete, and Sam was determined that Addie find the same happiness.

"So, who's the new man in your life?" The subject was great for many laugh filled evenings, and Addie never failed to surprise her with descriptions of love found, and love lost. Sam was curious to hear about her latest love interest, and looked across the table at Addie, waiting for an answer.

"I'll tell you after you tell me about Lyla," she answered in a teasing voice.

Sam sat her mug on the table next to her rocker, and took her time as she opened the basket of desserts.

"Hurry up," Addie said. "Just pick something. I really want to hear about this."

"Wait a minute. I want to get everything ready before I begin. No interruptions, well maybe a few questions, will be allowed." Sam smiled as she took out a fudgy chocolate brownie and set it on her plate. She knew Addie's curiosity was getting the best of her, and truth be known she enjoyed keeping her in suspense for a few more minutes.

Lyla had packed several varieties of cookies. Ginger, chocolate chip, and peanut butter. All were stacked neatly, along with a row of brownies, and each layer was separated by thin blue bakery paper. Thinking of everything, Lyla had included her favorite orange and cranberry biscotti. Sam left them in the basket for their evening snack and morning coffee. After rearranging the biscotti, she carefully placed the cookies and brownies on a large square white plate and set it on the table between her and Addie.

"Oh my God," said Addie. "These look so delicious I don't know where to begin. Now this was worth waiting for."

"I told you she was a great baker. Now you'll know what I mean. Let's eat and talk."

Sam took in a sip of coffee, wiped the brownie crumbs from her fingers, leaned back in the chair, and began the story about Lyla and GiGi.

# Chapter 24

She got straight to the point. "Lyla stole a Mini horse from a farm right here in Vermont."

"What? She stole a horse from a farm?" Addie almost choked on her coffee. "I can't believe your friend would do something like that. What kind of woman steals a horse and why would she tell you?" She was shocked. This wasn't the story she expected to hear.

"Wait a minute. Don't judge her yet. Wait 'till you hear it all, and then you'll understand."

"Okay, but this had better be good. I know how I'd feel if someone stole one of my horses," Addie's dark brown eyes narrowed and her voice was harsh.

"Promise you won't interrupt until I've told you the whole story," Sam asked as she leaned forward and looked into Addie's eyes. "You know I would never defend someone who stole a horse. Well, that was until I heard Lyla's story. I think you'll understand why she did it when I tell you everything."

"I promise," Addie said. "But I still can't believe one of your friends stole a horse, kept it a secret, told you, and then had the gall to ask you not to tell anyone."

"That's not completely true. She was a wreck worrying that someone was watching her all the time and she didn't know what to do. She agreed that I should tell Denver, but I couldn't burden him with this crisis. He has enough dealing with his family. So I asked her if I could tell you since you are really good at solving problems and very trustworthy. Honestly Addie, she's so weighed down with this secret. She needs help. Don't forget she has no family to go to. She isn't as lucky as you and me."

"Alright, if you care, then I guess I can at least listen," Addie said. But the concern in her voice worried Sam.

Sam leaned back in the chair, took another bite of brownie, and began the story about Lyla and GiGi.

"I met Lyla when I took in her horses after her barn was destroyed by the tornado," she said as she sat back in her chair.

Addie sat spellbound as Sam told her everything she knew from what Lyla had described. She began with Lyla's work at Pine Hollow, and went on to explain who Doc was, and finally what compelled her to take GiGi. She left nothing out. Addie only interrupted when she had a question she thought important.

When Sam finished, Addie looked at her in amazement. "I for once am speechless. Where in Vermont is this farm?"

"Barnsville. Do you know where it is?"

"I should hope so," Addie replied in amazement. "It's only about a half hour from me."

"What?" Sam was shocked to hear that the town was near Addie's. She was just ready to take another sip of coffee, and it spilled onto her hand. "I can't believe it. So, do you know where Pine Hollow Farm is?"

"Never heard of it, but I know someone who might. I was going to tell you about him, but that can wait until you finish the rest of Lyla's story. Catch your breath, and wipe the coffee before it drips onto your shirt," Addie said laughingly. "This sounds like the farm my friend Jace worked at."

Addie got up and stretched. "He never mentioned the name of the farm, but he did say they were testing some kind of vaccine on horses. He did the remodeling before the owner moved in." She shrugged her shoulders. "I can't believe how long we've been sitting here. Let's take a break. Do you want a refill on your coffee?"

"Thanks, but no. I'm coffeed out. I'm amazed at how this is falling into place."

"Not so fast. I still don't understand why she would steal the Mini. What made her think the foal was in danger?" Addie asked as she picked up the coffee mugs.

"Addie, it's what she saw in the black binder on Doc's desk. It frightened her so much that she impulsively took the foal. In her mind, she thought GiGi was going to be sacrificed in the name of science. Don't you get it? She thought she was saving GiGi, not stealing her." The more she talked about Lyla to Addie, the clearer Lyla's motives became. She hoped Addie would come to the same conclusion.

Addie, still stunned by everything Sam told her, was not quick to agree. She needed to digest the whole thing before she could find some clarity.

"Let me think about that one," Addie said trying to wrap her head around the whole story.

While Addie went to the kitchen, Sam stood and looked out the window. She was more puzzled than before. She couldn't believe how close Pine Hollow was. Although Addie said she knew someone who had worked at the farm, something about the place still didn't ring true.

Addie returned and handed her a glass of wine. "Time to change it up a bit," she said with a knowing smile.

"Thanks Addie. I agree." She took a sip of the cold wine and paused to pull her thoughts together. "Gosh now that you've told me you know someone who worked there, I guess it wasn't a secret about the farm's purpose. But I do know that Lyla was frightened to death working there. Honestly Addie, she's really a kind, sweet woman. I believe her when she told me why she did it and my gut feeling is telling me that the farm wasn't what they led everyone to believe. For Lyla to do something like that, she had to be desperate. I know her, and she isn't the type of woman to do this sort of thing."

"Jace said something about the foals being stillborn or dying soon after birth." Addie was still trying to piece together what Sam said and what Jace told her about the farm. "I thought it was cruel, and told him I could never work at a place like that, but he said the money was great and they were all informed that this is what happens at a research farm. They were working on a vaccine to save horses from some disease, and if some foals didn't make it, so be it. After all Sam, a lot of research labs use animals. Jace said people who worked there were happy to earn a lot of money, and they weren't as curious as it seems your friend Lyla was."

"So is he still working there?"

"No. His job ended when the renovations of the barns were completed. That took place before anyone moved onto the farm. But a couple of the guys told him how strange it was when the farm suddenly shut down. One morning they showed up for work and the only one there was the boss who gave them a final paycheck along with a large bonus. All of the horses were gone and the whole place was deserted. At first it was the talk of the town, but the job was done and eventually everyone moved on. They all went about their business and never thought any more about it."

"Did your friend say anything about the conditions at the barn or the foreman Bill, or the man everyone called Doc?"

"He did say that there was a vet who ran everything and he was very strange. Didn't talk to the help and only barked out orders. Always in a hurry and kind of a messy looking guy. They all stayed out of his way."

"From what Lyla told me, I don't think she knew what the farm was all about when she was hired, and it bothered her that so many foals died. She was afraid of Doc and his foreman Bill. I think she kept on working there because Carver, the man who hired her, reassured her that the vaccine would help all horses. And to tell the truth, I think she had a crush on him."

"That makes sense, but what does this have to do with the Mini horse?"

"Well, now that's where this gets interesting," Sam's eyes drew narrow and she took another sip of wine.

In the end Addie asked the same questions Sam did. Why had no one tried to find Lyla? They knew where she

186

lived. What about her Aunt Mamie? Lyla told Sam no one from Pine Hollow had contacted her aunt and there hadn't been any police officers knocking on her door. If the foal was so important to Doc, why hadn't he called the authorities and asked them to follow-up? Did the farm have so many horses that no one missed one foal? Was this foal as important to Doc as Lyla had thought? Who were these people, Carver, Bill, and Doc, and what was Pine Hollow really all about?

It was late in the afternoon when they finished talking, and it was time for Addie to begin evening chores.

She got up from her chair and went into the kitchen. Sam followed. They both were silent as they placed the basket of desserts on the table.

"Addie, I think it all comes down to this. I don't believe Lyla thought for one minute she was stealing GiGi. I still believe that she thought she was saving her. She didn't really know what was going on at the farm, but she had a feeling that if she didn't take GiGi away, she wouldn't survive. She did something spontaneous and now she doesn't know what to do. She can't go to the police, and she thinks that someone from the farm may be coming back for GiGi."

"I must tell you Sam. I am blown away by this. If anyone other than you had told me this, I wouldn't have believed it." Addie moved her shoulders back and forth to get the kinks out. "I'll tell you what. Let's not talk about it anymore until dinner tonight. It will give us both time to think about the whole thing and maybe something will pop into our heads we haven't considered. Agreed?"

"Agreed," said Sam. "Let's go. I need to stretch my legs and my mind is in a tizzy. I feel like I've been on a mental marathon and I'm exhausted."

They walked out the back door and the dogs hearing it open, took it as an invitation to follow. Addie picked up a stick and threw it as far as she could. The poodles and Lab dashed after the stick and pummeled into each other as they raced to see who could reach it first. Addie headed up the hill to the barn. She needed time to ruminate all of what Sam had told her. If she didn't know this had really happened, she would have thought she had seen it on TV. It was like something out of one of the CSI series. What to do was a question they both would need to talk about and for sure they needed a plan. She feared they were missing important pieces of information.

Addie picked up a bale of hay and tossed it into the wheelbarrow. Suddenly she had an epiphany. They could begin with Jace, her latest flirtation. Maybe he could fill in the missing pieces.

# Chapter 25

As tired as Addie was after the long evening talking with Sam, she found herself wide awake several times during the night. She got up, drank a glass of water, used the bathroom, went back to bed, but still couldn't sleep. Try as she might sleep eluded her, and thoughts of Lyla and her compelling story kept her tossing and turning all night. She plumped her pillow, kicked her blankets off, and at least a hundred times tried to will herself to fall asleep, but nothing worked. Each time she got up, Sam heard her footsteps, and the running of water in the bathroom sink. For a half a second, she thought of getting out of bed to join her, but she couldn't find the energy to do so. As with Addie, her sleep was fitful and restless.

By five a.m., Addie gave up. She got up, fixed herself a cup of coffee, and carried it to the family room. It was still dark outside, but she knew it was useless to try and sleep with so many thoughts swirling in her head. She now understood why Sam and Lyla couldn't figure out what to do. It was a dilemma that seemed to have no answers. Although, she couldn't fathom the anxiety Lyla had endured since she ran from Pine Hollow, she recognized the frantic state she must have been in to do so. Just imagining that night gave her chills. Lyla had been desperate enough to slip into the barn, take the foal, carry it to her truck, and make the trip back to Massachusetts. And she did it at the risk of being caught. Even now she was always looking over her

189

shoulder. Addie wondered if she would have had the audacity to do the same thing if she thought GiGi was in danger. Either Lyla was very brave or she was very foolish and although she had never met her, Sam's belief in her and her story, made Addie a believer. Not only was Sam her best friend, she was a woman who carefully analyzed a situation before she jumped into unknown waters. Even though the story seemed unbelievable to Addie, she trusted her friend's judgment. Sam was a woman who was steadfast in her loyalty to friends and this is what Addie admired most about her. It took a lot to rattle Sam. She loved to explore options, make plans, keep a daily list of things to do, and was very creative. She admired her for finally coming to terms with the fact that even her five-year plan could not be set in stone. Furthermore, Sam was not a woman easily led down a path without knowing the way back. Addie rubbed her eyes and yawned. She stretched, trying to shake off the cobwebs and leaned back in the chair. As she thought about Jace, she knew that she and Sam would have to be careful with their questions about Pine Hollow. They would have to think like detectives. She almost laughed out-loud as a picture of Sherlock Holmes and his side-kick Watson flashed through her mind. Was she suddenly thinking like a detective? She was more the Nancy Drew type, but if Sam thought they could unravel this mystery, so be it. Thinking of her and Sam as detectives was crazy, but maybe that's what it took to solve the mystery of Pine Hollow. And for that to work, they needed to use all of the tools that detectives did. She recalled that real detectives used deductive reasoning, and that's exactly what they needed to do. They must step away from Lyla, the person, and look at the whole situation not as a dilemma, but a case to be solved. That worked! And she and Sam would be ready for the task. It was time to make a list of what they knew, and make a plan to fill in the blanks. Now she was excited and she knew Sam would be too.

Addie drained the last of her coffee and walked to the kitchen. She felt like a woman on a mission and she would share her ideas with Sam when she came downstairs for breakfast. During the night, she heard Sam tossing and turning and she didn't want to disturb her this early in the morning.

"I may as well get an early start on chores," she thought. "When I come in I'll phone Jace and ask him to meet us for lunch. I'll tell him I want him to meet my best friend. He'll like that."

Thinking back she recalled that on several occasions Jace had talked to her about his job at Pine Hollow, but she hadn't been interested in anything except staring into his dark brown eyes. She knew he was infatuated with her and wanted to take their friendship to another level, but she held back. She wasn't quite ready to begin tying herself down with another man.

"I wonder what Sam will have to say about Jace?" Addie had wanted to talk to her about the new man in her life, but that would have to wait. Another thought ran through her mind. Sam and she would have to go over the questions they would ask him. They couldn't act too interested. Lunch would have to be casual, and they would have to ease him into talking about the farm. Jace would have to think it was his idea, and they would have to be careful not to appear too inquisitive. They both needed more information before they took the risk of bringing Jace into their circle. Until they learned more, Lyla and GiGi would be off limits in their conversation with Jace.

It was seven in the morning by the time Sam dragged herself downstairs for coffee and something to eat. Addie had already finished chores and was making a list on a white pad of paper. She had phoned Jace and asked him if he would like to have lunch with her and her friend from Massachusetts. Jace was more than happy to spend time with Addie and meeting her friend would be as he said "great." They would meet at noon at the Blue Cat Bakery and Deli in Barnsville.

By nine o'clock they had finished the last of the orange biscotti and downed more coffee than their kidneys could handle. It was going to be an interesting day and they were eager to meet with Jace. They completed the list of questions they would ask and went over them several times.

Most of the questions sounded innocent, and they could only hope that they would lead Jace to volunteer information about Pine Hollow that Lyla wasn't privy to.

Addie once again suggested they be upfront and tell Jace about Lyla, but Sam didn't want to involve anyone else in her debacle until they had more information about the farm to make that decision. In the end they both agreed that since Lyla was so afraid of Doc and the farm, the less people who knew her connection to them, the better. Doc was their biggest curiosity and it would be interesting to hear what Jace said about him..

Sam laughed when Addie told her they should think of themselves as detectives and on a mission to solve a mystery.

"So who's Sherlock and who's Watson?" she asked, amused at the idea.

"I think you can be Sherlock, since your name begins with an S and I will be Watson since I like the letter W." Addie chuckled at her ingenious idea. "If we're going to be detectives, we may as well find some humor in an otherwise scary situation."

"You are too funny," said Sam. "We'll have to be careful not to use these names around Jace. He'll really think we're crazy, plus it may give away the true reason for our interest in the farm."

"Agreed, Sherlock," Addie was now beginning to enjoy their nicknames and couldn't stop laughing.

"Okay Watson. Let's get going." Sam was laughing as hard as Addie. "Bring the pad of paper so we can write everything down when we leave the bakery. If we're going to be detectives we need to keep track of every detail of our conversation with Jace, and then go over our notes when we return."

# Chapter 26

The town of Barnsville, home to residents attracted by its beauty and quiet life, was fast becoming the gold standard for small town renewal. Barnsville was nestled in-between two mountain ridges and during good weather a slow flowing river hosted a picturesque collection of small boats. The river meandered lazily along on the outskirts of town, and in years gone by provided transportation for the delivery of necessary supplies to the early settlers.

Although Barnsville still boasted working farms and rolling fields of hay and corn, it was a retreat for artists and a second home for city dwellers looking for a quiet haven away from their busy lives. They had bought up many of the old farms and remodeled the antique homes to fit their lifestyle and needs. Although the new residents loved the beauty of the mountains and the ambiance of the small town, they also had a desire for the comforts of the city. Committees were formed to develop a plan to attract summer tourists and winter skiers. The citizens of Barnsville believed their town was a diamond in the rough and were in the throes of developing it into a honey spot for tourists. The rustic river town was still in the process of renovations, and many old buildings had been repainted with cheerful colors. Brick sidings had been cleaned and repaired and colorful flower boxes were filled with vinca vines and geraniums. Historically inspired street lamps bordered brick walkways and banners touting the shop names hung from the arms of the decorative lighting posts. Large trees with drooping leafed branches lined the street and old fashioned store fronts shaded with colorful awnings dotted the sidewalks. Flanking both sides of the street were several small boutiques and antique shops. A variety shop, aptly named "Gidgets and Gadgets" touted an assortment of toys and widgets that provided something for everyone. At the end of the Main Street a beautiful white church with a tall steeple held Sunday services, youth activities, and monthly dinners. Lots of thought and planning had gone into the aesthetics of Main Street.

Side streets running off of Main hosted a variety of bakeries, restaurants, and bookstores. Wooden benches sat under shaded trees and provided a welcome respite for tourists and weekends were filled with music, artist's fairs, and a large farmers market. Careful and deliberate planning had been fruitful and after ten years, tourism was thriving and new shops and restaurants were opening.

Barnsville was the town Addie came to when she felt the need for a break from her busy life. She loved the baked goods at the Blue Cat Bakery and Deli, and often met friends there for lunch or coffee. It was there she had first met Jace, and it was where Sam would meet Addie's latest flirtation. But this time Addie had a different agenda, and it was up to her to turn any conversation into information about Pine Hollow without Jace guessing he was an important part of a big puzzle. Even though she and Sam had talked about it for hours, she felt herself growing nervous as she wondered if she could pull it off without Jace becoming suspicious.

It was almost noon when Sam and Addie pulled into the parking lot of the Blue Cat. They parked their truck, looked at each other and smiled.

"Ok, Sherlock. Let's see what we can learn. But don't be surprised if my mind goes off track when I look into Jace's dark brown eyes. I tingle all over when he looks at me."

"Oh, really. You didn't tell me much about this Jace, but then I guess we didn't have a chance to talk about anything but Lyla. Even when Denver phoned me this morning, I kept it short; since he doesn't know about Lyla's secret, I was careful not to say anything. But he did ask if you had a new man in your life. Now I'm even more excited to meet Jace. Is there more than his brown eyes that you want to talk about, Watson?"

"Now I've got your attention," Addie said laughing as she opened the truck door and stepped down. "I'll tell you all about it later. And, by the way, I do want your opinion. You know my gold standard for men is Denver. I'll tell you about Jace when we get home," Addie said with a grin. "But for now it's all about Pine Hollow Farm."

Sam opened her door and stepped down from the truck. "Hmmm. I don't know if I'm more interested in Pine Hollow or Jace, but I guess we're going to be drinking lots of coffee when we get back to your farm."

They were still laughing as they walked up the sidewalk to the bakery. Changing the subject from Lyla to Jace was a welcome relief from the heaviness of Lyla's secret.

Addie paused at the bakery door and turned to Sam. "Well, Sherlock let's see if we can pull this one off. I thought we were going to spend the week riding on some of the trails you haven't been on, but now we're official mystery sleuths. And I have to use Jace to help us answer some of our questions. I don't feel good about this."

"I'm sorry, Addie. Try to think of it as an adventure. If Jace can't help, we may have to let it go, and I'll tell Lyla that her best plan would be to go to the authorities with the whole story."

"Ok," Addie replied. "I think we'll have a better idea after talking with him. If you think I'm giving him too much information, just kick my leg and I'll change the subject. Maybe you'll be better at asking innocent questions than I will."

Addie pushed open the door of the bakery and Sam was right behind her. As the door opened, Sam was engulfed with the delicious smell of freshly baked bread. A large display case was filled with all sorts of pastries and pies and an elderly woman dressed in a crisp yellow dress was busily waiting on customers. Covering her dress was a white apron decorated with a large blue cat with big black eyes. Tall racks were stacked with several varieties of warm bread, their crusty ends sticking out from white paper bags. It was a busy place and it looked to Sam like everyone in town came here for bread and desserts. Over the counter, a large menu listed the desserts of the day and the line of customers waiting to pay was wrapped around one side of the counter, while another line of people waited for a turn to order. To Sam

197

the whole place appeared to be in a state of organized chaos, and it reminded her of a Seinfeld episode where customers waited in line for the soup of the day.

Addie squeezed through the line, Sam following close by. An open doorway led the way into a room filled with booths and they stopped for a moment to let a waitress carrying coffee mugs go by. Sam was amused to see the streaks of red and blue on the dark hair of the waitress. She wore a light yellow shirt and bright yellow pants and her white apron with the blue cat logo, hung loosely around her thin body.

"Interesting color combinations," Sam thought. She was amused by the choice of colors for the wait staff. Although she saw no male waiters she wondered if they too had to wear yellow matching shirts and pants. The image of male waiters dressed in yellow with aprons adorned with blue cats made her chuckle.

As usual, anytime Sam found an interesting breakfast or luncheon place to eat, she thought about Minnie. "Minnie and friends would love this place," she thought as her eyes scanned the room. "Once Addie and I figure out what scared Lyla enough to steal a horse, I'll bring the ladies to visit Addie and we'll all come here for lunch."

For a moment she was so lost-in-thought as she gazed at the yellow wall with the large blue cat staring back at her, that she forgot why she and Addie were at the deli. She stopped and her eyes scanned the restaurant to find Addie. Another waitress excused herself and walked in front of Sam, tray held high, filled with deli sandwiches and desserts. Sam caught a glimpse of Addie as she walked full steam ahead. She saw her stop at a booth at the end of the room, lean down and plant a big kiss on the man sitting at the end of the table.

"That must be Jace," she thought.

Addie slid onto the seat across from the grinning man and she reached across the table and took his hand. Sam stopped for a moment and studied the man who leaned forward and said something to Addie that made her laugh.

Jace Andrew was a big man. His thick brown hair was tucked under a baseball cap with a John Deere label on it. He wore a denim shirt and his face was a bit scruffy from not shaving, but his smile said it all. He was smitten with Addie.

Sam walked up to the booth and for a brief instant felt like an intruder and that she had interrupted a special moment between them. Addie broke her gaze from Jace and turned to Sam. "Sam I'd like you to meet my friend Jace."

When Addie said that, Sam had all she could do to control the giggle rising in her throat. "Friend? She's kidding isn't she? He's more than that. I can feel the sparks just standing here."

Pulling herself together, she smiled and reached her hand out to Jace. He grinned and shook her hand. His hand shake was strong and steady. He looked directly into her eyes and said, "Glad to meet you Sam. I've heard so much about you and your adventures with Addie." His eyes twinkled, and Addie was right when she said he had beautiful eyes. Sam, like Minnie, thought she was a good judge of character and she immediately felt comfortable with the newest man in Addie's life.

"Yes," said Sam. "We've had our fun that's for sure. Thanks for meeting us for lunch. I've heard so much about you." She couldn't look at Addie when she said that. They both knew it was a bold faced lie. Addie had told her almost nothing about Jace. But then, they hadn't taken the time to talk about anything but Lyla.

Addie didn't miss a beat. "I've told you so much about Sam, and I wanted you to meet her. She's here for the week and we plan on doing some riding. I told her about the great trails in our towns. You know a lot of the mountain trails, so maybe you'll join us?"

Sam slid onto the seat next to Addie and was about to agree with the invitation, but the waitress with the purple streaked hair was there before she could say anything.

"Coffee?" she asked in a high pitched voice. Before they could answer she continued, "The soup of the day is broccoli baked potato and you can order it with a half sandwich. Or you can order a half sandwich, with either potato salad, coleslaw or a house salad. Are you ready to order?"

Sam felt a grin come to her face, and she had to look away from the waitress so she wouldn't embarrass anyone. The waitress was stick thin, with a large nose and her dark eyes were tiny and set close together. The tightly curled black hair looked like she had added a goop of gel to hold it in place, and the purple hair pieces clipped on the top looked like bird feathers. She had a large name tag pinned to her collar with the name Sparkle on it. Add that to the yellow uniform and tone of her voice and it was becoming too much for Sam to hold herself together. She glanced at Jace and Addie to see if they were as amused as she was, but they were too busy goggling over each other to notice anyone else. Sam could feel her silly gene kicking in, and it was taking all of her self-control not to laugh. The sound of Jace's deep voice snapped her out of a bad situation.

"No, we're not ready to order yet," Jace said with a smile. "We need a few minutes."

"I'll start with coffee," said Sam without looking up from the menu.

"Me too," Addie said, her eyes still locked with Jace's.

The waitress, a vision of yellow, turned and walked briskly away.

"Let's look at the menu and decide what we want to eat Sher---," and she caught herself, "Sam."

Sam rolled her eyes and then dropped her head to look at the menu. Addie had almost called her Sherlock.

Addie quickly added, "Then we can talk. Their deli sandwiches are delicious. The rolls are baked fresh daily and there are other soups on the menu if you don't like the soup of the day. And you can't go wrong with a salad and their house dressing." She would be careful not to make that mistake again with the name. She had to get serious about this.

"I think I'll try the soup of the day and match it with tuna salad on a croissant roll. I want to save some room for dessert."

"I'll have the same," said Addie. "What about you Jace?"

"Well, the soup sounds like a plan but I'll have a ham, cheese, and tomato on a bulky roll and a side of potato salad." He put the menu down and reached over and took Addie's hand.

Sam smiled as she watched the two love birds. This was going to be interesting.

# Chapter 27

Lunch was delicious and they were on their second cup of coffee and waiting for dessert. Sam looked around and spoke to Jace and Addie.

"Jace it's been a pleasure meeting you. Now I can put a face to the man that Addie has been talking so much about."

"Hope I've met your expectations and her description of me," he said as he winked at Addie.

For the first time since she had known her, Sam saw Addie's face flush.

"Let me say this," Sam said. "You're everything she described and more."

Now it was Jace's turn to squirm.

They all started laughing at the private joke and Jace trying not to get rattled even more, smoothly turned the conversation on to horses.

"You know, I really respect both of you and what you've accomplished with your horses. A rare breed of horse, and right here in front of me two women who themselves are rare breeds." Jace looked from one woman to the other and grinned.

"Why thank you. I'm flattered. What a sweet thing to say," Sam said.

Addie placed her hand on Jace's and leaned over the table and gave him a quick kiss. "Jace that is the nicest thing a man's ever said to me. I know Denver always calls Sam a rare breed, but you just melted my heart."

Sam saw Addie's eyes fill with tears. "Now that's the man for Addie," she thought.

She quickly moved to help Addie recover her emotions and said, "So, what do you think of Addie's farm and her Curly horses?"

"Well, Addie has taken me riding on some of her favorite trails and one of her Curly geldings is my favorite horse to ride. He's one of the best trail horses I've ridden. His name is Blackjack and I'm thinking of buying him. I own two Quarter Horses, but to tell the truth, the Curly horses have caught my eye. There sure is something special about them."

"Really, and did you know you can't own just one?" Sam asked teasingly.

Addie shook her head in agreement. "Yeah, I sure know that feeling."

"You don't have to tell me," Jace said. "I can see by the number of Curly horses on Addie's farm that's true, and from what she's told me Sam, your herd is building each year."

"Yes, I've been very fortunate. I've been careful in my breeding program and sales are up and now that Denver and I are getting married, we're thinking of increasing our herd. Of course Addie must have told you that she and I met through Curly horses. Actually, that's how I met Denver. He trailered some of my horses to shows, when I was just starting out."

"Sam's found true love with Denver and he's one special man. I can't wait for you to meet him," Addie said as she turned to Jace.

"Guess I have a lot to live up to," Jace said as he squeezed Addie's hand.

They were interrupted when the vision of yellow returned with dessert dishes filled with apple crisp, topped with vanilla ice cream. She set them on the table and asked if they would like their coffee warmed up. Coffee hounds that they were, they each said yes, and she added more coffee to their half filled cups.

Sam took another drink from the white mug trimmed in blue and smiled as she looked around. "Addie, I love this bakery, and especially the cheerful colors. It amazes me, but it seems to put everyone in a happy mood. The blue cat painting on the wall and the same print on the aprons is really fun," she said as she watched the waitress walk to the booth next to them and set plates filled with burgers and chips on their table. I can see why you and Jace enjoy coming here."

"Jace and I stop in at least once a week." Addie said. "It's our favorite place to eat, and sometimes we just order coffee and dessert. But, I want to tell you Sam, nothing can come close to your friend's home baked desserts. Jace, you have to try the biscotti that Sam's friend sent with her before we eat them all. We've already finished off all of the orange and there are only a few cranberry left," she laughed.

"Tell you what, how about if I stop by tomorrow morning and go riding with you? That is, if the offer still stands."

"We'd love it," Addie said. "I've been telling Sam about the mountain trails that connect my town to yours. And remember you were telling me about that old farm you and your friend worked at? Maybe we can ride by there. It sounded so interesting."

Sam took Addie's lead and asked, "What farm? I love to look at old farms and barns. Does anyone live there or is it a deserted?"

"Well," said Jace. "From what I was told by the guys who worked there, the owner suddenly upped and left. When they got to work one morning they were met by the barn boss who told them their job was over and the farm was being sold. He paid them and gave them a huge bonus. They were shocked but when they were hired they were told the job would last only six months to a year. The guys didn't much like the owner, but I never had a problem with him."

"So, you worked there too?" Sherlock had her thinking cap on.

"No, I never did farm work there. I was hired by the owner when he first bought the farm. He needed some remodeling done before he moved in. There's no house on the property. It burned down some years ago, but the new owner wanted to use the farm for a research facility of some kind. I fixed up the barns and built a new addition to house a lab and equipment. The new owner, he called himself Doc, also had me build a living area and office in a loft area

206

above one of the barns. That was the extent of my employment.

"Lab? What kind of Lab?" Sam asked.

"Don't know for sure. But they had quite a few Mini horses out there. Everything's gone now. Are you sure you girls want to go there? There are lots of other trails we could take that would be more interesting."

"I really would love to ride out to that farm," replied Addie. "Honestly, Jace. I've always been curious about the farm and it would be fun to see it with Sam."

"When did the owner move out?" asked Sam.

"Not sure, but only a short time ago. I still see one of the guys who worked there, and we play a game of pool several nights a week. He stayed behind after the farm closed up. He rents a house he's thinking of buying. Tells me his next job doesn't start for a few months."

"Wow, this is getting interesting," Sam thought. She still had a ton of questions, but she wasn't sure if she should ask any more.

Addie was spooning a bite of apple crisp into her mouth, when Sam cleared her throat to signal it was time to change the subject. They shouldn't act too curious. They could find out more when they got to the farm.

Addie raised her eyebrows and looked at Sam. Her mouth was full of ice cream and she reached for a napkin. "Oh my God. This is so delicious. What do you think Sam?"

Sam had just finished the warm apples drenched in ice cream. "This is the best apple crisp I've had in a long time. I wouldn't tell Minnie, but it beats even hers."

"Who's Minnie?" Jace asked as he scraped his bowl.

"Jace you have to meet Sam's Grandmother Minnie. She's the best, and so funny. You would love her and her friends. They make getting older look like fun. They wear the darndest bright colored shirts, and they dress in stretch pants and western boots. Sometimes they wear cowboy hats but the best part is when they wear matching sneakers." Addie was now laughing. "I love those women. I swear they are my role models."

"So, does Minnie live near you, Sam?" Jace asked.

Sam's mind was still on Pine Hollow and Addie had to take the lead. She knew Sherlock wanted to ask more questions, and she was mulling over how to ask them.

"Sam, tell Jace about Minnie and friends," Addie urged.

The question snapped Sam from her preoccupation with Jace's description of the farm. "Minnie is my mother's mom and she is someone if you met her once, you'd never forget her. She keeps me on my toes, and not a day goes by that she doesn't make me laugh. It would take a week to explain Minnie and her friends. My mom lives in Florida with my step-dad and I don't see her much, but Minnie has always lived close by me. Denver simply loves her and the feeling is mutual. Her friends, Dottie and Doris make-up the trio, and to know them is to love them."

"They sound like ladies I would get a kick out of. I hope I can meet them someday. That is if Addie keeps me around long enough."

Now, Sam knew for sure. This man really liked Addie and even though he said that in a teasing way, she knew he had Addie's number.

Jace placed his empty coffee mug down on the table and picked up the bill. "I hate to leave you ladies. Thanks for asking me to join you, but I've got to get a move on. I'm meeting a neighbor about a field he wants mowed. So, you two enjoy another cup of coffee. And Addie, bring home some of the bread. I think Sam will really like it. I'll see you ladies in the morning, say about ten?"

"Sounds like a plan," said Addie as she leaned over and gave him a quick kiss goodbye.

"Nice meeting you Sam. Enjoy the rest of the day and keep her in line, will you?"

That made Sam laugh. Keep Addie in line? Now the man is dreaming.

Jace left the booth, and Addie watched him as he maneuvered around their waitress carrying a tray to one of the booths. He spoke to her, and handed her the luncheon slip and money. Someone called his name and he stopped at a booth where a young couple greeted him. After a moment, he glanced back, gave a little salute to Addie, and made his way to the front door.

Addie waved back. "Well, what do you think?"

"He's really nice. Different than the other men in your life I've met. Are you sure he's your type?" Sam couldn't help teasing her friend.

"Better question Sherlock, "Do you think just riding to Pine Hollow will help us understand more about Lyla and how we can help her?"

"I don't know Watson," Sam said. "But, I guess we have to begin somewhere."

# Chapter 28

Sam and Addie agreed not to talk about the conversation with Jace until they were back at the farm. For now, they needed a distraction from Lyla and her problems. They spent the rest of the afternoon wandering through some of the antique shops in town. Sam, who could never resist searching through shops for Heisey glassware, came across a beautiful yellow glass pitcher. Addie asked how she knew it was Heisey, and she pointed out the raised capital H within a diamond mark on the bottom of the pitcher. Sam was thrilled as she watched the owner carefully wrap the latest addition to her collection. Now she had two bags to carry, one with a loaf of cheese bread she and Addie bought at the bakery, and one holding her precious Heisey glassware.

They left the antique shop and walked to the bookstore that Addie wanted Sam to see. It was tucked between a candy shop and a yarn store. The doorbell tinkled as they opened the door and the pleasant smell of books filled the air. A large sign hanging over a display rack drew Sam's attention. "Local Authors" was printed in bright red letters and a rack lined with books stood underneath. She walked over to take a look and was attracted by a book with an orange cover and the silhouette of a horse standing on a ridge. The title was, 'Spirit of a Rare Breed,' and she turned to the back cover to read the synopsis.

Addie joined her at the rack. "I love it when a bookstore features local authors and their books are as good as, or better than many well-known authors."

"Now this is what I want to do someday," said Sam. "I want to write a novel, but I don't have the time. And you know me; I would make myself crazy devoting every spare minute to work on it."

"But you are writing," Addie said as she picked up a romance novel. "Maybe you should think of your freelance writing as practice for the novel you'll someday have time to write."

"Now that's a novel idea, no pun intended," Sam said with a laugh. "I guess for now, being on the Oprah show with a best-selling novel will have to remain on my bucket list."

Addie's eyes widened, and she gave an exaggerated sigh. "You know what's on my bucket list? Finding someone special."

"You mean you're ready to find a man you can fall in love with?"

Addie stopped thumbing through the book and looked at Sam. "Sam, I'm serious. I really am."

The tone in Addie's voice convinced Sam she was.

"I know Andy was the love of my life and I've never allowed myself to fall in love, but I've been doing a lot of thinking about where I am in my life. Eden will be going to college in another year and then what? Since Andy died, my life has been Eden and my farm. I didn't tell you this Sam, but I finally admitted that I needed help with male relationships and I've been seeing a therapist. It's been

212

helping. She suggested that I was stuck in the past and I have never let go of Andy. He's remained such a big part of me that I've left no room for any other man."

"Wow, Addie. I'm so proud of you. You deserve the best that life has to offer. You're a young woman and you've got your whole life ahead of you. And as much as I wanted to, I couldn't tell you it was time to move on. You had to come to that realization yourself. I'm so happy that you've reached the point where you recognize that you need to change and have the guts to ask for help. Good for you."

"Well, even though the right man may not be Jace, at least I'm ready for a relationship that means more to me than a man who just fixes my tractor, or a man who delivers hay. Although, come to think of it, Chet has always been a man I think I could spend serious time with. After all, we're both horseaholics and that's a big thing we have in common."

Addie's last statement broke the philosophical tenor of the conversation and they started laughing. It was a private joke between Sam and Addie.

"Darn Addie, you had me for a moment," she said as she rolled her eyes.

"No, really Sam," Addie became serious again. "I want Eden to pick the right man. I want to be a good role model for my daughter. I've taught her all I can about horses and riding and now I need to prove that I can move on and find another man as good as her dad was."

"Addie, look I'm not laughing at you. I'm your best cheerleader. I think Eden wants you to have someone special in your life, just as the twins are glad that Denver is in my life. Even Lyla wants to find a man to share her life with. Maybe that's just the way it is. It doesn't matter who it is that fills that empty spot, only that we find the right one. Life is all about timing and choices. This time all of the planets are aligned for me, and maybe for you too."

"Enough with life's philosophy," said Addie. She put the book back on the shelf and took Sam's arm. "Let's go. I have things to do, and I have kids coming for riding lessons at four."

Sam closed the book she had been flipping through. She decided to buy it and after she paid for it she turned to Addie and said, "I remember reading something, and it made me think about my life. It went something like this 'If we want to change our lives we need to change ourselves first, and sometimes that's all it takes.' I've really had to do a lot of soul searching to make changes in my life. Getting stuck in the past isn't a good thing. Life moves on and if you don't move with it, the old baggage gets too heavy and blocks all opportunity. So, I'm working to be my own change agent rather than being forced into it. I think that's what you need to do, Addie. Take a chance on possibilities and don't wait for life to happen. Make it happen while you're still young enough to do it. You've been single long enough. I know there's not a man who will ever take Andy's place but you'll never know another love, unless you open the door and step outside.

"Uhhuh," Addie nodded as they walked down the street to her truck. "I love your tidbits of wisdom. You always have little sayings that fit the moment. Do you still live by your 'indecision is the key to flexibility?'"

"Sometimes, but I've learned not to be afraid of change. And I think indecision can be a roadblock if you fall back on it too much. I'm more careful about my adages, and try and find the humor in them rather than use them as an excuse. Especially the one 'when in doubt, do nothing.' I used that a lot."

"Okay Sherlock, and I have no doubt that we need to get out of here," Addie said as she put the truck in drive and pulled out of the parking place and headed towards home.

Driving back to the farm, they turned up the volume and sang along with Adele. The art of questioning Jace about Pine Hollow had been difficult for both women. It had been tough trying to be subtle, while at the same time wanting to learn more. They sang along with Adele to 'Someone like You' and 'Set Fire to the Rain.' Adele's CD ended and Willie Nelson's took its place. 'Always on my mind' filled the cab and when it ended, Chet Granger once again became the topic of conversation. Sam and Addie couldn't listen to a Willie song without talking about Chet, their good friend and fellow Curly horse breeder.

"Have you heard from Chet lately?" Addie asked Sam.

"He phoned about a couple weeks ago. Said he had met a sexy lady down there in Virginia, and she was taking up a lot of his time."

"That devil," laughed Addie. "He said he was saving himself for me. But then again, I don't picture myself selling my farm and moving south. As bad as the winters can be in Vermont, it's Eden's and my home."

"Chet's a great guy, and Denver always likes to visit with him. Those southern boys have a lot in common," laughed Sam. "Sometimes I wonder how a southern boy like Denver could find happiness in New England, but he's grown to love it here. Chet said he wouldn't miss our wedding for anything. Speaking of the wedding, Denver is supposed to be calling me around five o'clock. Says he has something to talk about before he comes home."

"That's a good time for both of us. I'll be busy with my riding students, and you can get dinner ready. By the time I finish with my last student, we'll be all set to eat and you and Denver will be finished talking."

The chit-chat ended when Addie's favorite song 'Lucky old Sun' began. Willie's voice blended perfectly with Kenny Chesney's and for the moment they forgot about Lyla and Jace and Pine Hollow Farm. They were almost home.

By the time the last song finished playing, they were heading up the long driveway to the farm.

The pickup stopped at the top of the hill and they parked beside the farm house. The dogs came running to greet them and several of the horses picked up their heads and called.

It had been a long day.

# Chapter 29

Addie went about her business, meeting the riders at the arena and Sam took the time to phone Denver. He answered right away and just hearing his voice made her think about how much she missed him.

"Hello darlin, good to hear your voice. I miss you."

"Hi cowboy," she said back. "I miss you more."

"How's my favorite cowgirl?" He asked in his teasing way.

Although they spoke daily, she was especially happy to talk to him after meeting Jace. She had a sudden urge to tell Denver everything about Lyla and Pine Hollow and had to hold herself back.

"How's your dad doing today?"

"He's fine and already working a few hours at the office."

"And your mom?"

"Mom is okay, and asking when you are coming for a visit.'

"When are you coming home? Have you made plans?"

"Looks like it will be another week. We'll be home about the same time. I take it you and Addie are having fun and talking up a storm? Have you done any riding yet?"

"Not yet, but we're going tomorrow morning. Addie has a new friend and he's going with us," she said with hesitation. Once again she had to fight the urge to confide in him.

"Another man in her life? Have you met him?"

"Yes, today at lunch and he's really nice. I like him. Maybe this will work out for her."

"Don't count on it. You know Addie. The fellow will show too much interest and she'll pull away, and wham--it's all over."

"I think this time it's different. I'll tell you about it when I see you. Addie's ready for a serious relationship and this new man, Jace, is very smitten with her as is she with him."

"Well, I hope you're right. You know how much I like Addie."

"Listen Sam, not to change the subject but I'm giving you a head's up, just in case you hear from my brother. My parents are putting the pressure on me to move back to Texas. I keep saying no, but they made me promise to ask you if you'd think about relocating to Texas after we get married."

"What, I thought we had already talked about this?" Sam was worried now. She knew Denver would not have mentioned it again if he were not giving it serious consideration.

"I know we have. But the twins are off to college and my parents think this is a perfect time for us to move here."

"And what about Minnie," Sam felt herself becoming agitated.

"Minnie can come and live with us."

There was silence at her end of the line. She tried to wrap her head around what he had just said. She knew without a doubt his parents were putting the pressure on him to convince her to give up her farm and move to Texas.

Now what? This was too much for her to think about right now. Lyla and Pine Hollow had taken all her concentration.

"Sam, say something," Denver said.

Sam took a moment and cleared her throat. She didn't want Denver to hear her sniffle back tears.

"We need to talk about this when you come home," she said quietly.

"Okay, I don't want to stress you. And it's not something I would even think about without considering your feelings. I just don't know if I'm doing the right thing living so far away from them. You understand don't you? I just want you to think about it."

"Yes, I understand how you feel, but as I said let's talk when you get home. This is too big to discuss on the phone."

"Okay, I'll talk to you tomorrow. Enjoy your ride in the morning. I love you."

"I love you too." Sam turned her phone off as her eyes welled with tears.

Her hands were shaking. This was not a good thing. She didn't want to move to Texas. It was a beautiful state, and she liked Denver's parents, but her home was in Massachusetts. This is where she built her farm and raised her children. It was where Minnie lived and Sam knew she would find it very difficult to leave her lifelong friends, Dottie and Doris. But was she willing to give up Denver, the man she loved, and start over?

Just the thought of losing him scared her, and she unconsciously smoothed her hair back and retied her pony tail as she walked to the kitchen to stir the beef stew and set the table. She removed the loaf of bread from the bag, her mind still troubled by the conversation with Denver. Addie would shortly be finished with students and ready to eat. Sam wanted her advice on how to handle the bombshell he had just dropped on her. She had a gut feeling before he left for Texas that this subject would come up, but she hadn't thought that he would consider it, never mind ask her to think about it. He was dead serious. She had already burdened Addie with Lyla's story, and now she needed her help with this delicate situation. Suddenly Lyla's problem didn't seem as important to her, now that Denver had suggested the move to Texas. Most of all, it wasn't fair to ask him to choose between his parents and her. She knew in her heart he would choose her, but at what cost?

# Chapter 30

Addie had finished most of her chores and was driving her tractor on the narrow path to the upper field when her cell phone rang.

"Hello," she said as she swerved to avoid a large boulder.

"Hi, Addie. I knew you'd be up early. Looks like a great morning for riding."

"So, what are you doing up this early, Jace? Going to cancel our ride?"

"Not a chance, but I wanted to ask you if it would be okay if my buddy joins us. You know the guy I play pool with who worked at Pine Hollow? I told him last night we were going to ride out to the farm, and he asked if he could come along. He's gone riding with me several times, and loves the mountain trails."

"Don't see why not," she replied as she put the tractor in neutral and jumped down to open a gate. "Does he have his own horse or should I bring one in from the field for him?"

"He'll ride one of yours, if that's okay with you. He's a good rider, so you won't have to worry."

"Okay, will do. See you around ten? Or if you get here earlier, we could have coffee."

"I'll try and get there earlier. I'll see how his schedule works out."

"Sounds good to me. I'll see you whenever," Addie said as she hopped back up on the tractor.

"Bye sweetheart," said Jace as he clicked off his phone.

Hearing Jace's voice, and his enthusiasm for the ride put Addie in a great mood. She was anxious to see him and wondered who his friend was. Jace must really like him, if he invited him to go riding with them. Maybe she and Sam could learn more about the farm from someone else who had worked there. They would have to be very careful not to sound too interested.

As soon as she finished chores and parked the tractor, Addie walked swiftly to the turn out area next to the barn to bring in the horses the men would ride. Jace's favorite gelding, Blackjack, was in the paddock with the other riding horses. Now all she had to do was decide which horse Jace's friend would ride. Lily would take only a few minutes to bring into the barn and Sam was already brushing Kahasi down. Lily and Kahasi had been moved to the same paddock last evening. Addie hated rushing and wanted everything ready when she finished chores. She took a quick look at the horses in the fenced area, and knew Morning Dancer would be the perfect fit for Jace's buddy.

Since Dancer was brought into the riding program, Addie had one youngster in particular who had bonded with the mare. A thirteen year old boy had taken an immediate liking to Dancer, and she seemed to be drawn to him, perking her ears towards his voice when he came into the riding area. Each time Addie watched them ride, she felt like cheering. Not only did they ride beautifully, they had grown to trust each other. Nothing gave Addie more pleasure than to watch youngsters with special needs, flourish in her riding program. Horses and kids. That's what life was all about for Addie. They filled the void left when Andy died, and gave her and Eden something to work together on. Addie believed that was all she needed, until she met Jace.

A slight smile came to her lips as she thought about how much she liked him and enjoyed the time they spent together.

Addie carried two halters and a lead line to the corral, and as she stopped to pull the gate open, she thought about Jace's friend.

"Wait 'till I tell Sam we're going to ride with someone who actually worked at Pine Hollow. I can't wait to see the expression on her face," she thought as she walked into the corral to get Dancer.

One of Dancer's pasture mates, Truro a gorgeous sorrel Curly, turned and watched as Addie placed the halter on Dancer and clipped the lead line to it. Blackjack, Jace's gelding as she called him, nudged her with his nose. She turned and ran her hand along his neck, then placed the other halter on him. Addie led Dancer through the gate, closed it, and walked her to the barn. Sam was still brushing Kahasi when Addie entered with Dancer. Addie clipped Dancer to the crossties in front of him, and mulled over whether to tell Sam now or when she returned, who the extra rider was. She decided to wait. It would be fun to surprise Sam.

Sam walked over to Dancer and ran her hand over her side. "Aren't you so pretty today?" she said to the mare that nuzzled her cheek as she scratched under her chin. "Dancer is looking really good Addie. Is Jace riding Dancer?"

Addie turned and smiled knowingly. "No, Dancer is for someone else. Jace is riding Blackjack and I'll get him now. After we have all three tacked, I'll bring in Lily."

"Who's riding Dancer?" Sam asked puzzled.

Addie lifted another halter from a hook on the wall and reached for a blue lead line hanging next to it.

"I'll tell you who, when I get back. You tack up Dancer and get her ready. After she's all set, move her to the last crossties so I can clip Blackjack here."

Before Sam could ask another question, Addie turned and walked away.

"Wait a minute. Come back here!" Sam yelled. But Addie never paused. She had a surprise for Sam, and she was grinning from ear to ear.

Dancer and Kahasi were tacked and ready to go when Addie returned with Blackjack. Sam took the lead from Addie and led the big Curly buckskin to the set of cross ties to get him ready. In a short time, Addie returned with Lily, clipped her to the crossties behind Blackjack and worked on her.

"Okay Watson," Sam said. "I'm not doing another thing until you tell me about the mystery person who's riding Dancer."

Addie was bursting at the seams with excitement. "Sam you're not going to believe this, but Jace called when I was out on the tractor and asked if he could bring a friend to ride with us. And guess what? It's the same friend he plays pool with, the one who worked at Pine Hollow."

"What? That's crazy. Do you think we can get him to tell us anything that will help Lyla? And how can we ask questions without him getting suspicious?"

"I don't know Sherlock. But this is perfect. Come on. We're clever women. We'll just think before we ask," she said as she turned to lift the bridle over Lily's head.

"Addie, this is totally different. We need a game plan. One thing for sure, we can't sound too eager when we ask questions," Sam said as she pulled the girth tight on Blackjack. "Shouldn't they be here soon? We don't have much time to talk about this."

"I guess we'll have to muddle along and hope our questions come naturally. You're the one who got us involved with this mystery," Addie laughed. "What would real detectives do?"

Sam admitted she wasn't sure. She had no idea how to get information from someone without making the person suspicious. They had already tried that with Jace. She hoped their conversations would flow smoothly.

"Well if we play our cards right, I bet this friend of Jace's will be a treasure trove of information," Sam said with a shrug.

Sam and Addie had the four horses tacked and waiting when they heard the dogs barking and the sound of a pickup coming up the driveway. Coffee would have to wait 'till after the ride. Jace hadn't been able to make it any earlier than the agreed upon time.

Addie headed down towards the house to greet the men. She was anxious to see Jace, but even more anxious to meet his friend.

The two men were out of the pickup and walking towards the barn when Addie reached them.

"Hi," said Jace as he gave Addie a quick kiss. "This is Carver. Carver, meet the love of my life," Jace said with a big smile.

Addie turned to the man, with the big grin on his face standing next to Jace. He held out his hand to shake hers. "Jace talks about you all the time and I thought it's about time I meet the woman he's clearly crazy about."

Addie gasped as she shook Carver's hand. "Pleased to meet you Carver. Jace has told me all about you and your pool games."

She felt like a young schoolgirl. For a moment she forgot about Carver and focused on Jace, the man standing next to her.

"Jace actually talks about me to his friends?" she thought with amazement.

For once she was at a loss for words. In a flash, that thought left and she fixated on the name Carver. Now she was worried. Did he notice the shocked look on her face when she heard his name? He must have noticed the blank stare, and she could only hope the expression on her face didn't give her away. Carver? Could this be the same Carver that Lyla talked about? Of course it was. Carver is not a common name. Jace never mentioned his pool buddies' name, and it never had occurred to her to ask. Before hearing Lyla's story, it wouldn't have mattered anyway. Addie quickly turned her gaze away from Carver and she moved closer to Jace. She felt her face flush, but composed herself enough to say, "I have the perfect horse for you to ride. My friend Sam is at the barn. We have the horses saddled up and ready to go. Are you all set to ride?" She felt like the words were coming too fast, but she couldn't stop.

The answer from both men was a unanimous "Let's go," and they headed towards the barn.

Addie needed time to think and walked ahead of the two men. She hoped Sam could hold her composure when she introduced Carver. Sam would be as shocked as she was. How should they handle this? She had butterflies in her stomach. What would Sherlock and Watson do?

"Enough already with this Sherlock and Watson thing," she thought. "We aren't detectives, and now what?"

Try as she might, to shake the uneasy feeling she couldn't. She had a gut feeling they were involved in something bigger than they could handle. Worst of all, there was no going back. Suddenly she became rattled. Why did Jace invite Carver to go riding with her and Sam? Jace had never asked anyone else along on their rides. Wait a minute. It was Carver who had asked Jace. Now she was really nervous.

Sam was rubbing Dancer's neck when Addie, Jace, and Carver approached the barn. Addie was in the lead, and Sam eyed the men walking towards her.

"Hey Sam," Addie said as she walked up to Dancer. "You can't stop fussing over her can you? Here, let me check her girth."

Sam was about to protest that the girth had been tightened enough, but the men, although they had stopped to look at the horses, were walking towards her.

Addie raised her eyebrows, caught Sam's eye and blinked rapidly trying to use Morse code with her eyes. It was a hopeless attempt to prepare Sam for the introduction to a man whose name they knew, but had never met.

Sam looked at Addie in bewilderment. "What the heck is going on with your eyes?" she wanted to ask.

Sam was just about to ask Addie what was wrong with her eyes, when Jace walked up to her with his friend. Jace's friend had a big smile and he looked directly into her eyes as he held out his hand. His striking blue eyes looked at her with interest and amusement. She studied him as she shook his hand. A black baseball cap covered his light brown hair and his clean shaven face was set off by straight white teeth and a dimple on his chin. The words, 'dimple on chin, devil within,' flashed through her mind. A tall man, he wore a denim jacket over a red plaid shirt and his dark blue jeans met the heel of his brown boots. She immediately sensed he was the type of man Jace would pick as a friend.

Jace, as jovial as ever said, "Sam I want you to meet my friend Carver."

For a moment Sam said nothing. She was too stunned to speak. Addie could see her visibly taken aback. Quick on her feet she regained her composure. "Hi Carver, pleased to meet you. I'm glad you're riding with us. This is Dancer and I know you'll love riding her." She was so flabbergasted at meeting Carver that the words tumbled from her mouth.

Carver's smile grew larger as he listened to Sam. The pretty woman standing in front of him was acting more startled than he expected.

Addie watched Sam as the realization washed over her that this Carver was the one who worked at Pine Hollow Farm.

Jace didn't notice a thing. He was too busy checking out Kahasi.

"I really like your gelding," Jace said to Sam as he ran his hand down the back of Kahasi. He's a very handsome guy. Solid looking and nice eyes. I judge most horses by the look in their eyes," he added.

Sam nodded in agreement. "I've heard lots of horse people say that. He does have a soft eye, but more than that he's strong and sound minded. I like the buckskin gelding you're riding and thinking of buying. He's gorgeous. Nice choice."

Horse talk was always a great diversion, and Sam was glad that this was a subject she loved to talk about. It was easy and gave her time to catch her breath. At the moment, she felt like she was part of an old-time movie that was moving in slow motion.

Sam could feel her heart racing and she needed to talk to Addie, now!

On impulse, she handed Carver the reins and said "Dancer's all set and ready to go. Why don't you walk her a little before you hop on?"

That's all she could think of to say. She needed time to absorb this whole turn of events and most of all she wanted to get this man out of her space. Carver took Dancer's reins and walked her away from the other horses. Jace unclipped Blackjack and joined Carver along the fence rail.

As soon as the men were far enough away Sam grabbed Addie's arm and mouthed, "Carver?"

Jace was adjusting the stirrups on his big buckskin, and Carver was tightening Dancer's girth. Then the men mounted their horses, and waited for Sam and Addie. As if on cue, Sherlock and Watson looked at each other and then at the men saddled up and waiting for them. Sam nodded to Addie. They knew what they had to do. It was imperative that they plan a strategy, and to do that they would have to let the men get a head start on them.

Sam took her time mounting Kahasi and asked Addie if she would adjust her stirrups for her before she mounted Lily. Addie, knowing Sam was stalling, yelled to the men to go ahead and they would catch up. Addie pretended to adjust the stirrups while Jace and Carver turned their horses towards the trail that led to Pine Hollow. When the men were far enough away, Addie placed one foot in the stirrup and swung herself up and onto the saddle. They were ready to ride.

"Oh my God!" Addie whispered. "It's Lyla's Carver. Can you believe it? Why do you think he wants to ride with us?"

"He looks just like she described him," Sam said. "I have no idea why he wants to ride with us," she continued in a low voice. "But something tells me he wants to know why we're interested in Pine Hollow. I'm sure Jace told him I was visiting you, and that I live in Massachusetts. I bet he'll ask me where I live, and then he'll ask if it's anywhere near Mansville, the town Lyla lives in. If he asks those questions, it will tell us more. It just seems too coincidental that he's here. Has Jace ever asked him to ride with you before?"

"No, he never even mentioned his name. Just said he plays pool with a guy who worked at the farm. He met him when he was doing all of the remodeling before anyone moved there."

"Well, Watson we need to play this carefully. Chances are he already knows where I live and that it is near Mansville. So, if he asks I'll admit that I live next to that town. And if he asks if I know Lyla, I'll say no. I don't think we can tell him otherwise unless we're sure that he has good intentions. I don't know what the penalty is for stealing a horse, but we can't take a chance on anything until we know more. What if Doc still wants GiGi back and is willing to turn Lyla in for stealing? I get the feeling Carver is a very smart man. For now, we'll need to be careful what we ask, and what we say."

"I agree," said Addie. "Jace is looking back wondering what's taking us so long. We've got to go. We'll talk more before we reach the farm."

Sam and Addie loosened their reins and their horses moved out in a slow walk. Jace and Carver were some distance ahead and Kahasi was eager to catch up to their horses. Sam murmured to him to slow down and held him in a walk.

"Let's enjoy the ride and see if Carver brings up Lyla's name. Maybe we're worrying for nothing," said Sam her face in a frown.

"Deal," replied Addie as she clucked to Lily to keep up with Kahasi.

They rode in silence, each rider deep in thought. Every now and then Jace looked back to make sure Sam and Addie were catching up. But catching up was not what they wanted to do. They had a lot more to talk about.

# Chapter 31

Addie's property was laid out in an irregular pattern of fields and fences. Horses ridden for her riding program were kept close to the indoor ring. She owned two stallions, and each was pastured with a band of mares Addie wanted bred for that particular bloodline for the next year. Mares and foals were held in a separate pasture, and weanlings still another. Addie always had a group of horses for sale, and they were kept in a large pasture with run-in sheds. They were well-trained and ridden frequently to keep them in shape. Besides Eden and herself, she had several women who routinely rode the horses and helped out at the farm and in the riding program. Addie always had a plan and she was careful to breed only the best Curly horses. Because she was so selective, sales were strong and growing each year. Since Addie had horses for sale at times when Sam didn't, she referred potential sales to her. Many sales were to horse people who were allergic to horse hair. Because of their unique gene, responsible for the Curly coat, their hair is hypoallergenic. It wasn't unusual for Sam and Addie to have horse lovers visit their respective farms to see if this quality made it possible for them to become horse owners.

A well-used bridle path ran between two fenced in pastures, and opened into a large hay field. The men were still a distance ahead of them, and Sam and Addie kept their horses in a walk. They were in no hurry to catch up to the men, who were now almost to the hay field. As Addie and

Sam rode by the horses grazing in the pastures, they raised their heads and whinnied. With a flick of their tails, they galloped towards the fence line and stopped short to greet the horses and riders. A flashy Curly black pinto caught Sam's eye and she asked Addie about him, as she pulled Kahasi to a halt to take a closer look.

"He's gorgeous," said Sam. "Who's he related to?"

"He's Kahasi's half-brother," Addie said as she pulled her horse alongside of Sam. "I thought you'd like him. I was going to show him to you before you left for home. Funny how you picked him out. You have a good eye. He has the same conformation and movement as Kahasi. Must be something you like about that line," Addie said with a grin. "Remember the first time you saw him?"

"How could I forget? I was absolutely mesmerized by him. He reminded me of a baby white unicorn. He was so handsome with his thick coat and curly mane. His body resembled fresh snow and his eyes were so big and beautiful. When he nuzzled my hand, I thought I'd melt."

"I think the most memorable moment I've ever had at the Equine Expo, was when I brought Kahasi to the show and you thought someone had bought him. You were so sad and disappointed. It was all I could do not to tell you that it was Denver who bought him for you. The look on your face when he handed you the lead line was priceless."

"Wow, what a surprise that was. I fell in love with Kahasi the first time I saw him in your field. When Denver handed me his lead line, I started to cry. That was the sweetest thing anyone had ever done for me. And you were in on the whole thing. You made me believe that you had sold him to a woman who was asking about him. And then you and Denver kept the secret until the last day. I don't know how you did it."

"Now that's true love," said Addie. "I was so impressed with Denver. You should have seen the look in your eyes when he handed the lead line and said, 'a rare horse for a rare woman.'

"Oh my God," said Sam recalling that day. "Never in my wildest dreams would I have thought he would buy Kahasi for me. He knew I hadn't planned on buying another horse. I had Kai, my black beauty, and even though I loved Kahasi, I didn't need another colt. He told me it was so much fun keeping the secret with you. Who couldn't love a man like that?"

"Speaking of secrets, I'm not the only one who can keep a secret. You're pretty good at that. Look at Lyla. Now that's what I call the biggest secret of all, Sherlock." Addie laughed as she moved Lily into a trot and left Sam to catch up.

Sam picked up the reins and clucked to Kahasi to trot on. Addie wasn't about to leave her behind. For a moment she forgot about Lyla and the man riding ahead.

"I want to take a look at your weanlings before I go home," she said as she caught up with Addie, and they pulled their horses into a walk.

"For sure. I had some really nice foals this year. Hey, I see Carver and Jace waiting for us. Must have wondered what took us so long," said Addie.

Jace and Carver sat on their horses and scanned the sun drenched field.

The mowed grass shimmered in the morning sun and spread out like a magnificent golden layer of plush carpet. Jace shaded his eyes with his hand as he scanned the field and Carver took a moment to remove his sunglasses from his pocket.

"Addie had a great year for hay." said Jace. "The season began early and we had the perfect amount of sun and rain. I helped with the haying and she has bales stacked to the rafters in her barn. Looks like this year she has more than enough to carry her through the winter."

"Maybe next year I can help," said Carver.

"Why, you planning on staying around?"

"Could be. I kind of like it around here, and it's nice to be able to beat a pool shark now and then," he said with a grin.

Jace was about to ask why he decided to stay longer, but the noisy clucking from a large gang of wild turkeys captured their attention. They turned in their saddles to watch them slowly peck their way through the field. Hens cackled to their chicks as the youngsters scrambled to keep up with the flock. One large male stopped now and then, puffed his feathers, spread out his tail and dragged his wings. He strutted and gobbled as he performed his dance to impress the hens. The turkeys didn't appear to be concerned about predators and their noisy clucking sound was either a brazen act or just plain dumb.

"Bet there's lots of nests along the wood line. Looks like the coyotes will feast this winter," said Jace. "I've never seen so many turkeys. They're all around my farm and Addie's field looks like turkey heaven," he chuckled.

"Looks like you won't have to buy a Butterball this Thanksgiving," Carver laughed.

"Rather the homegrown variety. Wild turkeys are not what I like to eat. They can be tough and gamey. Leave them to the coyotes. Keeps them fed and away from the deer, which I do like to hunt. Look towards the edge of the field," he pointed. "Addie and I usually see deer along the tree line. Quite a herd this year. And we've seen more than one moose out on the trail. Got to be careful of them. If they startle they can be dangerous. Good that our horses know they're around before we do."

"We've never seen any moose when you and I went out on the trails," Carver said. "Personally I'd love to see one, but not too close," he laughed.

Jace turned in the saddle and saw the women riding towards them. "Good they've caught up. Now we can run our horses to the edge of the field and cross the road to where the trail begins."

The five acre field gradually sloped down to a clump of trees that lined a dirt road. On the other side of the road, the trail curved through the mountainside and led to a valley with a slow moving river. It was part of an old stagecoach road and it would lead to Barnsville and Pine Hollow Farm. On horseback, it would take a couple hours of riding to reach their destination.

Addie and Sam brought their horses to a halt beside the men.

"About time you ladies got here," said Jace. "We were wondering what was taking so long. Your horses beat already?" he asked jokingly.

"You're too funny," Addie said as she pulled Lily alongside Jace's horse.

"Sam wanted to check out a few of the yearlings in the pasture. One of them is her gelding's half-brother."

"Which one?" asked Jace as he leaned over and gave Addie a quick kiss.

"The black pinto that I love, of course. Sam and I have similar tastes when it comes to horses," she laughed.

"I guess you mean men too," he winked. "You keep saying I remind you of Denver. Never met the guy but he must be great if we're anything alike," he teased.

Addie and Jace were so busy flirting with each other, they didn't notice the other two had left and were galloping towards the end of the field.

"Hey, why didn't they wait for us?" Jace asked as he pushed his heels into Blackjack's side and with a loud yahoo, raced to catch up with Sam and Carver.

Addie was right behind. Lily wasn't about to let Blackjack stay in the lead. The horses galloped across the short cut grass to where Sam and Carver waited and watched. Heavy bodied turkeys took flight as the horses raced by and chicks scurried for cover. Addie was in her glory. Nothing was more fun than racing her horse through an open field, and it was even better with Jace at her side.

Addie and Jace brought their horses to a halt alongside Sam and Carver.

"That was so much fun," said Addie as she pulled the strap of her helmet tighter. "Did you see the flock of turkeys?"

"Yes, and we saw them scatter as you rode through. It was so amazing to watch them take flight. They look so awkward and heavy, but all of a sudden, whoosh, they lift off the ground!"

Sam pushed a loose strand of hair behind her ear. She turned to Jace with a twinkle in her eye. "Looks like we beat you."

"Yup, you sure did, but I think I was a little distracted," he said as he grinned at Addie.

Addie raised her eyebrows as if surprised. Carver laughed as he clucked to Dancer to walk on. "Let's go you two love birds. The trail awaits us. We're off to Pine Hollow Farm. This should be a lot of fun."

Sam glanced at Addie. Their eyes connected and Addie nodded to her. They both wondered how much Carver knew about Lyla and silently speculated on when he would ask. Something told Sam that Carver was very interested in what they knew about the farm. Maybe it was the way his eyes met hers when he asked a question, but she was sure she would soon find out if her suspicions were right.

# Chapter 32

After running their horses through the field, they pulled them into a walk and crossed the road to enter the wooded trail. Each person was lost in thought as they made their way to the old stagecoach road. Addie thought about Jace, and her growing fondness for him. Jace was thinking about Addie and how pretty she looked this morning. Sam still wondered about Carver and how much he knew about Lyla, and Carver contemplated on how to bring up Lyla's name without sounding too interested. It was going to be a day of intrigue and a game a chess player would find fascinating.

The day was going to be hot, there wasn't a cloud in the sky but it was perfect for riding through the dense foliage of the mountain trail. The horses picked their way up the edge of the trail, and entered the narrow path that led through a rich green canopy of leaves. It was quiet and no one spoke. The riders were lulled by the sound of crunching leaves and the breaking of small branches from the horses' hooves. Every now and then one of the horses blew through its nostrils in relaxed contentment as they settled into a slow walk. The riders relaxed and sat deep in their saddles enjoying the rhythmic movement of their favorite steeds. They rode single file, Jace and Addie in front, followed by Sam and Carver. Sam rubbed her hand along the side of Kahasi's neck and spoke softly to him. It was during these moments that she most appreciated the strong, sturdy mount she rode on. He was solid and steady and did what she asked. Her black riding helmet sat snug on her head and although her hair was pulled back into a tight pony tail, as usual a strand kept coming loose and falling on her face. She looked down at her soft brown leather riding boots. They felt snug on her feet and very comfortable. Like Addie, she was dressed in jeans, a long sleeved jersey, and a light vest. Her thoughts wandered to Denver and she wondered what he was doing. She was missing him more with each passing day, and wished he were riding with her on this gorgeous morning. For a moment worry crossed her mind. Would he decide to move back to Texas even if she said no? All of her conversations with him alluded to the fact that his parents and siblings were pressuring him to do so. What would she do if he decided to do just that? She knew what a pull family was, especially when an illness was involved. And she also knew she didn't want to move to Texas and leave her farm and family. Denver was in a tough position. Her mind switched to Lyla. If only she had a chance to talk to him about Lyla before he left. He would know what to do and he would be able to analyze Carver better than she or Addie. He was a quick study of people, and she needed his input. For sure, she would call him when she got back to Addie's farm. The sudden urge to hear his voice came over her and she shook her head to push it away.

Her mind traveled over the list of possibilities for solving Lyla's dilemma and she was still thinking about what to do when Jace yelled out "Watch out for the low branch!"

The riders left the trail to avoid the large limb, and then continued on their way. The trail was now wide enough for two horses to ride side by side and Addie moved Lily up next to Blackjack. Jace leaned over and brushed a leaf from her shoulder.

Sam was riding next to Carver. She enjoyed watching the easy banter between Jace and Addie. She could see the connection and how happy Addie was with this gentle man. As she looked at Carver, he smiled knowingly. "They make a fine couple, don't they?" he said with a grin.

"Yes they do. I don't remember ever seeing Addie this happy. It seems they are perfect for each other," she replied with a smile.

A moment of silence passed, and then Carver broke it with, "So what part of Massachusetts are you from?"

Uh oh, here it comes. Her gut told her that he already knew she lived in a town near Lyla. She had better be honest with her answers. "I live in a small town called Algonquin."

"Is that anywhere near Mansville?" he asked.

"Yes it is. Do you know someone who lives there?" Sam asked trying her best to feign innocence.

"I do. A woman named Lyla worked at Pine Hollow for a bit. She was a pretty redhead. Hardworking, nice, and a great smile. I'd like to get in touch with her."

Carver's sunglasses were back in his pocket, and he looked directly into Sam's eyes, waiting for her reply. Her heart began pounding, and she took in a short breath, then turned her head away from his steely blue eyes.

"He knows," she thought. "He can see right through me. Does he see the worry dancing in my head?"

As if on cue, Addie's voice called out, "We'll be coming to an area where there are lots of trees down. Your horses will have to be careful where they plant their feet as they pick their way through."

Addie's warning was none too soon and it was just the break from Carver's questions that she needed. Now she knew what was meant by not being able to exhale. She finally caught her breath, and before he could protest or ask another question she said, "I'll wait for Addie. You and Jace can ride together. Kahasi likes to ride with Lily." Now that's a big lie, she thought. But what other excuse could she use so he wouldn't be more suspicious than he already was. She pushed Kahasi into a trot and left Carver to wait for Jace. Seeing Sam trot off, Jace brought Blackjack up alongside Dancer. He knew the girls wanted to ride together, after all Sam was here to visit Addie, not him or Carver. Addie put Lily into a trot to catch up to Sam and in a few strides they were once again riding side by side.

As soon as the men were out of hearing distance Sam turned to Addie and said hurriedly, "Oh my God, Addie. You called out just in time. Carver was asking about Lyla, and if my town is anywhere near Mansville. I didn't know how to answer. What do you think?"

"What?" Addie's brown eyes grew large with concern. "He already started with the questions. We figured he would, but not this soon. Let's try to stay away from him as much as possible. Jace knows I want to ride with you so we can talk. He thinks we're talking about your upcoming wedding. I told him I was going to bring him as my guest, I hope that's okay with you."

"Of course you can bring Jace. I really like him, but what are we going to do about Carver and how much should we tell him about Lyla?" she asked excitedly. "Do you think he'll try and find her and what then?"

"Well, Sherlock, we're in a fine mess aren't we?" Addie said with a fake twang to her voice.

"Come on Watson. Put your thinking cap on. I don't know what to say to Carver. He seems really nice and Lyla had good things to say about him. Maybe she had it right. He is one of the good guys. It was Doc and Bill who scared her to death."

"Yes, and of course what she saw in the black binder was the last straw," reminded Addie.

"We need a plan. How can we answer his questions truthfully without knowing for sure what his intentions are?" Sam clucked at Kahasi to move along a little quicker. Jace and Carver were left further behind.

"Okay," said Addie." Let's analyze the pros and cons of the situation and be prepared for his questions, rather than being left like two deer caught in headlights."

"Agreed," Sam said as she slowed Kahasi down to a walk.

# Chapter 33

Sam and Addie spent the next half hour discussing what their next move would be. Left in a quandary, the only decision they made was for Sam to admit she knew Lyla. She'd explain she met her because of the tornado, but she wouldn't mention the Mini. It wasn't perfect, but they didn't want to get tangled in a web of lies that may come back to haunt them. Besides, Addie had argued, Jace was a man of integrity and he knew Carver from the farm. If he thought he was dangerous, he wouldn't have picked him as a friend. Carver had surprised them, and they had no choice but to play the hand they were dealt. They would look around Pine Hollow and try and get Carver to talk about the farm and the man called Doc. When they got back to Addie's, they would call Lyla and tell her about meeting Carver and ask her what she wanted them to do.

Sam's head was spinning. She had so much on her mind. Between Denver and Lyla, she was feeling like any decision she made might not be the right one. Addie felt more positive. Once again, she reminded Sam that if Doc had wanted the foal back, he would have gone after Lyla right away. But he didn't, so maybe they were stressed for nothing.

The riders reached the slow flowing riverbed, dismounted from their horses and led them to the bank of the river. After the horses drank their fill, they walked them to a row of trees and used the lead lines they carried to tie them to some saplings. It was turning out to be a great ride despite their original misgivings about Carver. He was easy to talk to and enjoyable to be around, and he was a good rider and showed his love of horses by his gentle way with Dancer. The riders took a moment to stretch, and drank water from the bottles stored in their saddle bags. Sam shared the chocolate chip cookies and brownies that Lyla had sent, and they took time to relax and talk before continuing the ride.

"These are delicious," said Carver as he bit into one of the brownies. "Did you make them?" he asked Sam.

"No, I like to bake but my friend is the real baker, and she sent a large box of desserts with me to share with Addie."

"Well, be sure to tell her how much I've enjoyed them," he said as he reached into the box and took out another. "Does she own a bakery shop?" he asked.

Sam hesitated, for a moment the questions amused her but she quickly replied, "No, not yet, but she hopes to someday." Her eyes pleaded with Addie for help.

Addie took the signal and jumped into the conversation. "So how do you like riding Dancer?" she asked, changing the subject as she lifted the water bottle to drain the last few drops.

"She's great. Very comfortable to ride and quick on the response. I can see why she's one of your favorites," he replied as he opened his second bottle of water. "Is she for sale?"

Sam laughed. "All of Addie's horses are for sale. Isn't that true Addie?"

"Yup, as much as I would hate to part with her, she is. That's how I make a living, so every horse is for sale, well except for Lily," she nodded towards the mare standing beside the other horses. "I'll never sell her. I could never part with Lily."

"Well, I'm thinking of buying the house I've been renting for this past year, and if I do, I'll be looking for a horse. Now that I've ridden a Curly horse, I'd like to try out a few of yours. Would that be okay?" he asked as he pushed his hair back from his forehead and put his cap back on his head.

"That would be great," Addie said as she brushed off her jeans. "Any time is fine with me. Jace will bring you by. Right, Jace?"

Jace got up from the log he had been sitting on. "That sounds like a plan," he answered as he walked over to his horse to tighten the saddle girth.

Sam, pleased that the conversation had switched to horses, checked her saddle and put the rest of the cookies back in her saddle bag. "Okay, I'm ready to ride and excited to see the farm you fellows worked at. It sounds interesting," she said as she looked at Addie and grinned.

They mounted their horses and crossed the shallow part of the narrow river. Their boots got wet as the horses sloshed through the water but it didn't matter. It was fun to cross and the horses enjoyed the coolness of the water as much as they did. Once across, they picked up the last leg of the trail and urged their horses on. At times they had to move in single file, but often the trail widened and they were able to ride two by two. It was during these times that Sam and Addie, leaving a distance between the two men, talked strategy.

"Okay, Sherlock," Addie said as she leaned over and whispered to Sam. "Have you thought anymore about GiGi and what you'll say if Carver asks if Lyla has a Mini horse?"

"I'm praying he doesn't ask that but if he does, I guess I'll have to be truthful," she replied with a worried frown. "I say we keep avoiding any mention of Lyla but if he asks, we'll take it from there. So far we've been good at switching the subject to horses. Maybe it will continue to work," she replied as she rubbed the side of Kahasi's neck. "Good boy Kahasi," she murmured to the white horse.

"Well, we'd better come up with more than that if we don't want to get in too deep with explanations," Addie said, loosening Lily's reins and sitting deeper in the saddle.

"I know, but at this point, Watson, my mind is mush. I'm hoping that if he does ask any questions, one of us will get us out of any pitfall. We need to give honest answers without revealing too much. And maybe we're worrying for nothing," Sam said with an easy smile, trying to put Addie's fears to rest.

"I don't know, Sam. It seems too coincidental to me. I think he knows more than he's letting on and he's waiting for the right time to ask," Addie said with faint sarcasm.

Addie and Sam brought their horses to a halt to wait for the men, who were now out of sight.

"I agree, there's something about the whole thing that troubles me, but I just can't put my finger on it. Let's just wait and see."

It had turned out to be a gorgeous morning for a ride. The temperature in the air was just right and the horses had no problem with overheating even though they had been in the saddle for a few hours. The ride was peaceful and breathtakingly beautiful. But for Sam and Addie, the ride was only a means to an end. They were lost in their own thoughts and worried what Carver's next questions might be. It was too unsettling for them to enjoy what should have been an awesome trail ride.

Along the trail, they had watched a hawk soaring high above the trees looking for small animals, and on a twisted turn on the trail a red fox ran out right in front of the horses. Jace's horse jumped to the left as the sudden flash of fur darted in front of him, but he pulled him back onto the trail without incident.

The dense woodlands shielded most of the deer from the sight of the riders. Because of their keen sense of smell and amazing hearing, they knew the riders were invading their territory long before the horses came into view. The only hint that deer were close by, came when Jace heard the crackling of underbrush and saw the flash of a white tail as a large doe skirted away. Although they were on the lookout for bear, the only sign of any came when they had dismounted to take a short break and Jace noticed some claw marks on a tree where one had sharpened its nails. Sam didn't like that idea very much and had often said that bears were the one animal she hoped she would never run into. Several bears had been seen in her town and a den was found across the ridge from her property, but she had never confronted one and that was just fine with her. Coyotes were dangerous enough, but usually ran rather than attacked. Well, except for the one rogue coyote that had almost killed her filly, Kai. On inspection, the game warden had discovered that the coyote was old and said the coyote probably figured the foal was easy prey. But even he wasn't sure what triggered the attack, since coyotes usually hunt in packs. The coyote was tested and did not have rabies, so it still wasn't understood what caused the lone coyote attack. The only thing that made sense was that a calf had been killed around the same time and maybe the coyote got brave enough to try for a foal. Luckily Kai's dam had gone after the coyote and saved her baby. But Sam knew that even bears, if hungry enough after winter hibernation, would attack a foal if the opportunity presented itself, and she never felt safe with bears in her area.

Sam had a sudden revelation. "Why worry about bears when that would probably never be a problem. But right here and now was a scary problem and it was called Lyla and Pine Hollow Farm."

# Chapter 34

It was noon by the time the riders reached the edge of Pine Hollow Farm. They stopped at a fence line and looked across the meadow at the long barns now vacant. It was even more beautiful than Lyla had described. To their relief, Carver never mentioned Lyla's name again, and Sam and Addie considered the idea that just maybe he wasn't interested enough.

Carver and Jace pointed out the interesting parts of the farm and Sam and Addie both drooled over the open hay fields.

"I wonder if another horse person will buy the farm now that it's vacant." Sam asked as she shielded her eyes from the sun.

"I've heard from someone in town that several New Yorkers are looking at it," said Jace." Lots of New Yorkers are buying property around here for summer homes."

"Well," said Addie, "from what I can see it's truly a gorgeous piece of property. Whoever buys it is going to love it," she said with a smile.

"Everything still looks great," said Jace. "I know that someone is mowing the fields close to the barns and keeping up the place for resale. The only thing new owners would have to do is build a house," he said with a chuckle.

"If I were to build a house I would put it right over there," Carver pointed to a hill up from the barn."

"Yup, that would be a real pretty spot. Used to look at that small hill when I was doing the remodeling before the new owner moved in," said Jace as he turned his horse to move along the fence line.

Sam didn't say anything. Her mind was racing as she tried to merge how Lyla had described the farm and what she was looking at. Addie was silent in her own thoughts. For a moment they caught each other's eye, and looked knowingly at each other. Sam could see why Lyla was initially attracted to Pine Hollow. It looked serenely beautiful.

They turned their horses to follow Jace and looked for an opening along the fence line to enter the property. Most of the fencing was still in good shape but finally they found a small break and followed Carver as he trotted Dancer across the field.

Sam and Addie were amazed to see how large the farm was. For some reason they visualized it as a few long barns and some small paddocks, but it was huge and spread out over a large area. Several open fields, though overgrown, looked to be about five acres each and the red barns still looked freshly painted and glistened in the bright sun. Around the barns the grounds looked well kept, and several pieces of farm machinery were parked here and there. An old John Deere tractor stood outside a long red shed and a hay wagon that had seen better days stood parked against a barn wall.

They slowly rode past a long barn that was painted a deep apple red. The bright sun glistened on the roof top and it shimmered against the candy apple color of the barn. Carver brought Dancer to a halt at the second barn next to a sturdy hitching post. The riders dismounted and tied their horses to the post to get a better look at the inside. Sam and Addie didn't know what to expect, let alone what they should be looking for as they followed Jace and Carver into the coolness of a barn that would make any horse person drool.

Although the barn was vacant it only took a moment to know that it had once stabled horses, and it was only a short time ago. Everyone was silent as they slowly walked through taking in all that was around them. Sam pulled her helmet off and placed it on a stall rail. She pulled her wrap off of the back of her hair and smoothed it with her hands, then wrapped it tightly as she gathered the hair that had come loose. Addie removed her helmet and placed it alongside Sam's. She ran her fingers through her hair and the loose dark waves fell softly around her face as she shook her head.

Jace and Carver were walking ahead of them, and Carver flicked on overhead lights as they made their way down the long aisle. The dark barn was suddenly filled with light, and they could see how immaculate everything had been left. Sam had never been in a barn that was so impeccably clean, but there was no doubt that horses had been stabled there. The earthy aroma from hay, shavings, horses, leather, and grain still remained in the air.

"Oh my God, this barn is gorgeous," Sam whispered to Addie as she sniffed the air and felt immediate pleasure from the lingering smells.

"I've never seen a barn so pristine," Addie's eyes lit up with amazement. "Look at those beams," she said as she pointed upward.

Sam tilted her head back and studied the rafters above. The weathered oak beams were massive and they ran from one end of the enormous barn to the other. A cement center aisle, wide enough for a small tractor separated the wall of stalls. The barn was beautiful and she was amazed at how perfect everything was. A sudden unease came over her. She sniffed the air. Yes, that was it. Although it still held the smells of a barn once filled with horses, there was the faint aroma of bleach and other chemicals.

"Addie, does this barn give you the same funny feeling as it gives me?" she whispered as her eyes scanned the stalls looking for any remnants of horses.

"Yes," Addie replied in a hushed tone, "It's as if someone wanted to clean every hint of horses ever being here, and that's odd since it's being sold as a farm. What would make someone clean to the point of not leaving any evidence horses were here?" she asked. "You'd better put on your thinking cap Sherlock. I sense a bigger mystery here than we thought," she said as her eyes continued to scan the barn.

Sam moved closer to the wall of one of the stalls and looked inside the grillwork that lined the front of it. "How many stalls have you counted?" she asked Addie who was on the other side of the barn looking inside another stall.

Addie walked over to Sam. "I think there are about twelve stalls on that side and the same on this side. Notice how clean each one is."

"They look to be about ten by ten foot stalls. Nice size for Minis, that's for sure," Sam added.

"And look at these walls," Addie said excitedly. "They seem to be made of some kind of material that's not wood. I bet these cost a pretty penny. There are no knots or separations where dirt can gather. I've never seen anything like this. I'll have to ask Jace what this is," she said as she ran her hands down the side of the wall. "And the only thing a new owner would need to do is change the height of the feeders. Everything is set at a lower level to accommodate Mini horses."

Sam nodded in agreement. "That's easy enough to do. Wouldn't you love to have someone do a spring cleaning in your barn so it looked just like this?" Sam laughed as she ran her hand inside the corner feeder. "Not a speck of dirt!"

"Maybe when we win the lottery we could do something like this." Addie said with a grin, as she looked down at the stall floor covered with thick rubber mats. "But I don't think you or anyone else we know could afford this type of barn."

"I think it's too big for us anyway," said Sam in a conciliatory tone. "After all we're just regular horse people," she sighed. "But it would be nice," she quickly added.

"Not so fast," replied Addie. "We're not only horse people, we're both detectives Sherlock, and I think we need to start thinking like one," she reminded Sam. They were both so enthralled by the barn, for a moment they forgot why they were there in the first place.

"You're right Watson. Thanks for the reminder," Sam said as she saluted Addie. "Let's keep our eyes open and see if we can find just one clue."

She could hear the voices of Jace and Carver, as they opened the tack room door. She turned her head towards them and gestured. "Let's see what the men are up to."

At the end of the barn a wide doorway opened to a huge tack room. Rows of empty hooks lined the walls that once held halters, lead lines, and lunge lines. Long shelves, covered with drop down plastic covers kept brushes and grooming supplies free from dust. Everything was built with precise planning, to keep tack and equipment clean and neat. "Wow," was all Sam could say as she looked around.

Next to the tack room was a wash room for horses, also left spic and span. Across the aisle was a feed/storage room with washer and dryer plus a utility sink. Adjacent to that was a large open space reserved for hay, wheelbarrows, and forks.

Sam and Addie's voices filled with excitement, as they walked through each area. It was more than they could comprehend.

Jace and Carver watched the women with amusement as they oohed and aahed over each of the rooms they walked through. They reached the end of the barn and Carver pointed to a door that housed the bathroom. He opened the door and the women stepped inside. The large white tiled bathroom still glistened and Addie remarked that it smelled like a sterilized room that had never been used.

Carver answered her observations. "Remember this farm was used for research, and everything had to be kept immaculate," he explained.

"Where is the break room for the workers," Sam asked.

"That's in the second barn. There are three barns on this property. This barn was for horses, but the barn next to this was used by the workers for breaks and change of clothing. It also holds a few offices." replied Jace.

"So Jace, you did all of this before the owner moved in," asked Addie in amazement.

"Yes, and everything was built according to his specifications. No detail was left out and I was told that money was no object. He wanted it done as soon as possible, so I hired a large crew, and we completed the renovations within a month. After we were finished, the owner sent in his own team to finish up."

"Wow, this is really something. I had no idea that it would look like this. Whoever buys this farm won't have to do a thing to move in," Sam said as she looked around, fascinated by what she saw.

"Well, except build a house." Both of the men laughed.

"True enough," Addie joined in. "But if someone can afford this, I'm sure they will build a proper house to match."

Sam had stepped away from the group. She heard a small meow above her, and looked up to see a large grey cat sitting on a beam. "Whose cat is that," she yelled to Carver.

"Don't know," he said as he looked up at the beam. "Must be a stray since we didn't have cats during the time I worked here."

"Cats always find a home in a barn," said Addie. "Lots of free meals to catch if they're really hungry, although I did see a cat dish when I came in the barn. Maybe the man who keeps the place up leaves food here."

Sam almost let out a "Nice work Watson," but bit her tongue before the words spilled out.

"Probably so," replied Jace. "It's something I'd do."

Sam took advantage of the pause in the conversation. "By the way," she asked innocently. "If this farm was used for research, where was the lab?"

"I'll show you," replied Carver. "It's in the third barn. That was where Doc had his lab and also his living quarters and office."

Sam took in a quick breath. This was the first time anyone had mentioned Doc by name. She noticed when Carver said Doc; he looked straight at her and Addie and a small amused smile crossed his face. She felt a tingling in her gut and a shiver rolled down her arm. Without a doubt, he knew why they were there, and he was just playing along with their game. She looked at Addie in shock, as Carver and Jace turned to leave.

Addie mouthed the words, "He knows!"

After touring the rest of the barns, the riders mounted and rode back towards Addie's farm. Sam and Addie stayed out of Carver's way, hoping he didn't question them or see the guilt on their faces. They were happy to leave Pine

Hollow, and although they had found no clues that made any sense, they knew Carver had figured out that Lyla was connected to them. And if Lyla was, so was GiGi.

They rode the horses to the beginning of the field and then ran them through the short grass with pure abandonment, hooting and hollering as they raced each other. It was exhilarating to sit on the muscled horses and feel their power as they galloped across the field, kicking up dirt and grass, each one trying to leave the other behind. The tension at the barn melted away by the time they brought their horses to a halt at the end of the field and they marveled at how much fun they had. The playfulness of the ride pushed the list of questions and unresolved suspicions to the back of their minds as they made their way home.

The rest of the ride was uneventful and they took their time to admire the scenery and relax. Jace and Addie rode side by side whenever possible, and Carver and Sam kept their conversations to horses and the beautiful mountain views.

At times when they were riding single file, Carver reflected on the events of the day. He had not returned to the farm since the day of the move. Looking at it in the daylight, he was lost in his own thoughts. Everything appeared different, and yet the same. He recalled the months of work at the barn that was once filled with the low voices of people who worked there, and whinnies from the small horses. Mixed in was the sound of soulful country music that drifted through the barn from the radio speakers. It had been an interesting year, and now something new had been dropped on his lap. These two women were not only fine horse women; they knew Lyla. How well he didn't know but he was sure he would soon find out.

# Chapter 35

The day was late, and the sun was hidden behind billowy white clouds when the riders returned to Addie's farm. It had been a long ride and although they had started early in the morning, it had taken the whole day to ride to Pine Hollow and back. They turned the horses out to their paddocks, and watched as they dropped to the ground with satisfying grunts, rolled on one side, stood and shook the dirt off, then dropped and rolled to the other side. Then each heaved themselves up and shook again. After the all day ride, it was the horses' way of shaking off the sweat from the saddle, and getting the kinks out. Kind of like a human stretching, but more fun.

Sam and Addie walked the men to the truck to say their goodbyes. They continued to laugh and talk about what a great day it was, and how good it felt to be out of the saddles and stretch their legs. Sam leaned from one side to the other as she stretched her back and Addie did likewise, but the men didn't seem to show their need to stretch. Maybe they had more muscles, or maybe they didn't as most men, want to show any wear from the long ride.

"What's the matter honey? Not in shape for riding?" Jace said kiddingly to Addie as he massaged her shoulders.

"Funny, Jace. Maybe we don't have as much padding as you do," Addie gave back as good as she got.

"Hey Jace, I think you'd better quit while you can," Carver laughed. "You're no match for her, I can tell."

"You'll learn, Jace," said Sam as she started towards the house. "Addie is quick with the comebacks and she will always be one up on you," she chuckled. It was nice to laugh and not be on guard for fear of more questions about Lyla. She was thinking that maybe Lyla was right. Carver was one of the good guys.

Addie gave Jace a big hug and a long kiss goodbye. Carver and Sam stood by the door of the truck and talked more about Dancer and how much he enjoyed riding her.

"Although I want to ride a few more of Addie's horses," he said, "I'm thinking Dancer is the mare for me. I can see why you like her so much."

"I knew you would like riding her. She's a great mare and if you buy her I know she will have a good home and you'll have lots of fun riding her," Sam said as Carver opened the truck door.

Carver hesitated a moment and turned to Sam. "Before I forget, I'd really like to get in touch with Lyla, and if you can manage that in some way, I'd really appreciate it. So will you help me?" He stared directly into her eyes with a knowing look.

Sam's eyes met his gaze. Taken by surprise, she paused for a brief second and said, "If I ever talk to Lyla, I'll be sure and tell her what you asked."

Carver closed the door and winked. "You do that," he said with a grin. "I'll see you soon, and thanks again for letting me join you for the ride. Pine Hollow Farm is one fascinating place."

Before he could ask anything more, Sam turned on her heels, and walked swiftly towards the door of the house. She could feel his eyes on her back, and her hands shook as she opened the door and walked to the sink for a cold glass of water. As the water ran full force, she leaned on the counter and watched it swirl around the sink and pour down the drain, all the time trying to make sense of Carver and his interest in Lyla.

It was only then that the smell of chicken stew, slowly cooking in the crock pot, caught her attention. She had put it together early in the morning, while Addie did chores and the fragrant smell of the stew comforted her for a brief moment. As she clicked the controller to off, she heard Addie say goodbye to Jace, and she walked to the door to meet her.

"Well, that was a fun day," Addie said. "How did you like Carver?"

By the look on Sam's face, Addie knew immediately that something was wrong. "What's going on?" she asked with concern.

"Well, I thought everything was fine and we didn't have to worry about any more questions from Carver." Sam's eyes grew big.

"And?" Addie asked anxiously.

"But then, just as he was getting in the truck, he asked me to help him to get in touch with Lyla?"

"He what?" Addie gasped. "What did you say?"

I was taken by surprise and at first I couldn't say anything. But the words spilled from my mouth, that if I saw

263

her I would let her know he was asking or something like that. Honest, I didn't know exactly how to answer one way or another, and when he looked at me he winked. He could see right through me. Addie if we had any doubt, for sure he knows that we know Lyla. But why didn't he just call her himself?"

"Let's call her right now," Addie said. "This can't wait any longer. We need to tell her about Carver and ask her what she wants us to do."

"I agree. It's up to her how we handle this," said Sam as she pulled her cell phone out of her jean pocket and tapped in Lyla's number.

Lyla answered her phone on the fourth ring.

"Hi Sam, how's it going up there in Vermont?" she asked as she set the manure fork down.

"Hi Lyla, where are you right now?" Sam asked.

"I'm cleaning stalls and finishing up chores," she replied.

"We need to talk. Can you take a break and sit down for a minute?"

"Sure, I'm walking towards the house right now," she replied as she made her way up the path, dogs scooting after her.

"Lyla, I'm putting you on speaker phone so that Addie can listen to our conversation," Sam said.

"Ok, I'm almost at the porch."

"Well sit down. This is going to surprise you." Sam said with a steady voice. She had a habit of talking too fast when she was excited.

Lyla opened the screen door to the porch and sat down on the rocker. "Okay all set. What's going on?"

Sam spoke non-stop for the next ten minutes. Occasionally Lyla interjected with questions and Addie added her thoughts. Lyla was shocked, and close to tears after listening to Sam and Addie tell about riding to Pine Hollow with Carver. Nothing was left out.

"So what do you think, Lyla? Should we tell Carver that we spoke to you? I think he knows more than he lets on." She waited for Lyla to answer and the silence was deafening.

"Sam, I've got to go to the police about this. I don't know what else to do. Although I trusted Carver and still believe in my heart that he's a good guy, I don't know why he didn't just call me rather than go through all this intrigue. Why didn't he just come out and ask you directly if you know me, if he already knows the answer?" Lyla was close to tears and was trying to hold herself together.

Addie chimed in, "That's what we can't figure out. He seems like a really great guy and looks just like you described him, but if he knew where you lived, why wait till he meets us to see if we know you. It doesn't make sense."

"That's why I need to confess and have the police find out what was going on at Pine Hollow," Lyla said with a shaky voice.

"Lyla, don't do anything yet. Stop and think for a minute. He didn't scare us or try and intimidate us. I have the feeling he was having fun watching us squirm." Sam said as she thought about her last encounter with Carver.

Lyla paused. "Well he does have a great sense of humor, but this is too crazy for me to wrap my head around, and now I don't know whether to be scared or excited."

"Okay, just tell me this. Do you want me to contact him again and give him your cell phone number, or do you want to think about it some more? And, please don't go to the police until we get some more answers." Sam said.

"I agree with Sam," Addie added." Don't do anything until you've made up your mind about Carver. Would it be alright if I confided in Jace? He knows Carver and I'm sure he would have some solid advice."

"If you think it will help, I'm fine with that. You both have been so good to me and I can't thank you enough. Do whatever you need to. I don't want to talk to Carver unless your friend Jace thinks it's okay. I'll wait for your call before I do anything. I promise."

Lyla was relieved she didn't have to make a decision on the spot. This was a lot to think about. She grew quiet and then mustering all the bravado she could, said in a shaky voice, "I'm sorry I brought you both into my mess, and I'll do whatever you say."

"Okay," Sam could hear Lyla's voice crack. "Don't feel bad about asking us for help. Don't worry. We'll figure this out. I've got Watson working with me," she smiled at Addie as she tried to lighten the mood.

"Who's Watson?" Lyla asked.

"Addie and I are now unofficial detectives so we named ourselves Sherlock and Watson. I'm Sherlock and she's Watson," Sam giggled.

266

"That's right Lyla, Sherlock and Watson are on the case," Addie said as she nudged Sam.

"You both are too funny. I love it," said Lyla smiling for the first time.

"We'll phone you as soon as we talk to Jace," Addie said.

"So, for now, try and relax Lyla. We've got it under control," Sam replied reassuringly. "Talk to ya soon."

"I'll be waiting," Lyla said as she clicked off her phone.

"What now?" Addie asked as she walked to the cabinet and reached on the shelf for the bowls for dinner.

"What now?" Sam asked with a smile. "Let's eat. I'm starving."

# Chapter 36

Sam and Addie agreed not to talk about anything until they finished dinner. Then, they would take their wine to the porch and try and figure out their next step. This gave them time to reflect on everything that had transpired and come up with a new strategy.

After dinner, Addie grabbed a pencil and pad and Sam took a bottle of Riesling from the refrigerator.

"Let's itemize what we know, what we don't know, and the players involved," she said as Sam set her glass and the bottle of wine on the side table next to her.

"Okay," Sam replied. "I like to organize my thoughts and this is the best way to do it. I guess great minds run in the same direction," she said kiddingly as she sat down.

For the rest of the evening, they drank wine and wrote down everything Lyla had told them and listed all the questions and theories they had about Pine Hollow, Doc, and Carver. Addie filled a platter with cheese and crackers, and after a short break, they went over each point and wrote down their observations and conclusions. They were careful and exact, and found that when one remembered something it piqued the other's memory. The pad began filling with more and more tidbits of information. The pieces of the puzzle were coming together.

As Sam looked at the list, she suddenly had an Aha moment. "I just thought of something," she said excitedly. "Right after Lyla brought her horses to my farm, I had my vet come and check them out and he told me something very interesting."

"What does it have to do with Pine Hollow?" Addie asked as she refilled her glass with wine.

"Well, until now nothing." Sam said as she reached for a cracker and chunk of cheese.

Sam filled Addie in on the visit from Doc Mike and what he told her about his visit from Homeland Security and their interest in sudden equine deaths.

"I don't see what this has to do with Pine Hollow, but if you do, why?" Addie asked as she got up from her chair and stretched.

"I don't know but let's add it to the list and think about it," Sam replied as she pushed a strand of hair behind her ear. "Maybe there's no connection, but at this point everything is suspicious to me. Maybe there's a link."

"Now you're thinking like a real detective," Addie laughed. "Let's complicate things even more. But who knows? Maybe there is connection, but this is one clue that I'm not sure fits in."

Sam's cell phone rang. She looked at the time and couldn't believe how it had passed so quickly. Her face lit up as she answered. "Denver, I'm so glad to hear your voice. How's your dad doing?" she asked as she walked towards the kitchen, yawning.

Addie smiled. The phone call was a welcome relief and she didn't see any sense in continuing tonight. It was late and they needed some rest. The list could wait until tomorrow. It was another day and maybe they could come up with more answers when they reviewed it all with a fresh look.

After the long day riding, Carver was left with his own decision to muddle over. He reached into the microwave and removed a plate of leftover Chinese food and set it on the counter as he popped open a cold beer. That was a risky thing he had done. He couldn't tell Sam, Addie, or his friend Jace about Lyla. All he could do was hint and see what the ladies would do with the information. Of course, he knew that they knew Lyla. Even though he had convinced Doc not to do anything about the theft of the Mini or the young woman who took it, he had been well aware of where she lived and everything else about her. He knew that the tornado had brought her into Sam's life. That was his job and he knew how to do it. What he hadn't bargained for was the attraction he felt for the woman with the curly red hair.

He took a drink of the ice cold beer while he mulled over the day. Even he wasn't sure what Pine Hollow was all about and he had used all of his expertise to do so. Doc had hired him at an extraordinary salary and one of the provisions in the contract was that he was forbidden to ask questions about any of the research. It was easier to believe what Doc had told him after his own investigation turned up empty. Doc was adamant when he hired him that was not to get friendly with any workers and he was to avoid any questions about the farm. His job was to review all of the camera feed daily, report any suspicious conversations between the workers, and be vigilant about trespassers. When he had questioned Doc about what to do if

270

trespassers broke through the security fence, Doc said it was nothing he needed to concern himself with. He had someone to take care of that end of it. He was just to report it to him immediately.

Doc had him do a thorough background check on every person who worked on the farm, including Lyla. He often wondered why Doc had let the situation of the stolen foal go so easily, and didn't push to pursue it. He couldn't fathom why Doc had allowed himself to be talked into that one. There must have been an important reason for him to drop the matter, but the answer eluded Carver.

What to do now was the question. Doc had phoned him several times with questions about security and he had been ordered back to the farm a few weeks after it was vacated to check on one thing or another.

He finished the beer and opened the refrigerator, deep in thought, and took out another. As he walked back to the table, he decided to think through everything before he phoned Doc and informed him about Lyla's friends, and their visit to Pine Hollow Farm. The whole thing needed to be presented in an understated way to alleviate any concerns Doc would have. He knew Doc would be aggravated, and it was his job to reassure him that he would take care of the situation and not let it go any further.

# Chapter 37

Early the next morning, while working at the barn, Lyla heard the sound of a vehicle coming up the driveway. She stopped cleaning the stall, leaned the fork against the wall, and moved the wheelbarrow out of the way. Although she half jogged to the vehicle, the dogs were at the red SUV before she could stop them from smothering the person with slurpy, drooly doggy kisses, and overly robust greetings.

The driver was out of the car and bent over petting each of the dogs, and as she reached the car he stood to greet her. Denver was home.

"Wow, looks like you've missed me," he said to Ranger as the dog leaped and bounced in the air almost knocking him over. "Hi Lyla, I know I should have called but time got ahead of me," he said as he scratched Ranger's ear. He gave the order 'off!' and Ranger headed across the field to find his ball. His friend was home and he was ready to play.

"Gosh this is a surprise," Lyla said as she hugged Denver.

"Yup, couldn't take it any longer. They didn't need me even though they tried to convince me otherwise, so I headed home." He picked up the ball Ranger had dropped in front of him and tossed it as far as he could for the shaggy dog to retrieve.

"Sam will be so happy to know you're home," she said as she walked him to the house. "How was your trip?"

"Tedious," he said as he ran his fingers through his hair. "I'm glad to be home. Two weeks is long enough to be away from Sam," he said. "I thought I'd check on the farm and see how you're doing then drive to Vermont and surprise her."

"Well, I was just finishing cleaning the barn, but I can use a break and looks like you could use a coffee," Lyla said as they walked into the kitchen.

Denver reached for a K-cup and popped it in the coffeemaker. "Now this is what I need," he said as he placed a mug under the lid and pushed the button.

"I've got some fresh biscotti," Lyla said as she walked over to a large plastic container filled with desserts sitting on the counter.

"I'm telling you Lyla, the man who marries you will have to workout at the gym every day," he laughed. "He won't be able to resist your baking," he said as he lifted the orange pastry from the container.

Lyla filled her mug with coffee and sat down at the table across from Denver. "He's going to Vermont?" she thought. "Oh, no. He's walking into a mess that he knows nothing about, and I know he's had enough worry with his dad's health." She could tell by his tired eyes, that he had a lot on his plate and he was anxious to see Sam. Her eyebrows furrowed as she contemplated what to say.

She had to tell him about GiGi, and what Sam and Addie had been up to. It was now or never and she knew what she had to do. Tell him everything now before Sam has to. It wasn't fair to have her explain the whole sordid thing.

Her eyes settled on the coffee mug, as she thought about how to begin.

She cleared her throat and looked across the table at Denver. "Before you go to Vermont, I need to fill you in on something," she said as she clasped her hands together to stop them from shaking.

Denver stopped eating and studied the woman, visibly upset, sitting across from him.

"Nothing's happened to Sam or Minnie or Addie?" he asked as he took in a quick breath. "And the twins are okay?"

"No, no, nothing like that, thank God. This is all about me. Sam and Addie both know about this, and now I need to tell you. Sam was going to talk to you before you went to Texas but she knew you had enough on your mind and decided to wait until you came home." For a flash of a second she wanted to take back her words, but she had already started and she was frozen to the chair as she tried to pull herself together. Now she had his total attention.

"I know this is sudden and you are probably too tired to listen to my drama, but it does involve Sam and Addie." The words poured from her mouth. She could feel the tears easing out from the corners of her eyes, and she squeezed them tight to stop the flow.

"Slow down. Take a breath. It can't be that bad. Just spit it out." He took a drink from his mug, while he studied the distraught woman, not knowing what to do or say. He felt awkward and didn't know how to help her, but something told him to give her a moment, and she would be okay.

Lyla tilted her head back and then leaned forward. "Alright, give me a minute and I'll try and put it all in order," she said as she drained her coffee mug, got up and went for a refill.

Lyla talked non-stop for the next hour. Unlike Sam, Denver didn't ask many questions or attempt to slow her down. He got up once to fix himself another coffee, and then sat down. Lyla didn't skip a beat, and continued talking until she was emptied out.

When she was finished, she met Denver's eyes. "You must think I'm a horrible woman. I am no better than a common horse thief." Lyla began crying in earnest. The tears flowed down both cheeks and she started to sob.

Denver, as with most men, didn't know what to do except get up from his chair and give her a hug. He left for a moment, went to the bathroom and retrieved a box of tissues.

Lyla pulled herself together and waited for Denver's reaction. He took a minute, tilted his head back and rubbed the bridge of his nose, then leaned forward and looked directly into her bloodshot eyes. "Lyla, I'm not judging you. First of all, I think you're a fine, honest woman. Sam and I both like you very much. Sounds like you got yourself into something that you don't understand, and fear drove you to do something completely out of character. I can tell the good guys from the bad guys," he grinned, "and as far as I can see, you're one of the good guys. To tell the truth this whole thing not only shocks me, it puzzles me. I just don't get it, but I think it's time we both head to Addie's and talk this whole thing over with her and Sam." He got up from the chair and stretched, tired from the flight home, but intrigued by Lyla's story. He felt the sudden urge to walk outside and throw a few sticks for Ranger. It was time to clear his head and think.

"Should I phone Sam and tell her we're coming?"

"Naw, don't do that. I want to surprise her. First call Addie and tell her you're coming to try and work this mess out and then call Pattie and see if she can take care of things for today and tomorrow. Get an overnight bag together and after we finish chores and have lunch, we'll head to Vermont," he said without missing a beat.

As usual, he was quick to make a decision, and once made he was ready to go.

Lyla phoned Addie to tell her she wanted to come to the farm and talk over the meeting with Carver. Addie and Sam thought it was a good idea. They were running out of answers, and decided that Lyla had to either face Carver or go with them to the authorities to explain what she had done and why. They would support her either way, but this was too big for them to solve. Even though they had fun with the titles of Sherlock and Watson, they knew they were way out of their league, and neither knew what a real PI would do. The mystery had grown too deep, and now that Carver was aware that Sam knew her, Lyla needed to be there in person to decide their next step. The web was becoming more and more tangled, and what to do next couldn't be decided over the phone.

Lyla didn't mention to Addie that Denver was home and wanted to surprise Sam, although she was tempted. She said she would stay overnight and would bring a chicken and squash casserole for dinner, and of course a loaf of baked bread and a dozen biscotti. Assortments of desserts, already prepared for the Farmer's Market on Saturday, were packed in a basket and Lyla also added several of Denver's favorite apple muffins. Everything was arranged for the trip. Patty and two of Sam's friends would take care of the farm while they were in Vermont, and Lyla made up her mind to face what needed to be done. Somehow she had to make this right.

# Chapter 38

Since Lyla wasn't expected until late afternoon, it was a perfect time for Sam and Addie to go on an early morning ride. Addie had promised to take Sam on a trail that led to a beautiful view from the top of one of the mountains. Once again they rode through the field where mares and foals were pastured and they stopped to take a closer look at Kahasi's half-brother. It was a welcomed break from the stress of the day before, and they took their time evaluating the foals and talking about their breeding programs. The morning air was soft with the scent of greenery and flowers. Addie's potbelly pigs were rooting in the warm soil, and scattered when the horses rode next to them.

"I think I'd like a few potbelly pigs for my farm," Sam said as she clucked for Kahasi to move out. "There's something about them that is so charming. Maybe I should replace a few chickens with pigs. No eggs from pigs, but a lot more entertaining," she said as she watched the pigs follow one another to a new rooting spot.

Addie grinned as she watched the pigs. "I really have taken a liking to them," she said. "Now that I have them, I think I'll always keep a few potbellies on the farm. You should try them. Wonder how your goats would like them?" she laughed.

"Rudy and Roger would probably find them amusing to be around. They are like big dogs, but much more mischievous. Got to watch them or they'll think they can run the farm and boss every animal on it."

"That's why I gave up goats and only have horses and pigs. Been there done that," said Addie as she trotted alongside Sam.

They came to the end of the field and crossed the road and onto the mountain trail. It was the same one they had rode on with the men the day before.

"Where does the new trail leave this one?" Sam asked as she walked Kahasi along the cool dirt path.

"We'll head towards the river and pick up the trail to the ridge before we cross. Just follow me."

After an hour of riding along the shallow river, they crossed over and picked their way through trees and moved out onto a trail used by snow mobiles. The wide dirt path ran along the side of the mountain where a single trail broke away into some tall pines and low shrubs. They followed the trail for a distance, as it meandered up and wound along the ridge. At the end of the tree lined ridge, an open sloping field of tall grass laid out the most spectacular view Sam had ever seen. They drew their horses to a halt, dismounted, and walked them over to some young saplings where they wrapped lead lines carried on their saddles around low branches. Brushing themselves off, they walked through the tall grass to the edge of the long sloping hill that led to a valley below. The only sound that broke the silence was the nicker from their horses as they blew through their nostrils. They stopped talking and listened. The trill of birds filled the air and the buzz from a honey bee flitting from flower to flower provided nature's symphony. Their eyes scanned the valley. They were high above the tree line and Sam took in an audible breath.

"Oh my God, Addie. This is the most beautiful place I have ever been."

"I think you can see New Hampshire from here," Addie replied as she pointed her finger.

The view was spectacular. The vista was dotted with trees of various shades of green and the valley danced with color. Slow moving white puffs of clouds crept slowly across the deep blue sky, and a large hawk soared high above catching the upward draft.

"This is an artist's dream," Sam said as she pointed her camera up towards the hawk. It was breathtakingly beautiful, and Sam's camera clicked away taking picture after picture as she pointed it in each direction.

"A little piece of heaven I wanted you to see while you were here. Eden and I found this trail some time ago, and we come back here when we want to commune with nature," Addie said with a smile. "There are so many trails through these mountains we have yet to discover. I'm planning on buying a GPS system so that when we ride on a new trail it will help us find the way home. One of my friends told me that there is also an App for my I Phone. Of course, the horses would probably find their way, but I'd feel safer with a system that will show our location and keep track of the miles we've ridden. Wouldn't that be neat?" she asked as she shielded her eyes with her hand from the glaring sun.

"Uh, huh," Sam replied as she sat down on the grass and marveled at the beauty around her. She tilted her face to the sun and closed her eyes.

"Give me your camera and I'll take a photo of you to show Denver," Addie said.

"Okay, and then we'll face the valley and hold the camera in front of us and take a picture of you and me," Sam said as she handed the camera to Addie.

Time slipped away, and although hesitant to move on, the women mounted their horses for the return ride home.

"I want to bring Denver here some time. He would love this," Sam said as they left the ridge and rode down the mountainside. "I feel like we just sat at heaven's door," she laughed.

Addie nodded in agreement. "It would be fun to ride up here with Jace and Denver and bring a picnic lunch. Let's plan on it as soon as we get through this Lyla thing," she said as she clucked to Lily to head for home.

By mid-afternoon, Lyla and Denver were on their way to Vermont. The conversation continued about Pine Hollow and Lyla had Denver's full attention. Now instead of just listening, he asked questions and by the time they arrived at Addie's farm he had a better understanding of the people involved and about Lyla's brazen theft of GiGi.

It was almost five o'clock when they pulled into Addie's driveway. The black poodle reached the vehicle before the women did. Denver and Lyla bent down to pet the jumping ball of energy. The yellow lab greeted them in a nonchalant way. He sniffed their legs, smelling Sam's dogs and then calmly strolled away.

The door opened and Sam and Addie walked out to greet Lyla. Sam's eyes grew wide with surprise when Denver looked up and said, "Hi darlin." She ran straight into his arms and Lyla and Addie stood and watched as Sam behaved like a young teenager hugging him and smothering him with kisses.

"You devil, you," she exclaimed as she stepped back and looked at him. "Why didn't you tell me you were coming home? I've missed you so much," she said as she hugged him again.

"I wanted to surprise you, but after talking to Lyla, I thought it was a good idea for both of us to come. I think we have some really big talking to do," he grinned. He had stayed away too long and even though going to Texas was something he had to do, it wouldn't happen again soon.

"Okay you two," Addie chimed in. "Let's go inside and by the way cowboy, where's my hug?"

Denver turned to Addie and wrapped his arms around her. "You're looking gorgeous as ever," he said in his charming southern drawl. "Been taking good care of my girl?" he asked teasingly.

"What's to take care of, and that would be the day she'd let me take care of her. You've learned that yourself," she laughed.

"Oh my gosh," Sam said as she looked at the red haired woman standing watching the scene. "I'm sorry Lyla; I didn't mean to ignore you. Addie this is Lyla."

Addie held out her hand. "Hi Lyla, not to worry about introductions. I feel that I already know you, and I must say I loved all of the desserts you sent."

"I've brought more," Lyla laughed as she reached into the back of the SUV to take out the basket of desserts and the covered casserole pan. "I think it's going to be a long evening. I've told Denver everything, which is why he suggested I come along with him."

"I'm so glad you told him yourself. Now we can all sit down and talk about some kind of plan," said Sam as she reached over and squeezed Denver's hand.

"That's why I'm here darlin. You don't think I would let you worry about this any longer do you?" he said as he put his arm around her shoulder. "Not only that, I couldn't stand one more day without you," he grinned.

After a leisurely dinner and coffee with desserts, they sat on the porch to discuss everything and try and come up with a strategy. Denver looked at the list that Sam and Addie had put together. Lyla added more facts as questions from each of them stirred her memory.

At last, Denver put down the pencil, stretched his arms over his head and yawned. It had been a long day. He had been on the go since four in the morning. All it took was two glasses of wine and he was ready for bed.

"Enough is enough," he said to Lyla as he got up from the chair. "It's time to take the bull by the horns and face Carver. It sounds like only he can take the mystery out of Pine Hollow and end all of the worry and suspicion that you've had to live with."

It was that simple. Denver had made a decision, and the women were glad that he had. They were weary of the whole thing.

He said goodnight to Addie and Lyla and headed upstairs. "Come on cowgirl, it's time to tuck me in," he said to Sam with a wink.

Sam got up from the chair and turned to Addie and Lyla. "I'll be back as soon as he falls asleep," she said with a yawn.

Lyla and Addie smiled knowingly at each other.

"You two have a lot of personal issues to talk over. Don't worry about us. We're going to finish the bottle of wine and hit the sack. We need to be up early to put our plan into action," Addie said.

The plan was made. Addie would phone Jace in the morning, and invite him and Carver to the Blue Cat for lunch. She would tell him she wanted them to meet Sam's fiancé. He had surprised Sam and returned home earlier than expected. She would not mention Lyla. A lot would be learned when they watched Carver's reaction when he saw her. What would he say? Would he explain to Lyla why no one had contacted her? Would Carver finally fill in the missing pieces? They had purposely chosen the deli because it was a public place and they had questions that only Carver had the answers to. Denver was certain that he was the key to the mystery at Pine Hollow. Only then would Lyla have enough information to decide whether to go to the authorities and admit what she had done, or to finally--feel safe. If Carver cared anything about her, he would advise her on what she should do. Not knowing Carver, Denver had a hunch about what might happen, but he didn't want to share it with Sam or Addie, and most of all Lyla.

# Chapter 39

Addie was up and out doing chores before any of her friends were stirring. She enjoyed getting an early morning start and finishing before the sun beckoned her to take a coffee break. Jace was always up early, planning his work schedule for the day, and she had phoned him and invited him and Carver to meet Sam and her at the Blue Cat for lunch. As much as she wanted to, she didn't tell him that Denver and Lyla would be joining them. After all, he didn't know how Carver fit into the picture with Lyla. Jace phoned Carver and passed on the invitation and as Sam and Addie expected, he jumped at the chance to see them again.

As Carver hung up the phone, he breathed a sigh of relief. He was trying to figure out how to see Sam again before she left for home. He could always say he wanted to look at Dancer again, but now it was all taken care of. It was perfect. After his conversation with Doc he knew what he had to do and the questions he needed answered. It was now or never, and he was glad that he would finally be able to be done with Pine Hollow Farm.

Lyla was giddy with anticipation. On one hand she couldn't wait to see Carver, but on the other she feared facing him. Her concerns were not the same as Sam and Addie's. They weren't sure about Carver and what part he really had in Pine Hollow. Along with Denver, they didn't believe Lyla knew the whole story about Carver and his job. Last night they had reviewed all of the notes and talked over every possibility about the mysterious farm. But there were too many holes in the story to be able to come to any conclusion. Carver was the only one to fill in the blanks. But would he?

Sam and Denver were in the kitchen, when Lyla came downstairs. Although sleep deprived, it didn't take away her natural beauty. Her curly tossed red hair hung in ringlets around her face, and her green eyes although showing lack of sleep had a softness that could melt any man's heart.

Denver and Sam were at the counter fixing their coffee. His arm was draped over her shoulder and they spoke in hushed tones, preoccupied with what they were talking about, so they didn't hear Lyla come into the kitchen.

Sam nestled her head on his shoulder. She couldn't get enough of him, and was ever so happy to have him back with her. "Are you sure that you don't want to move back to Texas?" she asked for the fourth time. "I don't want you to have any regrets."

Denver tipped her head up and looked into her eyes. "Listen darlin. You are my life and I promise I will never have any regrets. And I don't mind repeating myself a hundred times if that's what it takes to convince you how much I love you and how glad I am that you and the twins are in my life."

She kissed him again. "I love you cowboy," she said with a smile. "And don't you forget it," she teased as she brushed his hair back from his forehead.

Lyla cleared her throat. She was embarrassed for interrupting a special moment.

287

They both turned and smiled.

"Don't worry," Denver said seeing her embarrassment. He winked at her and said, "We're always like this."

"I should be so lucky to have someone in my life that makes me this happy," Lyla said as she walked to the counter to fix a coffee. She reached up in the cupboard and took out a purple mug with the outline of a horse on it and placed it under the coffeemaker.

Sam walked to the table and set her mug down. Denver took an apple muffin from the plate and sat down.

He looked at Lyla and said teasingly, "I'm thinking you'll find someone who one day will sweep you off your feet. You're not only gorgeous, but you can bake a mean apple muffin," he laughed as he swallowed the last bite, and reached for another. "This is delicious. How many did you bring?"

"Enough for you I guess," said Sam who was wiping her mouth with a napkin. "Honestly, Lyla, Denver's right. Given half the chance a lot of men would be beating down your door. You know the old saying 'the way to a man's heart is through his stomach' and right in front of you is a man ready to give a testimonial on your behalf."

For the first time, the tension of the matter in front of them was broken. There was something about the coffee and the breakfast pastries that set the mood. Sam studied Denver as he drank his coffee. His dark hair was tousled and ready for a cut and his white tee shirt fit snug around his shoulders, showing his muscled arms. He was a very handsome man and she realized how fortunate she was. It was going to be a good day.

By noon they were ready to meet Jace and Carver at the deli. Each one was looking forward to resolving the missing parts of Lyla's venture. Sam was certain that today would bring closure to Lyla's conundrum and finally settle her doubts as to whether she would be able to keep GiGi or go to the authorities and admit her wrongdoing.

Lyla on the other hand, was not as confident about the meeting. Her anxiety was spilling over and her heart was beating so fast it felt like it would jump out of her chest. As she washed her face, she stared in the mirror. A flushed face stared back, and her usually sparkly eyes looked tired and scared.

She must have brushed her hair at least ten times and pulled it back into a pony tail, only to undo it and start again. The anxiety and wonder made her want to run as she had at Pine Hollow, but her friends were with her and she felt protected and supported by them. Denver was strong and in control and Addie and Sam promised not to leave her side.

"Don't worry Lyla," Sam reassured her. "You're not alone and together we can do this." Sam and Addie wrapped their arms around her and she could feel their strength and support. She couldn't believe how fortunate she was to have found these wonderful friends. It was as her mother often told her, "If you want to have a friend, you need to be a friend."

There was nothing she would not do to repay their kindness and support. For now it was through her baking and cooking, but she had other ideas to show them how much she appreciated their faith and trust in her. One thing for sure, when Sam and Denver went on their honeymoon she would stay at their farm for as long as needed.

By noon they were at the Blue Cat. It promised to be a warm day and the anticipation of meeting Carver after fleeing the farm was almost too much for Lyla to bear, but the continual prattle between Sam and Addie took away a lot of her misgivings.

They entered the deli and just as before the wonderful smell of baked bread filled their nostrils. Lyla was in heaven, and if not for the anticipation of meeting Carver, she would have been able to appreciate the wonderful aromas and ambiance that surrounded her.

Addie asked the waitress Pearl, dressed in a bright yellow uniform, if Jace had arrived. Addie and Jace, regular customers, knew everyone by name.

Lyla's eyes grew big as she looked around the room. This was how she pictured her bakery looking and smelling. Everything was cheerful and people seemed happy. It must be the colors she thought, or the background music, but something made this deli different. And Blue Cat bakery! What a wonderful ring to that name. No time to figure out what made this deli special, because the waitress was leading them past the counter and down the aisle to a booth at the end of the long room. Just as the last time, the room was crowded and the waitresses were busy filling orders. Addie led the way, followed by Sam, Lyla, and Denver. She weaved in and out as she made her way with focus and determination.

A waitress stepped in-between them and they lost track of Addie, who was on a mission. The waitress moved on and as they scooted past her, they saw Addie stop at a booth against the wall.

Carver stood to let Addie in the booth next to Jace. It was then that he saw Sam, followed by a woman with red hair. His eyes locked with hers and his jaw dropped in surprise. Could it be? Yes it was. It was Lyla.

# Chapter 40

*One Month Later*

*Alexandra Science Center, New York City*

"May I have your attention please?"

A hush fell over the large room. The sound from the low baritone voice stopped all conversation and guests who were sipping wine, lightly placed their glasses back on the table. All eyes turned towards the stage.

The moderator, Geoffrey H. Loos, was an impressive figure. As CEO of Larkspur Pharmaceuticals, his demeanor and poise implied; affluent business man. His wavy blonde hair, streaked with grey, was slicked back at the sides allowing small wisps to turn up at the nape of his neck. A member of the Fortune 500, he exuded the picture of success. His tailor made black tuxedo completed his polished image, and he looked like he had just walked off a fashion runway.

The name of the scientist to receive the distinguished science award, sponsored by Larkspur Pharmaceuticals, was ready to be announced.

The large room was filled to capacity with world-acclaimed scientists and smartly dressed company executives. Vases of yellow roses were elegantly placed on the center of tables, and invited guests had completed a fabulous dinner of lobster and prime rib. Small footed dessert dishes were now empty of heavenly Crème Brule and delighted guests had finished bottles of expensive wine. Empty wine glasses were being replaced with crystal fluted glasses filled with champagne. Scientists and executives were anxious to toast the highly regarded scientist who had made Larkspur Pharmaceuticals the victor in a huge government sponsored research project.

It had begun with a raid on an apartment where suspected terrorists had lived. Bells and whistles went off when the anti-terrorist unit found a small piece of paper in an apartment vacated by unknown persons. The information was passed on to the authorities in the biological terrorism unit of Homeland Security, and an immense amount of resources and money poured into the research for development of a vaccine for a deadly strain of Botulism. Pharmaceutical companies set-up specific labs for highly intensive research, and the best Biomedical Research Scientists were recruited to work round the clock in an effort to develop a vaccine. There was an imminent danger to entire populations, and the race was on to prevent what could be a biological terrorist attack.

As they sat waiting for the award to be given, several of the scientists sat poker-faced, but many smiled broadly as they listened with anticipation for the moderator to ask the celebrated recipient to come forward.

The room grew quiet as they waited for the speaker's announcement. The prestigious event was the culmination of a year's investigative work that took place in small laboratories throughout the country. The coveted honor was not only monetary; it would anoint the beneficiary with worldwide prominence and respect. Everyone in the room knew that the man to receive the coveted award deserved it. Most scientists in attendance had been a part of the competition, but there was only one winner and it was Dr. Nicola Petrovic. His vaccine was now in production and ready if needed for distribution to protect American citizens against the latest biological threat. Although the monetary award was hefty, each scientist knew that the greatest honor for Dr. Petrovic would be the accolades bestowed on him by his peers in the science community.

Now that he had everyone's attention, the CEO cleared his throat and began. "It gives me great pleasure to recognize and introduce the esteemed scientist Doctor Nicola Petrovic. Dr. Petrovic is the master of many disciplines. He is a highly acclaimed scientist in the world of biochemistry, genetics, physical science, and bacterial research. He has been sought out by many government agencies for advice on biological warfare, and has published his theories and research in Nature, the Science Journal, and the American Association of Science. His many contributions for scholarly research are too numerous to list. As you know, several pharmaceutical companies took part in the race to develop this vaccine. However, there is only one man, Dr. Petrovic, whose determination and perseverance, and I might add his long hours of work, accomplished the task set before him. Now, without further ado, let me introduce the man of the hour.

"Dr. Petrovic, will you please come forward," the CEO grinned broadly and the audience responded with loud applause.

Dr. Petrovic rose from his seat. He was dressed in a black suit and tie. He pulled his shoulders back, took in a deep breath and buttoned his jacket. A slight smile crossed his lips. He hesitated briefly, and then reached over to shake the hand of the man who sat across from him, Morton Ridgeway. Morton, better known by his colleagues and employees as Doc, reached out and shook his hand. He gave Nicola a quick wink. Nicola smiled, turned, and walked toward the stage.

Doc's small brown eyes lit with amusement as he watched his friend step up and onto the stage. Beads of perspiration dripped from his forehead, and he reached for his handkerchief to wipe his brow.

As he appraised his friend and colleague, he could not help but admire the distinguished stature of the man he knew he could never be. Their personalities were as different as day and night but in spite of it, they had built a friendship based on mutual respect, and collaboration. While Nicola was humble and sincere, Doc was a narcissist, who thought of himself as intellectually superior to most people, and was intolerant of those who failed to perform to his expectations.

"Oh well," he mused. "I know most people think I'm a backwoods, rude man, but so be it. I don't care what other people think of me. Truth be known, I don't give a damn about other people's opinions. If they don't like the way I look or speak, it's not my problem. Why can't people just do the job and not ask stupid questions? Thank God I've been able to work with Nicola. No questions and he's brilliant and resourceful. He has faith in me and knows I get the job done. Nicola is someone I can respect."

Doc reached up and wiped his brow again. "I can't wait to get out of this suit," he thought as he turned his attention to the stage. A smile curled his lips upward ever so slightly. "They had done it!"

He sat back and listened to the accolades hosted upon his friend and bathed himself in the thrill of their success.

The CEO continued. "With the gratitude of our country and the commendation from our company, it gives me great honor to present this award to Dr. Nicola Petrovic. Our Botulism vaccine is only one arrow in our quiver to fight the war on biologic terror. Many scientists worked tirelessly to produce a vaccine for treatment of this strain of Botulism, but you are the one who succeeded. Thanks to you, Larkspur Pharmaceuticals is now in the production and the distribution stage of supplying this vaccine to our government. Doctor Petrovic; the scientific community, our company, and the world at large are grateful to you for your service and dedication. I would like to present you with this award from Larkspur Pharmaceuticals. Enjoy and thank you."

The moderator stepped aside and handed Nicola the microphone.

Nicola hesitated for a moment and cleared his throat. Acutely aware that his command of the English language was not fluent, he chose his words carefully. "Thank you Larkspur Pharmaceuticals for this award. The quest we were charged with has been all consuming." He paused and began again. "Although I was able to develop the vaccine, the clinical trials were conducted by my friend and colleague, Dr. Morton Ridgeway. I would like to share this honor with him. All of my research depended on his expertise to take it to its final stage of testing. Although he and I were in constant contact and I visited the research facility on several occasions, his dedication to our research was invaluable. This colossal undertaking of managing our clinical trials was carefully and methodically carried out at a farm in Vermont. My dear colleague spent untold hours and months to bring this project to fruition. The American people can be proud of the scientific community and the work that unknown scientists perform. They are safe today because of these dedicated men and women. Morton would you please stand?"

The pudgy man pushed away his chair from the table and took a slight bow. Applause filled the room. He eased himself back onto his chair and dabbed his lip with the corner of his handkerchief.

"Damn," he thought. "I can't wait to get out here."

He took a sip of water from the glass sitting next to his plate. The moderator had the microphone again and continued talking about the vaccine and the science that went into its development. Doc's eyes glazed over and his mind wandered back to the journey that had brought them to this prestigious event. He recalled the exact moment when he and Nicola made the decision to pull the biggest caper of their lives.

They were both working in the Project Green Lab and it had been an exhausting week. They had worked fourteen hours that day, and Nicola invited Doc to his apartment to share a cold beer and talk about his research.

Doc leaned forward in his chair and met Nicola's eyes. "So, Nicola, tell me about your latest findings."

"I have done it, my friend." Nicola's face showed the seriousness of his statement. "I have completed my research and validated my results. My vaccine is ready for clinical trials."

Nicola spoke in a tired, resigned tone. He sighed deeply, leaned back in his chair and tipped his head back.

Doc placed his glass on the table and studied his friend.

Nicola had a strong foreign accent and his words were measured and slow. Doc was keenly aware of Nicola's unease and trepidation about his research. On one hand he was excited about his findings, but on the other, he was concerned about sharing his results with the slick opportunist and project manager, Calmar Jackovich.

"So," Doc said, "Jackovich gets the money and all the glory for your hard work and what do you get my friend?"

"I know." Nicola sat up and rubbed his chin. He looked down at his hands and said, "Jackovich has contributed nothing but cruel words and our research has been exhausting. We all know he has this job because of his marriage to the sister of one of the company executives. If I had known what a tyrant he was, I would never have agreed to work for him. I'm sorry that I didn't look closer into his background, but I'm not sorry to help my adopted country. That has been my goal. I will give back to the country that has embraced me and given me a home."

"That is an honorable thing to do my friend," replied Doc. "But I remind you that honor means nothing to Jackovich."

Doc paused and looked directly into the scientist's eyes and held them for a moment before he looked down. His brain was working on over-time. The black sheep of a wealthy family, he had never fit into the mold his overbearing father had expected from each of his children. Doc's two siblings were successful business men. They were well respected in the community and belonged to several upscale country clubs and played golf on the best courses. However, nothing in business interested him. Doc didn't look anything like his brothers, nor did he think like them. He was the oddball of the family and after successfully completing a degree in science; he left home and never looked back. A loner and cranky man of few words, he was a perfect fit for the cloistered environment of Project Green Laboratory.

"May I have another cold beer, my friend?" Doc reached for his handkerchief to wipe his forehead.

"Of course," replied Nicola as he got up from the tattered leather recliner to walk to the refrigerator.

Doc leaned back in the faded red velvet chair and closed his eyes, deep in thought.

Nicola returned and poured the foamy liquid into Doc's glass.

Doc opened his eyes, took another sip of the dark cold liquid and placed the glass on the table beside him.

"I have been thinking. What if we took your research and performed our own clinical trials?"

"That's crazy." Nicola's eyes were open wide. "How could we do that and what if someone found out?"

Doc spoke slowly as he shared his thoughts. "Right now your research is yours." As he continued to speak, his plan became clearer and clearer. "You own your work and it's all on your lab computer. Jackovich has constantly reminded us not to come to him with any observations or theories unless they are conclusive and ready for testing. He allows no talk between us and no sharing of information. He is an ass."

"True, but how would we be able to remove my research from the Lab?" Nickolas' voice showed signs of apprehension and his speech was becoming less clear.

"Slow down, my friend. You are mixing your language. Let me think."

Doc took another drink from the glass and looked directly into Nicola's eyes. "Listen, Nicola. First of all, Jackovich should not profit in any way from your research. He will never give you the credit. He deserves nothing. And he is obsessed with fear. He doesn't own us or our work. He hired us under false pretenses. He can do nothing if we begin our own clinical trials. He believes he owns your work, which is why nothing can be brought in or taken out of the lab. That is except for our music CDs."

Nicola nodded and leaned in closer to Doc. They both came to the same conclusion at the same time. They knew they had found a way to remove Nicola's research. It was daring, but yet so simple. They would bring into the lab, a blank disc covered with a music label. Then, they would transfer Nicola's data from the computer to the fake music CD.

As he recalled that moment, a big smile spread across Doc's face. It was one of the few times he did so. But as he thought about that moment when they devised a way to back door Jackovich, he almost burst into laughter.

Loud applause broke in on his daydreaming. People were now standing. Doc stood and applauded loudly. They had done it!

Seated in the back of the room at a round table, three beautifully dressed women and three men dressed in black tie, stood and applauded with the rest of the guests.

Samantha smiled at her friend standing next to her. She reached down and picked up her wine glass. Addie did the same. They tapped each other's glass and Sam gave a 'thumbs up.'

"To science and horses," Sam said.

"To Lyla and GiGi," Addie beamed.

Lyla, Carver, Denver, and Jace turned to Sam and Addie. They smiled broadly as they lifted their glasses and saluted.

"To Sherlock and Watson," Lyla said as Carver placed his hand on her shoulder, leaned over and kissed her cheek.

# Ginger Cookies

Temp/time: Oven 350*
Bake time: 8-12 minutes

**Ingredients:**
2 Cups Sugar
1 ½ Cup Soft Butter
2 Eggs
½ Cup Molasses
4 Cup Flour
1 Tbsp Ground Ginger
2 Tsp Cinnamon
4 Tsp Baking Soda
1 Tsp Salt

**Directions:**
Mix together sugar and butter; Add eggs, beat well; Add molasses
Combine flour, ginger, cinnamon, baking soda, and salt
Gradually add to wet ingredient
Mix well, scoop with small cookie scoop onto cookie sheet
Bake 8-12 minutes
When cool drizzle with white chocolate

The Upper Crust Bakery
Tea & Coffee Shop

# 25 Main Street, Monson, MA

01057 theuppercrustbakerymonson@gmail.com

# Minnie's Welsh Cookies

Ingredients:
4 Cups Flour
1 ½ Cups Sugar
1 Cup Shortening
2 Tsp Baking Powder
¼ tsp Baking Soda
1 Tsp Nutmeg
½ Tsp Salt
2 Eggs
1/3 Cup Milk
1 Cup Raisins

**Directions:**
Combine dry ingredients
Blend in shortening; Add beaten eggs and milk mixing thoroughly; Add raisins
Roll into 1/8 inch thickness
Cut with round cookie cutter
Lightly grease fry pan and preheat fry pan to around 350* degrees
Place cookies in pan and fry (yes, fry) for about 5 minutes on each side

# Therapeutic Riding

Therapeutic riding uses equine assisted activities for the purpose of contributing positively to the emotional, cognitive, physical, and social well-being of individuals with disabilities. These equine activities have been shown to be beneficial to the child with physical or developmental challenges while presenting itself in a fun rewarding manner. Studies show that therapeutic riding can increase flexibility, balance, coordination, memory, sequencing, attention, and body awareness.

All Therapeutic Riding programs are made available through the generosity and support of readers just like you. You can help a child or adult with these challenges as they grow and develop self-confidence through the fun of riding and caring for horses.

Donations for Therapeutic Riding Centers provide opportunity for all children and adults with special challenges. Some of these centers are also working with our disabled veterans.

To learn more about the 'Dream on Curls Riding Center' located in Vermont and featured in my novel, please go to www.dreamoncurls.com.

Photography by Caryn Paradis
www.beadsofparadis.com

Sandra J. Howell is a retired college professor. She and her husband live on a farm in Massachusetts. Her Curly horses have been showcased in area shows, newspapers, and Equine magazines. A foundation breeding program was established in Sweden with one of her Curly mares.

www.westridgefarmpublishing.com

www.ingramcontent.com/pod-product-compliance
Lightning Source LLC
Chambersburg PA
CBHW020254200626
46816CB00001BA/285